GÖRING'S GAMBLE

DAN O'ROURKE

ISBN: 978-1981641789

ACKNOWLEDGMENTS

I have many to thank here and the first one is my wife Kate who, along with one of my daughters, is the inspiration for my heroine. Kate also took me twice to Thoor Ballylee, where I learned about Yeats.

The story itself has dozens of beginnings, some relating to family ties to Oxford and to a trip there years ago and to the nearby Cotswolds. As a fan of detective fiction, historical fiction, and to a much lesser extent, alternative history, I have tried to combine the elements of each. At the same time, I tried to keep the history changes to a minimum. The use of science fiction is the best way to new stories in my view.

Many thanks to Jack Close for listening to the developing plot as we played golf, Steve Haight and his son for their enthusiasm about the project, and Art McGiveren who dared me to put down The Killer Angels once I opened the cover many years ago. Reading history has been so enjoyable while being illuminating.

Thanks also to Kevin and Theo in New York, and to Michael who introduced me to the publishing business while there at a pitch conference.

Dan O'Rourke

November 2017

PROLOGUE:

GÖRING'S GLIMMER

The blood-dimmed tide is loosed, and everywhere
The ceremony of innocence is drowned;
The best lack all conviction, while the worst
Are full of passionate intensity.

—W.B. Yeats, from "The Second Coming"

THE REICHSMARSCHALL ENJOYED THE SOUND *his beautifully-shined shoes made upon the spacious, marble-paved hallways of the New Reich Chancellery. He enjoyed the familiar tightness of his crisply-pressed uniform, the dignified weight of the medals pinned to it, the heavy ivory baton—as long as a man's thigh—he carried to mark his rank. Glancing out the many stately windows that lined the hallway, he enjoyed the way the golden May sunshine glowed along the street that bore his name. He paused outside a particular door and checked his watch: he was precisely three minutes early. His scientists and hand-picked commandos were already inside: they knew better than to keep the Führer waiting. The Reichsmarschall had a trickier balance to maintain. He used thirty seconds to mentally review the briefing he had received on the Führer's plan: air strikes against Britain would cripple the Royal Air Force, paving the way for an amphibious invasion—if the*

Brits held out that long. *Probably they would beg to sign an armistice. But the Angles were a stubborn race, and their new Prime Minister might not know the difference between audacity and suicide. A good backup plan, the Reichsmarschall reflected, would be wise.*

He spent another thirty seconds choosing the words in which he would introduce Direktor Schumann's intriguing device and the stratagem he and Oberstleutnant Cordesmann had woven around it. *The Führer would be skeptical, but he was a reasonable man—or at least a rational one. Yes. The Reichsmarschall could reason with the Führer; that was a certainty he would stake his life on.*

Finally, the Reichsmarschall spent thirty seconds thinking of nothing at all. He took the spring air into his large sturdy lungs and let it out again. He squared his big square shoulders and stiffened his ramrod spine. He ran his thumb over one of his baton's diamond-inlaid gold-and-platinum end caps and let a sense of his own power and importance suffuse him like the warmth from an excellent Eiswein. Thus fortified—and still ninety seconds ahead of schedule—the Reichsmarschall opened the door. With a nod to pretty Frau Schroeder, he crossed the anteroom, opened the inner door, and did one more thing he enjoyed: he made an entrance.

The Führer's office was virile, imposing: four hundred marble-lined square meters. The Reichsmarschall didn't have long to spend on his admiration and envy, though: "So kind of Herr Göring to join us," the Führer murmured in that voice, which though quiet, somehow carried crisply across the fifteen me-ters between them and silenced the soft conversations of the other five people in the room.

The Reichsmarschall silently noted that his watch was still synchronized with the enormous built-in wall clock over the door he had just entered. Then he saluted and the room came to order, saluting back. The Führer did not invite them to sit; he occupied the room's only chair. The Reichsmarschall cleared his throat. "Gentlemen. Thank you for joining me today, and I appreciate your patience." He looked around the room and made eye contact with each man. He saw that Erich Schumann had set up a series of diagrams on an easel. "Mein Führer, my heart swells when I read of your plans for the destruction of the British Royal Air Force and the subsequent invasion of that island which owes so much of what is best in it to its Teutonic heritage. Nothing would give me greater joy or pride than to see Mein Führer ascending the steps of Westminster Abbey to be crowned King, unless it would be to see Winston Churchill being marched up the same aisle in chains to kiss Mein Führer's boot."

The Reichsmarschall paused here. There was still time. He hadn't said anything yet to which the Führer could possibly object. Still, he reflected, fortune favors the bold—and so he pressed on. "However, we here are all well-read men; we know that history is made in the howevers. The weather over the English Channel is notoriously treacherous. And the English are a famously unreasonable people—a condition arising, no doubt, from the insidious admixture of Celtic blood over the centuries with the noble Anglo-Saxon. They may refuse to surrender. Even after our Luftwaffe has demonstrated its superiority, the R.A.F. may cling to cowardly guerrilla measures and continue to pester us. In fact, no one is more aware than we are of just how much of his brilliance Mein Führer owes to his masterful habit of preparing for every eventuality." There—the first hurdle was past. The Reichsmarschall could see tension in the Führer's face—and was that a nigh-imperceptible twitch of displeasure in the Führer's mustache?—but no alarms had gone off, no axes had fallen. The Führer was still listening.

"Mein Führer recalls, no doubt, the yellow uranium dioxide powder he procured last summer from the Belgian Congo and provided to Direktor Schumann's team for research and development. The strides that Herr Direktor and his men have made are nothing short of remarkable. I will let them tell you themselves about the new substance they have synthesized and the implosion device it has allowed them to design."

The Reichsmarschall only half-listened to the presentation Schumann and his colleagues had rehearsed with him twenty times over the preceding days. The locking components in their coffin-shaped cases, yes; the custom-designed trucks and Heinkels; the trigger assemblies to be armed with seven hundred fifty kilos of TNT apiece, yes, yes, yes. What the Reichsmarschall was paying attention to as his knuckles whitened around his baton was the Führer's face. At the beginning of Schumann's speech it was distorted with distaste; the Reichsmarschall half-expected him to cry a halt to this display of "Jewish science." The Führer had a visceral distaste for anything connected with "that libelous rat Einstein." But as the Direktor spoke, the Führer's features softened and relaxed into a contemplative attitude. He leaned forward, elbows on his desk, chin resting on his clasped hands. His bright eyes took in every detail of Schumann's diagrams and schematics. And when Schumann explained, "This waste product of the absorption of slow neurons by uranium, which our device employs in its radioactive core, we have tentatively named Teutonium," did an approving smile flicker momentarily across the Führer's face? The Reichsmarschall confessed to himself that he was not sure—but he was hopeful. Fortune favors the bold!

When the scientists had finished speaking, the Reichsmarschall asked and received the Führer's permission to dismiss them. The whispers of their slacks and lab coats filled the marble room, then were gone. "The device Direktor Schumann has just shown you," the Reichsmarschall asserted, "is the centerpiece of our ultimate backup plan—the Über plan, if you will. Imagine the Prime Minister and King George removed at a blow, leaving Britain free for your leadership, either directly or through the Reich's unjustly dethroned friend Edward." He squared his chest to the Führer's and looked him authoritatively in the eye. "I have no doubt that the British cowards will capitulate and that the invasion will be a glorious success. However." The Reichsmarschall allowed the word to hang in the air for a moment, giving the Führer time to remember his earlier bon mot. *"If anything should go wrong, shall we wait for spring, when our foes are well-rested, and try the same strategy again? Or shall we rather strike the Über blow, take England, and at the same time send Roosevelt scurrying to sign a non-aggression pact? Oberstleutnant Cordesmann and I have developed a strategy to provoke shock and awe. It will paralyze with terror all those who may have thought to stand against us."*

The Reichsmarschall savored another significant pause, gripping his baton, but before he could cede the floor to the Oberstleutnant, the Führer broke in. "Yes, tell me about this strategy of yours, Herr Reichsmarschall," he murmured, his voice dripping with sarcasm. "You have shown me a prototype device, untested. You have shown me little trucks, little planes. Even supposing you can produce this Teutonium explosion, which of your toys can deliver a payload that, all told, weighs—what—twenty tons?" The Führer let out a dismissive little puff of air from under his mustache. He unclasped his hands, let them hover on either side of his face. "Shall we load everything onto the Bismarck and sail it up the Thames?" The Führer's sneer lasted another split second, then broke as he was gripped by genuine merriment at the absurdity of his own suggestion. He chuckled genially; the Reichsmarschall and the commandos laughed with him, politely. Silence returned abruptly, though, when the Führer's eyes returned to the Reichsmarschall's face, his expression attentive.

The Reichsmarschall smiled, then cleared his throat. "Closer to twenty-five tons in all, Mein Führer," he said, "and we did consider U-boats as a means of transport. But I hope you will find Oberstleutnant Cordesmann's plan even more ingenious." Cordesmann's pitch had required only one rehearsal with the Reichsmarschall. Max Cordesmann was a military man through and through, precise, steel-nerved, loyal to the end. "With Mein Führer's permission," the Reichsmarschall said, nodding towards the Oberstleutnant and preparing to enjoy the commando's speech. If he had been seated, he would have leaned back.

Truly, although Cordesmann did not embody the racial ideal nearly as closely as himself, the Reichsmarschall couldn't help but admire the man. His slender, compact physique belied the massive strength the Reichsmarschall had seen him display. With his soft though close-cropped salt-and-pepper curls, his thoughtful demeanor, and his unaccented fluency in a half-dozen languages, he had more the air of a Jesuit than a soldier. But the Reichsmarschall had seen him move like a cat, had seen him complete a no-penalty twenty-kilometer biathlon in under an hour when he hadn't slept for days, knew details of the many operations in which he had cheated death. Where others noticed apple cheeks and sadly smiling eyes, the Reichsmarschall focused on the silvery vertical lines of scar tissue that cut through Cordesmann's eyebrow and the corner of his mouth. He'd gotten those scars from a British bayonet in '18, when he was practically a boy. Cordesmann wasn't likely to forget.

The Führer listened, rapt, as the Oberstleutnant detailed the operation he and the Reichsmarschall had designated Über, how it would dovetail with the already-planned Luftwaffe offensive, for instance, and take advantage of the predictable holiday plans of the American Ambassador to the United Kingdom. When Cordesmann finished his presentation, the Führer asked detailed, penetrating follow-up questions: an excellent sign. Then he leaned back in his seat and lapsed into thoughtful silence. The marble room echoed with it. After a minute or two, the Reichsmarschall's left knee creaked audibly, but if the other men took any notice, they were too disciplined to show it. He adjusted his stance imperceptibly, ran his fingers lightly along the golden eagles and black-enameled crosses that adorned his baton's ivory shaft. He pictured the scene from the point of view of an imaginary photographer standing just in front of the office's main door. To balance the composition, he shifted a couple inches to his right.

"You must test the device," the Führer said finally. "I expect a test detonation report by the end of October, and then I will decide whether you may *deploy our precious store of Teutonium. Regarding the rest of the components, I hereby authorize you to proceed with your plan." He fixed the Reichsmarschall with stern eyes. "We are taking a serious risk here, you understand. I would prefer that London be undamaged when I arrive. And we do not want to give the world premature notice of a technology with which we might otherwise surprise Moscow—or even Washington." He paused for a beat or two. "But as you say, we cannot know the future. Let us prepare for all eventualities." The Führer stood. "Gentlemen. Secrecy is paramount if your Operation Über is to succeed. Strictly need-to-know—you understand, yes?" He looked around, made eye contact with each man. "Yes. There is to be no mention of any aspect of this project over the wireless—not even in code. If there is any breach of security, we must abort immediately." Again he gave each man a stern look in the eye. "Well," he said then, and gave a tight little smile. "Thank you, gentlemen, for your dedication to the Fatherland." He saluted; they saluted; he dismissed them. The Reichsmarschall and his soldiers turned towards the door, the Reichsmarschall with a courtly little "after-you" gesture. He was feeling positively cheerful. Just as he reached the threshold, he was stopped by the Führer's voice.*

"Hermann," the Führer murmured. "I will hold you personally responsible for this project's success. Or its failure."

CHAPTER ONE:

HOME FRONT

I had a thought for no one's but your ears:
That you were beautiful, and that I strove
To love you in the old high way of love;
That it had all seemed happy, and yet we'd grown
As weary-hearted as that hollow moon.

—W.B. Yeats, from "Adam's Curse"

ON TOP OF EVERYTHING ELSE, Ian's egg was underdone. Maggie wanted to cry—no, to scream—but instead, as always, she simply sat up a little straighter. She reached for the bell to summon Zofia, but Ian placed his hand over hers. "Don't worry her, love," he said in his I'm-patient-and-longsuffering voice, "it's just all too much for her. She'll learn." Maggie wondered when it would occur to Ian that it might all be too much for *her*, too.

I'm being unfair, she chided herself. Ian really *was* a kind man—it wasn't just for show. And there was so much to be grateful for: the sweet little deal breakfast table that had been carried into the garden to take advantage of the May sunshine; the garden itself, bursting with primroses, bluebells, and violets, ringed round with a froth of elderflower and shaded here and there by tender first leaves of apple;

even Zofia, a good-natured girl and clever, though who could ever fill the shoes of the late, lamented Mrs. Phipps? "You're right, of course," Maggie conceded. "And you're right about the other, too—of course there's no keeping up the scholar's life while the war is on, even I've seen that, not since the young men have all—"

Maggie caught herself, but of course she'd said too much already. A tear ran down Ian's cheek and lost itself in stubble that once would have seemed out of place there. In recent months, though, Ian appeared unshaven at breakfast more often than not, and the pink, raw rims around his eyes had become habitual. Was his dark hair thinner than it had been just half a year ago? Surely it was greyer. "Bother," Maggie muttered to the linen serviette she held bunched on her knee. "I can't seem to say more than three words this morning without putting my foot in it, can I?" In an automatic gesture, she caught at the wisps already escaping from her sensible bun—the soft gray-brown of a dove—and hooked them behind her ear. "He'll be all right, you know." She sought Ian's eye; he wouldn't lift his face to meet her gaze, but when she took his hand across the table, he didn't pull away. "Allie's always been a tough one, ever since he was a little boy. Remember the scrapes he used to get into, in Dublin? Remember when he climbed up and sat on old Lecky's shoulders in Library Square?" A light seemed to come into Ian's eyes, and he let out a little breath that might have been a chuckle. Encouraged, Maggie continued, "That fine old statue was so covered in pigeon leavings, Mrs. Phipps never could get Allie's little trousers clean. Had to toss them out. Remember that?"

Ian smiled, really smiled. His big dark eyes finally met hers. "Or when he took it into his head to be a pirate, and pinched Sean Reilly's old green rowboat?" he said. "We heard the little Reilly girls shrieking, and out we ran—"

"—and there went Allie, off down the Liffey with only one oar. And d'you remember how pleased with himself he was when that fisherman brought him back?"

"Been minding his own business, the chap said, and next thing he knew he was being boarded by Nobeard!"

"We never did get Reilly's boat back, either," Maggie added with a laugh. "Remember how hard he squeezed us? That new one we bought him was well nigh the Queen Mary."

"Allister O'Hare Brooke," Ian growled in a fond mockery of scolding. The merry crinkles around his eyes held for a moment, faded too soon. "How hurt his feelings were, though, when we sent him off to bed without his tea. Do you remember that?" A note of pleading entered his voice, and he seemed to search Maggie's puckish face. "The little scoundrel never could bear to let cooler heads prevail. Adventures he wanted—an adventure every minute. He's on the adventure of his life now, all right, and God knows what it'll cost him." Ian let go of Maggie's fingers, laid his hand on his bad right leg, and tossed a bitter glance at the cane leaning against the table's end.

"Oh Ian. You did your duty and now he's doing his, and it's too late to fight about it. Besides, war's different now—"

"Different, yes," Ian broke in. "Everything's different. For one thing, I was a man, old enough to—"

"—to know better," Maggie put in quietly, but Ian didn't seem to hear. Just as well.

"Old enough to decide," Ian was saying. "Allie's practically a boy, and a brighter one than I ever was. His duty's in Cambridge with the other scientific men, and you know I told him so. Professor Kapur—"

"Professor Kapur taught Allie a great deal at the Mond Lab, yes. But Allie was done at Caius. He finished his degree. He wanted to fight Hitler, he wanted to serve his father's country, he wanted to fly.

Could you deny him that?"

"And send him to bed without his tea, too, in a heartbeat." Ian was angry now. "You don't know what war is, Mags. Oh, sure, you knitted gloves, you sat with the veterans at Dr. Steven's Auxiliary, but—" Ian dug the heels of his hands into his eyes. "You can't imagine the things a man sees in war. The things that can happen to a man. You can't imagine what it was like when that mortar hit us—not knowing if I'd lose the leg—oh, how can we go through it again, Mags? How?" His voice broke. He dropped his hands into his lap and kept his gaze on them. "Churchill is a bloody fool if he doesn't sign an armistice."

Maggie's voice was steady, quiet. "Finish your breakfast, Ian. Your toast'll've gone all hard." She picked up her fork, waited for him to take a bite, then went on. "You know I'm no great admirer of the daring Mr. Churchill." She snorted gently. "But darling, we've all got our own battles to fight. I was just Allie's age when I graduated from Wellesley and went to Trinity, and you know what my parents—what everyone—thought of that. And if I'd told them up front I wanted to study Yeats! Not Virgil or Aeschylus! They'd have laughed in my face. I mean the Trinity people, too. It was good of him to win the Nobel—now I'm prescient, not potty." Ian started to interrupt, but Maggie plowed on. "Besides, if there'd been no mortar, there's no telling when you finally would have found your way to Trinity. Some other fellow might have snapped me up"—she winked—"and there'd have been no Allie. So let him fight the fight he feels he must. If Hitler knew him like we do, he'd be shaking in his jackboots."

Zofia came out just then with Ian's train ticket on a tray. It was a gentle reminder, Maggie knew, that Ian needed to get a move on. She was a good girl, Zofia; what she lacked in English she made up in old-fashioned courtesy. Maggie was even getting used to doing without help on Friday nights—Zofia's diligence on Sundays certainly made up for it. They both were silent until she'd gone, and then Ian said, "So off I go to Hambleden, to fight the fight I feel I must. I'm sure Mother's left things a mess. Machine parts never were her strong suit."

"I'm afraid you're right there, rest her soul," Maggie agreed, crossing herself absently. "But I know Malcolm will be pleased to have his brother in the family business at last, and I'm sure he's done all he could to keep things in line."

"And you'll stay in Oxford—for how long?" Ian asked, using the chair back for balance as he stood and reached for his cane.

Maggie stood too. "You'll scarcely have time to miss me. A few weeks at most. I've some things to wind up, though, at the university, and closing up the house. And there's the Home Guard Women's Auxiliary—I'll have to see how busy they keep me. But then to Hambleden, as I must." Maggie smiled, but Ian saw her eyes sweep along the wall of the house she loved, then dart in the direction of the university where she toiled so diligently. She'd been a Reader for ten years now; Ian was a full Professor here, as he had been at Trinity, though his wife had published twice the work he had at least. That was Maggie, though—never bitter, but also never giving up. It was easy to see where Allie got his fool hardheadedness. "I'll drive you to the station," she offered.

Ian consulted his watch. "Thank you, love, but I've time to walk." The station wasn't far. "It'll do me good." His mouth smiled, but his eyes still were haunted. They embraced a little stiffly, a still-handsome couple in tweeds of brown and green: both of them long-limbed, she slender and straight, he comfortably soft, leaning on his cane. Then Ian was off, walking with surprising speed given his hitching gait. When he reached the front walk, Zofia was waiting with his valise. He took it without breaking his stride, and soon he was out of sight.

Oxford's many bell towers were just striking eight when Maggie arrived, pink-cheeked, at the cozy little shared office under the eaves of St. Hugh's college. The hall was bustling already, though, with brisk young nurses consulting lists and issuing orders to porters, who lugged cartons of supplies here and set up cots there. On the lower floors, the lecture hall had already been scrubbed and draped for a temporary operating theatre, while the classrooms had been transformed into wards. Outside, the college's handsome gardens were full of construction equipment: cottages housing more wards were to be constructed. Maggie's heart rose to her throat to picture all those rooms filled with injured men—boys, really—no older than Allie.

The porters had already taken away most of her things to be stored at St. Hilda's. All that remained to take home were a few personal effects: a copy of *The Winding Stair*, inscribed to Maggie by Yeats personally; a sickly potted fuchsia; a framed portrait of the blind bard Antoine Ó Raifteiri plying his fiddle; a fiercely mustachioed bust of Irish President Douglas Hyde. As she wrapped this last in newsprint and laid it gently in a crate, Maggie said a silent prayer for the health of that "fine and scholarly old gentleman," as Roosevelt had called him. It warmed her heart to think of the President of her native land complimenting the President of her chosen one, the land of her parents' birth and her son's, the wild island that ruled her blood and her imagination. She was dreaming of Ireland as she took down her framed Trinity degree, of the magical Ireland Yeats had brought to life for her as she laid her hand on the matching frame of her Summa Cum Laude from Wellesley, and she was standing caught in that green dream some minutes later when a hand touched her shoulder and a jovial voice teased, "Who was this Margaret Mary O'Hare, then, of Massachusetts?"

Maggie blinked a couple of times and seemed to come to herself. She laughed gaily, "Just another Irish girl from South Boston, surely of no more relation to the scholar M.M. Brooke than my friend Jack Lewis is to the noted novelist C.S." The novelist chuckled and gave Maggie's back a comradely pounding. "What brings you this way, Jack?" Maggie asked, placing the degree in her crate and closing its lid.

"Curiosity, in part," Lewis admitted. "I'd heard that St. Hugh's was to be a war hospital, and I needed to see it with my own eyes. One can't quite imagine a familiar place so changed—one needs to see the cots for oneself, somehow. It all seems quite out of place—as if one opened one's wardrobe one day to find a forest growing there—doesn't it?"

"It does, at that," Maggie agreed, looking around the now-bare little office, its desks and shelves empty, its tiny casement window thrown open. She affixed her address label to her crate, and Lewis chivalrously hoisted it from the desk and set it in the corridor to be delivered to her at home. "And yet," she mused, "there's also something about it that's all too familiar, isn't there?" She allowed Lewis to take her arm, and they descended the stairs together.

"Too true," Lewis agreed. "I'm only grateful that this time I'm too old to see the front lines." His long face, with its drooping brows and playfully flashing eyes, was perfect for affecting exaggerated mourning. With the homburg he clutched in his free hand, he gestured towards the bald patch just beginning on his crown. Becoming serious, he added, "Tell me, though. What do you hear from your boy? He's gone for a—let me remember now—"

"—A bomb aimer with the R.A.F.," Maggie supplied. "Since October. And we haven't heard from him, not for weeks. It's liable to send Ian right round the bend." She shook her head.

"We do worry about our young people, don't we?" Lewis murmured sympathetically, patting Maggie's hand. "As much joy as our child evacuees have brought to The Kilns, I must admit I've been all worry since the moment the first one arrived." He echoed Maggie's headshake. "I'm certain young Allie is right as rain. They do keep a man busy in the service. He probably hasn't had a moment to pick up a pen."

They emerged, blinking, into the sunlight of the college's erstwhile garden. Men with barrows and tractors bustled around like ants. Lewis momentarily let go of her arm in order to arrange his homburg, and Maggie changed the subject deftly. "What's this about your being too old for service? I'd have said you were half a boy yourself. Surely you didn't exaggerate your age just to stay here with us in Oxford?"

"To tell you the truth, I tried to volunteer, but I was declared entirely too decrepit. If you ask me, it seems Britain is rejecting its best resources. Never fear, though," he said with playful bravado, "The Oxford Home Guard has graciously accepted me. Oxfordshire, at least, I shall keep safe! And I hear that you, my dear lady, will also be serving."

"I shall indeed, in the women's auxiliary. Mustn't allow us ladies to think we're *too* useful. Next thing you know we'll be insisting upon entry to all sorts of men's-only organizations." She arched her eyebrow meaningfully as they neared the poplar-shaded intersection at which their ways home would diverge.

"Heavens! One would almost suspect that you were needling me about the Inklings again!" Lewis exclaimed with a twinkle. It was so

like him, Maggie reflected, to wear a merry face in troubled times—
or when gently rejecting a friend's request. It gave the writer no
pleasure to see feelings hurt. "Madame, I am certain that we would
only disappoint you. We are a most staid group of literary men, most
traditional. Why, even now you can probably smell the cigar ash of
our proceedings lingering about me. Surely a mind such as yours can
find livelier company?"

"It sounds to me," Maggie rejoined, "as if your literary club needs
me. After all, 'Though pedantry denies,/ It's plain the Bible means/
That Solomon grew wise/ While talking with his queens.' That's your
countryman Mr. Yeats, you know."

"I seem to have given that country up, dear lady, and become
thoroughly Anglican."

"Much to my despair, and Ronald Tolkien's. Tell me, will you never join us for one of our Sundays at Westminster?"

"High mass and then luncheon with the Cardinal? You may well
convince me one of these Sundays. Though it seems rather out of the
way, doesn't it? Don't they miss you at the Oxford Oratory?"

"I believe they get along just fine without me once every month
or six weeks. And London's not so far to go to keep up with friends as
kind—and as fascinating—as the Cardinal, is it?"

"You tempt me, madam. Ronald tells me your conversations are
quite spirited. But for now"—and here Lewis released Maggie's arm
and gave a jovial little tip of his hat—"I'm afraid I must leave you.
Good morning." He began to stride away, then turned back to her and
pressed the fingertips of her left hand between both of his palms.
"And Maggie, I meant what I said." His face, though still warm,
had become serious, and his eyes met hers directly. "I'm sure your
boy is just fine. But if you should need anything—anything at all—
you know where to find us." His mischievous smile crept back, and

releasing her hand, he finished, "Au revoir for now, dear lady."

Maggie watched his retreating back while filling her lungs deeply with the sweet spring air. Larks sang among the neighborhood's many boughs, and between them, sunshine filtered down like honey. In Hambleden, Malcolm would be showing Ian the business's books by now; she hoped that new work and his brother's company would bring Ian solace, or at least distraction. And Allie, she told herself, was no doubt skimming like a young falcon across the skies of France. At home, her book-lined study, with its gracious view of the garden, awaited her. Her review of *On the Boiler* was nearly done, and she knew now just how she wanted to finish it. As she strolled towards her pleasant task, her fingers idly trailing along a fragrant yew hedge, her eyes scanning the poplar and linden branches for songbird nests, she thought how impossible it seemed that the world should be at war on a morning as beautiful as this one.

CHAPTER TWO:

CONSPIRATORS

Too long a sacrifice
Can make a stone of the heart.
O when may it suffice?
—W.B. Yeats, from "Easter 1916"

"WHATEVER LINE MR. CHURCHILL may draw between evacuations and victories," Cardinal Hinsley opined, his voice wavering, yet still sonorous, "I believe he had it closer to right when he called last week's events at Dunkirk a miracle of deliverance. A third of a million men seemed doomed, but were spared. As Christ teaches us in the Gospel of Saint Matthew, 'Will not the shepherd leave the ninety-nine on the mountain and go in search of the one that went astray? It is not the will of my Father in Heaven that any of his lambs should perish.'" With a lace serviette he dabbed gravy from the corner of his wrinkled mouth.

Signaling with her chin to the footman to refill the Cardinal's water glass, Sister Angela Curran wondered what Mr. Churchill had thought of all the lambs who had perished by his order at the Cup and Saucer. Churchill had been Secretary of State for the Colonies and bent on crushing the Irish Republicans when he'd ordered the British and Free State Forces to shell Millmount Fort, as outsiders called the Cup and Saucer. Angela had been a wee thing, her first Holy Communion just past. She had huddled with her mother and five sisters in the root cellar of their little house in Priest's Lane—in the Cup and Saucer's very shadow—while it seemed the whole world shook. And shake the Curran girls' world did: their father didn't come home that day, and when finally he did it was to lie on a door across two sawhorses in the front parlor with silver coins on his eyes.

"Amen and alleluia," assented Mr. Bellerby, the florid-faced local organist, from the foot of the table; murmurs of agreement ran in a little fugue up and down among the luncheon party, somewhat smaller today than usual. The Cardinal had celebrated Mass, along with several baptisms and confirmations, at the tiny Chapel of St. Genesis in Warborough, and in lieu of his customary gathering at London's Archbishop House he had assembled a few of his nearest and dearest in the dining room of his country estate just outside the village. Hare House was a rustic whitewashed stone place, much smaller than a manor house but comfortable, and its grounds featured orchards, apiaries, and a dairy—all opportunities for the Church to provide employment for the locals. The first few times the Cardinal had dragged her out to this remote waypost, Sister Angela had been annoyed, but today she welcomed the opportunity to observe the work going forward at Hare House.

"We must rejoice at every life saved in this wretched war," put in Mrs. Brooke, who always had something to say. It was her many thoughts on poetry, in fact, that had made her a great favorite of the Cardinal, though Sister Angela failed to understand how a woman who claimed such devotion to Ireland could so blithely marry an Englishman and support the British war effort. With her quick, bright eyes and her drab plumage, Mrs. Brooke put Sister Angela in mind of a great gray heron, though with her constant prattling, perhaps she was more like a myna bird.

Beyond Mrs. Brooke sat Mr. Tolkien. If Mrs. Brooke was a bird, then her colleague Mr. Tolkien, with his childlike cheeks, narrow mouth, and long teeth, was a mouse. He mused, "I agree wholeheartedly. We must strive to preserve life and to perceive and celebrate all that is beautiful within it—and yet we must also not neglect our duty to oppose evil." As Sister Angela pushed creamed chicken aside to reveal the Cardinal's coat of arms emblazoned on her plate—on a field gules, an archiepiscopal cross gold surmounted with a pallium proper—Mr. Tolkien continued, "We must thwart the philistine Hitler, with his murderous perversions of the noble northern spirit—and yet if we make of every German soldier a ravening animal to be slaughtered, are we any better than he is? It is a conundrum that breaks my heart." Mr. Tolkien appeared genuinely to have upset himself, which in turn distressed his wife, who sat across from Sister Angela, at the Cardinal's left hand.

Sister Angela watched creases of worry appear next to Mrs. Tolkien's large, limpid eyes. The woman must have been fifty, but it was still quite evident that she had been a raven-haired beauty. "Ronald," she said in a gentle, musical voice, "Darling, you'll make yourself ill." To the rest of the company, Mrs. Tolkien said, "Our Michael's an anti-aircraft gunner, you know. He's not seen combat yet—he wasn't sent abroad—but now that the fight is coming, as Mr. Churchill said, to our own beaches, our fields and streets, it's terribly unnerving." She fought to regain control of herself and cast a kindly look at Mrs. Brooke. "Mr. Tolkien and I so admire your courage. And, oh! It must be especially hard for you just now, with the loss in your family. How *is* Mr. Brooke?"

While glancing up and down the table and nodding to the footman and maid to clear away the course, Sister Angela asked herself just what it was that made her find Edith Tolkien so gracious. Surely the woman was as effete an English snob as her husband—perhaps worse. At least *he* was from a Catholic family. Somehow, though, Sister Angela's heart always softened for Mrs. Tolkien as it couldn't for Mrs. Brooke, who went on about her late mother-in-law and about her husband's family business in Hambleden while Sister Angela kept a close eye on the servants. As they prepared to bring in the cheese plate, conversation turned to the recent illness of England's Apostolic Delegate. "His symptoms are unaccountable. Simply ... unaccountable," insisted portly Dr. Tibbets. He was the Cardinal's nephew and had recently been elected a Fellow of the Royal College of Physicians; nothing gave him more pleasure than supervising another physician's practice. "Dr. Greenway has ruled out cancers, polyps, and ulcers. He is a careful, thorough man, but he has been unable to diagnose Monseigneur Godfrey's condition; moreover, His Excellency has on several occasions given every appearance of effecting a recovery, only to relapse with little warning."

"You can imagine what consternation it gives the Church finally to establish an Apostolic Nunciature to Great Britain only to have our Nuncio fall too ill to perform his duties. But our own Sister Angela," Cardinal Hinsley put in, "has been a veritable angel of mercy in this, the hour of Monseigneur Godfrey's need." He patted Sister Angela's small smooth hand with his wrinkled and spotted one. "She has visited him every day; she has read to him and tempted him with delicacies she baked herself. You all know how indispensable she is to me, but I fear His Excellency may steal her from me."

"Never, Your Eminence," Sister Angela promised stoutly. Monseigneur Godfrey would have his own assistance soon enough, and frankly, the Cardinal kept Sister Angela's hands quite full enough, thank you. For instance, just now the servants were hovering in the doorway as if uncertain whether to bring in the next course or fly north for the summer. Sister Angela gave them an impatient little nod, and they served each guest a small wedge of Wensleydale studded with blueberries and topped with a dab of golden honey.

Mr. Bellerby emitted a joyous little cry when his plate was set before him. "Your Lordship, how *do* you manage such exquisite cheeses?"

"I don't think I've seen a Wensleydale since before the rationing began," gushed Mrs. Tibbets. "Truly, Your Eminence's dairy is a marvel." Sister Angela would have sworn that whey-faced Mrs. Tibbets was a Wensleydale herself.

"Thank you for saying so, my dear," the Cardinal beamed. "As a matter of fact, I've just begun expanding it. My fond hope is to supplement rations for as many of the children of the diocese as I can. As always, of course, Sister Angela has been my good right hand. Figures, planning, supplies—she is truly gifted, and a gift."

Sister Angela turned her cherubic countenance—full cheeks, beatific blue eyes, golden frizz escaping around her wimple's edges—on the company at large. "You must allow me to offer you all a tour after our meal," she said. "Hare House is His Eminence's pride and joy, and justly so."

Outside, the estate was just coming into its June glory. The apple and plum trees were thickly set with small green fruit and bees hummed busily among the spotted cows grazing in meadows crammed with wildflowers. A large addition to the dairy barn had been framed out, and lumber for finishing it was stacked neatly in preparation for the coming week's work. "In deference to petrol rationing," Sister Angela explained, "we're using traditional building methods." The site was thick with donkey tracks, though Maggie

Brooke, looking closely at the mud and bent grasses, silently noted that at least one truck had driven here recently. "I see Stevens has brought the car around," Sister Angela continued. "He'll drive you to the station. Mrs. Brooke, have we lost you?" The woman was dawdling around the construction site. It wouldn't do to have that sharp beak pecking too inquisitively.

"Heavens! Daydreaming again. Do pardon me," Mrs. Brooke said brightly, trotting to catch up with the group. Sister Angela felt pleased with the show of openness she had made about the construction project, as she felt pleased with the progress that had been evident upon her inspection early that morning. Still, she had to make a conscious effort to ignore the tug of anxiety in her stomach as the Cardinal enjoyed his guests' inane chitchat and she fielded their demands upon his social calendar. She wasn't really able to breathe properly until Stevens had driven the last of them out between the two large archiepiscopal crosses that marked Hare House's entrance.

In Rome it was already hot. The train compartment into which the false priest guided Father DiGangi was even stuffier than the Vatican apartments in which Pope Pius XII had received him that morning. Slats of sunlight had pierced the ancient shutters of the room, illuminating somber wood, threadbare red velvet, and what felt like two millennia of dust. "Bless you, my son, and bless our ailing William," the Pope had intoned, his hands gentle on DiGangi's bowed head. "May God keep and strengthen you both, and may He sanctify this our fledgling diplomatic tie to Great Britain." Father DiGangi lifted his face to Pius's. His Holiness looked grave and tired. His little round glasses echoed the dark circles under his eyes. "The news from

German-occupied lands is very troubling—Jewish businesses confiscated, Jews dispossessed of everything they had, ghettoes being built, rumors of deportations to work camps ... Hitler seems to believe that Christians are superior to Jews, but my son, you know this: the true heir to our Father's Kingdom sets himself above no man. We follow Christ's example when we humble ourselves, and when we serve."

The Pope took both of Father DiGangi's large, square hands in his own. Though DiGangi was a scholar in the Jesuit tradition, he was descended from a long line of Adriatic fishermen. His long, spare frame, his walnut-colored skin, his stiff brush of grizzled hair and the thick crop of stubble his jaw sprouted by early afternoon no matter how carefully he shaved each morning gave him a rough and rustic air that belied his gentle, discerning spirit. Indeed, it was DiGangi's loving monographs on peacemakers—Martin of Tours, Hildegard of Bingen, Erasmus of Rotterdam, Baruch Spinoza—that had prompted His Holiness to choose him for this mission. "Your Holiness," he promised, "I will serve William Godfrey in his illness and assist him in health. I will promote our Church's ties with Great Britain, and above all, I will seek Christ in all things." He bowed his head again, and then, feeling His Holiness's hand under his elbow, he stood.

"Then, Roberto DiGangi, it is with great confidence," Pius said, "that the Holy Roman Catholic Church names you Assistant to the Papal Nuncio to Great Britain, and Acting Nuncio until William's recovery, which we pray will be swift and full. We will remain in close contact regarding the church's response to this disturbing conflict; we must consider the views of the British government and our Anglican brothers and sisters. You have been briefed on the use of the Diplomatic Pouch?" DiGangi inclined his head affirmatively. "And of the Seal that will guarantee diplomatic immunity for you and confidentiality for the messages you and our other official messengers carry between the Holy See and our Apostolic Nunciature in London?" Again the Jesuit inclined his head to indicate he understood, and the sad-eyed Pope kissed him on both cheeks.

Emerging into the sunlight and fresh air along Via di Porta Angelica, DiGangi felt delight at the Pope's trust and curiosity about London crowding out the dread and anxiety provoked by war and by his old friend William Godfrey's illness. Orange and yellow butterflies swirled around the window boxes and planters that lined the street; though automobile traffic was heavy as ever, the sidewalk was spacious and his limbs felt young and energetic. He loped with great verve towards his small office at Sant'Agnese in Agone. Not only would he enjoy life abroad, he would ease poor William's burdens and work for peace and compassion. If Pius XII believed he could make a difference, then it must be so. DiGangi pulled a stiffly-starched handkerchief from his pocket and was just wiping perspiration from his eyes and brow when he felt a heavy, dull blow on the crown of his head. Then everything went dark.

He came to in the broiling backseat of a large sedan. It took him a moment to orient himself even that much—the backseat was dark, its window curtains tightly drawn. DiGangi didn't feel much inclined to pull them back to see where he was—his head was splitting, his eyes squinting as if to push out even the weak light in the car. Anyway his wrists were tied awkwardly behind his back, his full weight pinning them against the seat. His shoulders screamed—were they dislocated? The knot of his hands dug punishingly into his right kidney. He coughed and struggled to sit up but was rewarded with a blow that filled his mouth with blood. "Don't move," a low-pitched quiet voice said, very close to his ear, in an Italian accented only with the faintest traces of German. "Listen very carefully. Your new diplomatic status is more important than you know. Luisa is in grave danger, and you are going to use it to save her life."

His only sister's name went through DiGangi like a knife. She was the youngest of his siblings, newly married, living alone in Termoli since her husband had been deployed to help hold Albania. Big-hearted, joyful, and profoundly innocent, Luisa was the darling of all her brothers' hearts. Danger to her was danger to them all; to protect her was not only DiGangi's desire, it was his duty. "Where is Luisa?" he demanded, earning another blow. The world was spinning; if he could have craned his neck from where he was slumped to see the man next to him, he would have seen him double. And yet when a black-gloved hand appeared before his eyes, holding, in a bloodied handkerchief, a dainty finger ringed with Luisa's delicate wedding band, DiGangi knew it at once. He would have known it among all the fingers of the world. His heart and stomach lurched and he could not suppress a cry that ended in choking sobs.

He expected to be hit again, but the other man refrained. "We had to show you we were serious," the quiet voice went on. "But you can prevent any further harm from coming to her. You must be my partner. If we are to protect Luisa, I must have your full cooperation. If you betray or undermine me in any way, she will pay for it with her life." Several moments of silence followed. DiGangi struggled to take calm, deep, even breaths; he shut his eyes tightly, then opened them, chose a speck of lint on the sedan's curtains on which to focus while the world slowly became single and still.

The voice resumed: "To protect Luisa, you must cooperate with me. Completely and absolutely. Nod if you understand." Di Gangi nodded. "Good. We must be partners. I will accompany you to London, and you will introduce me as your associate. I will share in your work at the Nunciature. From time to time we will extend hospitality and support to certain of my professional contacts. I will—and this is very, very important—I will have full use of your Diplomatic Pouch. You will give me unrestricted access to your Seal for sending confidential messages between London and the Holy See. Your diplomatic couriers will be my diplomatic couriers. Nod if you understand."

Roberto DiGangi's gorge rose. He had not even begun his diplomatic mission and already it was compromised. The prospect of betraying the Church and His Holiness Pius XII—of betraying the causes of peace and human unity—made him feel ill and weak. But he knew that there was nothing so repugnant that he would not do it for his poor, maimed little sister. He imagined her wide, black, liquid eyes—as they had looked when he counseled her against marrying a soldier, and then again as they had looked when she was four years old and skinned her knee. If she were hurt again, he could not live with himself. He could barely live with himself as it was. Fat tears rolled down his cheeks as he nodded once more. "Herrlich. Here, let me help you." A warm, wet cloth gently bathed DiGangi's face. A cuspidor was held beneath his chin. "Spit," the voice said; DiGangi spat. A cup of water was held to his lips, then the cuspidor as the voice directed, "Spit again."

The other man leaned across DiGangi, hoisted him by his armpits until he was sitting up straight. He held the cup to his lips again and DiGangi drank deeply. The man straightened DiGangi's lightweight black suit coat, then directed him to lean forward. "We must be partners. Luisa is counting on you, Roberto. I know you will earn my trust." The rope around DiGangi's wrists tightened until they were almost numb, then abruptly fell away, leaving them free. He raised, lowered, then rolled his shoulders; he chafed life back into his wrists. "Our London contacts will identify themselves when we meet them. Some, I think, will be familiar to you." Now the man reached for DiGangi's hand and shook it as if they were meeting for the first time.

"My associates took the liberty of packing and shipping your bags for you, so we will go directly to the station. I know it will be a pleasure working with you, Father DiGangi. You can call me Father Antonio DiClemente."

The two men rode the remaining five minutes to Roma Termini in silence, DiClemente ostentatiously polishing the lightning mark on the grip of his Walther PPK, loading the gun and stowing it in his coat pocket. He was dressed identically to DiGangi—lightweight black trousers, suit jacket, and shirt; white clerical collar; silver and onyx rosary—though DiClemente looked more natural in priestly garb than DiGangi, who had worn it his entire adult life. Despite the powerful blows he had dealt DiGangi, DiClemente turned out to be a small, elegant man with curling salt-and-pepper hair and a gentle, apple-cheeked face. Not until they got out of the sedan—DiClemente taking DiGangi's elbow solicitously and propelling him to the proper platform, car, and compartment—did DiGangi see the silvery vertical lines of scar tissue that cut through DiClemente's eyebrow and the corner of his mouth on one side.

CHAPTER THREE:
IT'S A FULL TIME JOB TO WIN

Those that I fight I do not hate
Those that I guard I do not love ...
—W.B. Yeats, from "An Irish Airman Foresees His Death"

"BLOOM," THUNDERED LIEUTENANT DAVIES in a voice that rattled the flyspecked light fixtures of the tiny basement office in St. James's Street. Stephen Bloom knew from long experience that Davies's bellowing was intended to be hearty and jovial, but given the frazzled state of the nerves throughout MI-5 this summer, a softer voice might have been kinder. Davies landed a series of pats—whacks, really—on Bloom's right shoulder, already sore from hunching over this desk fifteen hours a day for months.

Bloom blinked up at his superior. Behind his round faux-tortoise-shell glasses, his large dark eyes were red-rimmed and sleep-deprived, and he could see that Davies's looked no better. Both men were equally careworn and unshaven. He started to rise politely, but Davies rumbled, "Morning, old son. Don't get up." Davies cast about for a second chair, but Bloom's was the only one in the police-box-sized office. Neither was there an uncluttered corner of the desk Davies could perch on. He settled for leaning against the filing cabinet that took up the other half of the room. "I've a job for you, Bloom. Strategy's changing around here. Orders of Harker himself." Davies swelled importantly for a moment, then sagged. A rueful smile appeared on his broad ploughman's face. "Or so I was told at morning briefing by my superior, who was told last night by his superior. And so on." He shrugged. Despite his propensity for high-volume bravado, Davies really wasn't a bad sort. "At any rate," he went on, "word is, the House of Commons is kicking up a ruckus about the enemy aliens we've got interned on the Isle of Man. Too many internees, lots of them Jewish, no motive to sabotage the war effort, blah blah. You know the argument." Davies jumped a little, focused a bit more intently on Bloom. "Come to think of it, I suppose it's an argument you've made yourself. A good bit more persuasively than our esteemed MPs, I might add." He shook his head. "Bloom, old boy, I'll never understand why they're wasting a chap as bright as you down in this basement. Nor why you stand for it, year after y—decade, really."

"Oh, well, that's simple enough," Bloom said, managing a twinkle despite his fatigue and jerking his thumb towards the deeper end of the basement corridor. "I stay on because of the typist in Sealed Archives."

"Mrs. Fitzwilliam? The deaf grandmum with the mole on her chin?" Davies asked with evident incredulity.

"That's the one. Don't tell, but she makes the best cup of tea in London. Shh!" he pantomimed looking around for eavesdroppers, "it's a deep secret. I'll not have the whole agency down here competing with me for my cuppa." The men shared a chuckle, and then Bloom asked, "So what's Harker's new plan?"

"Well. That is. It has come to his attention that the enemy is engaging the R.A.F. right here in His Majesty's airspace."

"He's noticed that, has he?" A meaningful look passed between the two weary agents. They were hardworking, capable men, tired of being embarrassed of the agency where they were employed. Privately they'd murmured their relief when Churchill sacked Vernon Kell, but Oswald Harker's bumbling had become, if anything, worse. To remark on it aloud, however, was somewhere between morale-lowering and downright treasonous, so Bloom and Davies limited themselves to meaningful looks.

"Mmm. We would seem to be next on the Führer's invasion list. So the Home Guard's role will be increasingly significant. The long and the short of it is, you'll be working with the Home Guard to gather intelligence domestically. This will involve verifying facts, coordinating with our wireless-interception teams, that sort of thing. And to start, recruiting talent. Ah, here are the first dossiers now." To make room for the dolly overloaded with file boxes that nosed into Bloom's door, Davies retreated into the corridor. "Back to catching spies for me, I'm afraid. Preliminary report by Friday? Good man!" he bellowed, and was gone.

Sighing, Bloom started to shove the mountain range of dossiers already cluttering his desk into his dustbin. The first to leave the desk's edge bounced off the bin's rim, though, and fell open to the floor. Picking it up, Bloom was arrested by the profile it contained: a nationally competitive rower, twenty-one years old, who had just taken high honors in meteorology at Newnham College. If she were a young man, the navy or R.A.F. would have snapped her up as an officer. Instead, the dossier indicated that she had spent May and June at her parents' farm in Wales, patriotically knitting socks for the boys at the front. Her reported rate of sock production, Bloom reflected, ought itself to have been award-winning—and yet this struck him as a criminal waste of the nation's human resources.

At random, Bloom began opening other dossiers from his desk, quickly flinging most of them into the dustbin. He saved the files of a Girl Guide leader who had trekked across the German Alps and a young mother who had filed a patent for an ingeniously improved washing-machine wringer. Bloom tore open the top two file boxes from the dolly parked in his doorway. As he'd suspected: the dossiers within belonged to men and boys only. Looking back at the three files left on his desk, Bloom picked up his heavy black telephone. "Yes, Lucy?" he said, recognizing the voice at the switchboard. "I hope your mother is feeling better. Ah, that's good news! Listen, be a love and connect me with Records, won't you?"

It was hours before Bloom paused from his skimming and sorting of dossiers. He stood, stretched, and consulted the only item of his dress that was not utterly plain: his pocket watch, a lovely silver antique embossed with an elaborate Star of David. Ten past eight in the evening. On his desk, next to a tower of unread files, two more towers were growing: healthy, currently interned men who were likely still angrier with Hitler than with Churchill, and robust, intelligent young women whose talents seemed to fit them for responsibilities beyond knitting or scrap metal reclamation. Bloom withdrew a soggy packet of cheese-and-cress sandwiches from his desk drawer and leaned back in his chair.

From a bit too high on the wall, a poster of Max Aitken Lord Beaverbrook's bald head, heavy and gray, loomed down at him. The new Minister for Aircraft Production's cheeks were drawn back in a grimace that Bloom could only assume was intended to make him look friendly or avuncular, but Beaverbrook's heavy, arched eyebrows, combined with the drawing's leaden complexion and the word *urgency* scrawled across its center in blood red, gave him a vampiric aspect—though perhaps Bloom was only projecting. As a newspaper baron, Beaverbrook had screamed, "There will be no war!" from every headline, right up until the moment Churchill had appointed him Minister. Now, the rumor was that Beaverbrook was pushing his men to produce planes at a rate he himself knew was impossible. A great gray smudge stained the poster behind Beaverbrook's shoulder just as the factories of industrial warfare were staining the British summer sky. The slogan that stretched across the bottom band of the poster was distressingly accurate: "It's a full time job to win." But who would shoulder that burden? Famous, powerful men like Churchill and Beaverbrook? Nameless nobodies, toiling away on assembly lines and in cramped basement offices? How much difference could be made by the added strength of Britain's women? Doffing his glasses, Steven rubbed his eyes hard, then lightly slapped blood back into his cheeks. He took his glasses up again and, sandwich in hand, resumed his perusal of the tower of dossiers.

Typing the final full stop of her first report, Maggie Brooke stood and pulled the page from the typewriter with a triumphant little puff of breath. The rest of the typewriters were neatly covered for the evening, the rows of tables tidied and vacant. Maggie brushed a few eraser crumbs from her calf-length khaki uniform skirt. Standing, she was eye to eye with the pencil-gray image of Max Aitken Lord Beaverbrook, whose poster hung among a rank of posters. Their presence in this erstwhile schoolroom was no doubt intended to motivate the Oxford Home Guard Women's Auxiliary. Personally, Maggie preferred the poster next to it, a bold red-on-white cartoon of a comically shocked Hitler standing in a rowboat while a torpedo labeled "The Junk on Your Farm" bore down upon it. "Make Sure They're

Sunk—Bring In Your Junk," proclaimed the headline. Maggie added the final page to her stack of papers, eased the report into a cover, then placed it in the box on the Oxford Home Guard director's desk. She made sure all the lights were out, donned her uniform cap, and locked up the Home Guard Women's Auxiliary room for the evening.

As she strolled home through the rose-scented July dusk, Maggie reviewed the scrap reclamation project she had planned for her unit. The three galvanized steel grain bins that Lord Mitford was donating would yield twenty-two tons of scrap, she estimated. The bolts, nuts, and washers alone would be nearly as valuable as the sheet metal itself. And if Lord Mitford could also provide scaffolding for her girls, they could easily loosen the bolts and cut the metal into manageable sheets. Her report had also included a roadmap of Lord Mitford's estate, listed the equipment the Home Guard would have to provide (blowtorches, visors, wrenches, three lorries, a crane), and estimated that twenty capable girls could have the bins down and on their way to munitions plants in just a week.

Maggie had labored over every detail of the report as lovingly as she ever had over an analysis of Yeats's prosody, and she meditated upon it in her mind now. As long as she could think of man-hours and petrol usage and the safety training Gladys Grimmesby's old father had agreed to give the girls, she needn't think of the silence. But the silence managed to intrude anyway, as always: the aggressively empty mailbox, the telephone's deafening refusal to ring. Maggie had to appreciate the irony: how she'd fought for space and time to herself, to think and work, for all the long years of her career. The discipline it had taken to close the study door, saying, "Not now, Allie. Mummy will play with you after supper." For four long weeks, sons had been writing, ringing, even visiting their mothers to reassure them they had made it home safe from France. And as the four weeks had gone on, other mothers had received telegrams and visits in a more somber key. Maggie held her breath each time a dark sedan, driven by a grim-faced officer, passed along her street—and yet she began to wonder whether it might be a relief to know. What if he had been taken prisoner? Would it be hard labor, or something worse? She couldn't bear it. Counting under her breath, Maggie rechecked her report's figures from memory. Somehow they had lost their power to soothe, though. As she hurried up her front walk, she could feel her face becoming hot. She bustled through the door, pressing her hat and bag into Zofia's hands and ignoring the girl's expression of mingled alarm and concern as she rushed into her study and shut the door.

Maggie wasn't one to stay disarranged for long, though. By the time a quiet knock came on the study door, followed by Zofia edging around it with a tea-tray, Maggie was once again composed. "Thank you," she said, and meant it heartily; she hoped Zofia wouldn't notice the handkerchief lying crumpled atop her unabridged dictionary. Maggie was preparing to take her first sip—Zofia wasn't even out of the room yet—when the quiet was broken by a loud trill from the telephone. The two women looked at one another wide-eyed. The phone rang a second time, but they were frozen. On the third ring, Maggie rose and Zofia hurried out into the corridor to answer.

"Yes … Good evening, sir … yes … one moment … " Zofia covered the handset's receiver and whispered, "Is Professor Brooke." She handed Maggie the telephone and withdrew tactfully.

"Hello, Ian," Maggie said, and then suddenly heard herself burst out, "How I've missed your voice!"

"Oh, my dear, of course," Ian stammered, never one for emotional displays. Then, too, his mother had never had a telephone installed in the house at Hambleden, so he was likely standing in the corridor of his brother Malcolm's place at Henley-on-Thames, with the servants and Malcolm and Eugenia and their son Colin all trying not to eaves-drop. "Hambleden will be much cheerier when you can join me here. Business is strong, though. Malcolm really knows what he's about. And of course, demand at the moment is high. It's all rather bracing, really." Beneath his display of sturdy optimism, Maggie could hear strained threads in his voice.

"But that's not what you rang to tell me, is it? Oh, Ian, please say you've learned something about Allie."

"Nothing definite, I'm afraid. I was hoping you'd have heard from him since you wrote me last."

"Not a word," Maggie groaned.

"Well, listen, my dear. I've made some inquiries. The R.A.F., I'm afraid, has tentatively listed him as missing in action—his Blenheim didn't return from a raid at Sedan on May 14. But"—Ian pressed on quickly over a muffled sob from Maggie—"there was such chaos after Dunkirk, you see. M.I.A.s are still turning up all the time, including airmen. The troops were all shuffled around. He could be in any num-ber of hospitals, or simply deployed to another unit—the paperwork hasn't all had time to catch up. Likely he's just fine, I was assured over and over." Ian made his very best effort to sound as if he believed this last, but Maggie knew his brave front when she heard it. "There's an office in Dover—that's where most of the men coming back landed, if he came back on a boat instead of a plane, and he might have! He really might have. So. There's an office in Dover that did their best to document the men who came through. It's not perfect, you under-stand, but they might be able to help us. Anne is headed down first thing—"

"No. Tell Anne no, to wait. I'll go." Her sister-in-law lived in Can-terbury, no distance from Dover at all really, but this was something Maggie felt she must do herself. She consulted her wristwatch. "I can still make the night train. I'll call on Anne tomorrow evening, when I'm finished in Dover. You don't suppose she'd mind billeting me for the night, do you?"

"She'll be delighted. I'll ring her back at once. But are you sure you can make the trip? Will you be all right, my dear? And can the Home Guard spare you?"

Maggie paused only for a moment to take mental stock. "It couldn't have come at a better time, really. I've just ordered the supplies I need for my first project, but they won't be in until Monday at least. And as for my feelings—it will be a relief to go looking for Allie. I can't stand to sit still and wait a moment longer. Thank you, Ian. Thank you for this."

After Ian rang off, it took Maggie less than ten minutes to pack a valise and dash off a note for Zofia to deliver to the Home Guard office in the morning. As passionately as Maggie wanted to do her bit, she couldn't help suspecting that the Women's Auxiliary was mostly being given busywork to keep worried wives and mothers occupied. She was certain they could spare her for a day or two. Giving her home a last-minute glance-over, Maggie's eye came to rest on a hinged double frame that rested on the parlor mantelpiece. In it were two recent formal photo portraits of Allie: one in his Cambridge graduation regalia, and one in his R.A.F. uniform. Impulsively Maggie snapped the hinged frame shut and thrust it into her valise. Then she let Zofia shepherd her out into the night.

By Saturday morning, both Anne and Maggie were exhausted and discouraged. They'd made the rounds of offices and read lists until their eyes watered; they'd showed Allie's picture to everyone from the clergy of St. Mary's church to the staff below Dover Castle. A pair of hospital nurses thought they might have cared for a young man who looked like Allie, but they couldn't swear to it—and anyway, the patients who couldn't be discharged for immediate duty had been parceled out to hospitals all over England and Scotland. Maggie rose with the sun, early indeed on these long summer days, but she found she couldn't contain her nervous energy. She slipped on her sensible Oxfords, her brown tweed skirt suit. Like Maggie and Ian, Anne kept only one servant—Mrs. Lanspeary, a jovial grandmotherly type—and even she was not yet stirring when Maggie slipped out for a morning stroll. She expected she'd be back in plenty of time for a leisurely breakfast with Anne before the ten o'clock train took her home.

Anne's snug cottage was one among a cluster of ancient white-washed stone cottages on the eastern edge of Canterbury. After only a few minutes of ambling past gardens thick with dog roses and fox-gloves aswarm with butterflies and bees, Maggie found herself in the countryside. Hawthorne and crabapple made tidy hedges along pas-tureland and cereal fields. The air smelled of mist, but the sky was already warm and blue; the only sounds were insects' industrious hum and the occasional far-off tinkle of the bell of a cow or sheep. Maggie stretched luxuriously, beginning with her arms—out, then skywards, her back arched—then moving to her lower back and some deep knee bends. She felt alert; she felt heartsick about her son, anx-ious about the war, the disarray into which her lovely life had been thrown—and yet, this beautiful morning, she also felt alive, fit, al-most young. Among the hedgerow brambles, wild raspberries peeked out invitingly. Maggie helped herself to one here and there as she walked, careful of stinging nettles.

She rambled for half an hour, then set her nose back towards Anne's cottage as the sun mounted. Likely the household would be stirring when she returned. Somewhere far off a cuckoo called, as if to remind Maggie of the time; nearer, chaffinches sported in the hedge and dust-bathed on the road's shoulder. She was in sight—only just—of the roofs of Anne's cluster of cottages when a rumble, as of thunder, made her turn her head to the clear sky. Behind her, far off still but coming fast and flying low against the sun, she could make out the silhouettes of airplanes: three—no, four. She squinted against the early-morning glare. The birds went quiet; again the sound like thunder came, but louder, closer—and then the planes swept over her with a sound like locomotives. As they passed and she turned, she could see that they were dark gray-green, could make out the Luftwaffe's black crosses on their wings. Her blood seemed to freeze in her veins. The Germans, here! It seemed unreal.

As quickly as the planes' sound had died down, it rose again. At the edge of her field of vision, Maggie could see the four shapes banking together, graceful as a flock of starlings, towards the south, then back east. A new whine rose in her right ear until it was all but unbearable: three Hawker Hurricanes appeared from the north in pursuit of the invaders. It was all Maggie could do not to cheer. Instead she stood frozen like a deer on the road's shoulder, her hands clasped under her chin, her face to the heavens. The air was quiet again for thirty seconds—sixty—ninety—and then from the north came three more British planes, the spots on their flanks and wings striking Maggie as proper, natural, almost friendly.

She couldn't have said how long she stood waiting after the sky cleared—two minutes? five?—but when the excitement seemed to be over, Maggie started walking again. She didn't want her absence from the cottage to cause Anne or Mrs. Lanspeary any alarm. But hardly had she taken a step when the distant thunder and whines began again, and then the sky seemed to split open. From the south the four Luftwaffe planes returned, three Hurricanes in hot pursuit. Maggie could see little explosions happening on the Hurricanes' noses and understood that this meant that they were shooting. The two hindmost gray-green planes peeled away from their formation, circled back to engage the Hurricanes—but those, too, were turning, the whole arrangement becoming chaotic, planes chasing one another like quarreling crows but thunderously loud. Where were the other three Hurricanes? Just as Maggie thought to wonder, they appeared from the west, banked south practically over her head to join the fight she could no longer follow with any certainty. It didn't occur to her to run away, to seek shelter, to cry a warning. She simply stood, transfixed.

The fighting went on what seemed like forever—later she reckoned it was twenty minutes or so. Sometimes the planes drew closer to her, sometimes farther off to the east, north, or south. The planes reminded her of young dogs, running and nipping one another's flanks; she had to remind herself that this was a game played in deadly earnest, one she prayed her Allie was playing now, would play again. She was finally shaken out of her still posture of watching when, in a burst of orange light, one of the planes caught fire. The whole pack of them were too far away, too east-south-east in the morning glare, for her to tell which one, which side it was on. But they were coming closer, all of them, their thunder roaring louder and louder in her ears until it looked to her as if the fireball were going to descend on her very head. Only then did she fling herself into the ditch on the north side of the road and cower there, her knees and chest and elbows in muddy water, her hands shielding her head. She waited for the world to stop shaking.

After a while she realized it was she who was shaking. She took a breath, as deep as she could in her crouched position, and listened.

Silence—the petrified silence she'd heard each time the dogfight had moved out of earshot—was replaced slowly by the natural noise of the morning: crickets chirping, bees and birds going about their business. Somewhere close by, a frog croaked, and Maggie nearly jumped out of her skin. Then she laughed, stood, and made what effort she could to slough the worst of the mud off of her skirt and lightweight jacket. There was mud in her shoes: one at a time she took them off and emptied them. Only then did she look around her.

In the big pasture to her north, not three hundred yards northwest of where she stood, the crumpled remains of a green German plane lay burning. Half of that distance was tracked by a long gouge, like a scar, running deeper and deeper into the ground until it reached the crash site. Maggie followed the gouge until she was within fifty feet of the burning plane. She could feel the heat of it against her face as if it were a campfire. She could hear sheep somewhere to the west, but within her field of vision nothing moved. In a few minutes, she could hear steps approaching along the same path she'd taken. A portly fellow about Ian's age appeared at her elbow. "All right, then, madam?" he asked. He was an inch or two shorter than Maggie and wearing all khaki as if he expected to go lion-shooting. On his head he wore a black steel helmet, and on the helmet were stenciled in white the letters O.C. A lanyard around his neck held a pair of field binoculars. "Are you all right?" he asked again.

"Fine, thank you," Maggie said. "Fine." She breathed in, out, in again, steeling herself against her trembling. "Are we being invaded?"

He chuckled. "Oh, I don't think so, ma'am. Not if the R.A.F. have anything to say about it." He motioned behind them, towards the field on the other side of the road, with his chin. "That one's not invading anyone. He and his parachute, full of bullet holes." He shook his head. "Still, it's an unsettling thing. More and more of them flying our way the past few weeks. Me, I'm Observation Corps," he added proudly. "Got a post just yonder, on that little rise. The telephone line comes right to me. I spot 'em, I call 'em in, and our boys in the R.A.F. take it from there. Well, and the fire brigade. I expect they'll be here shortly."

"What if more come? Should you be at your post?" Maggie asked, hugging herself. Despite the July sunshine and the roaring fire, she suddenly had a chill.

"No, ma'am," he said cheerfully. "Joe Fagan relieved me at oh five hundred hours. I'm on my way home for a kip. But I could hardly turn in without having a look at this, could I? Messerschmitt Bf one-oh-nine. The most modern fighting plane there is, this. It's a thing of beauty. Makes you right proud of our boys, doesn't it? Shooting one of these down."

Maggie couldn't pretend to follow his logic, but it didn't matter. She was thinking of something else, her eyes wandering up and down the craft's gray-green body, barely hearing the fire-brigade siren approaching fast from town. "How much steel would you say is in one of these?"

CHAPTER FOUR:

IS LOOSED UPON THE WORLD

Turning and turning in the widening gyre
The falcon cannot hear the falconer;
Things fall apart; the centre cannot hold;
Mere anarchy is loosed upon the world …

—W.B. Yeats, from "The Second Coming"

IT'S A GORGEOUS SUMMER AFTERNOON, and Oxfordshire spreads out beneath the custom-built Heinkel He 111 like the Land of Counterpane: here a bright patch of rye, there a dark patch of forest, the streams all silvery seams running through. It flies toward Chipping Norton in formation with several regulation Heinkels, buried in an unobtrusive position on the flank. The engine purrs smoothly despite the 2-ton payload in the specially-designed hold and the tremor in the hands of the hostaged Czech pilot. Against his heart he can feel the cool of his Svatý Václav medal, the Good King Wenceslaus of his occupied homeland. He moves to raise it to his lips, but the blond navigator growls something at him in German and he returns both hands to the controls. He banks in unison with the other planes, drifts downward with them. The bucolic landscape looks shades of gray through the dark tinting of the Heinkel's custom canopy. Land of the dead. The pilot can smell death, and he knows it has come for him.

Sure enough, from the south and west, British Hurricanes and Spitfires appear on the horizon, closing fast. The Heinkels close ranks, protecting the custom bomber from being shot out of the sky. The formation breaks apart as the dogfight intensifies, but only to draw away the enemy planes. From outside, the custom bomber looks no different from the others: mottled green, crosses on the wings, swastika on the tail. The canopy is a little darker, maybe, though who can be sure? But inside, the German navigator is waiting for his chance. When the fight's confusion reaches a peak, when the bullets are thick, he flips an overhead switch and smoke begins to pour from both wings. The plane descends quickly but smoothly: the pilot is still in control, but only just. Now comes the moment he has trained for, the moment when success will safeguard not his own life, but at least, he prays, those of his captive wife and child. The fields go by beneath them, close and fast. He must land the plane gently enough to preserve the cargo intact, but without putting down his landing gear—it must appear to be a crash.

The Heinkel's belly nearly brushes the uppermost oak branches of the last hedgerow, then sets down and sleds in, digging a gouge deep and short into the pasture. From a nearby coppice rushes a refrigerated lorry, cheerfully decorated with the smiling face of a cartoon cow. "Hare House Dairy," its panels read, and smaller, "Archdiocese of Westminster." It reaches the plane almost before it comes to a stop, backing carefully up to dock with the plane's custom bay. Three men spring out, two of whom are dressed in dairymen's coveralls. They set immediately to work. The third—a priest in clericals, a silvery scar running through one eyebrow and the corner of his mouth— watches them for a moment, then moves towards the plane's nose. A shot rings out, and then the blond navigator swings down into the knee-high grass. He salutes the priest, who salutes back, then places a fatherly hand on his shoulder. The priest is carrying a third coverall; he hands it to the navigator, who zips it on over his flight suit. Then the navigator hastens to help the other two men transfer the plane's heavy, fragile cargo to the lorry. The loading equipment is engineered precisely for this job; the men's movements are swift and practiced.

When the refrigerated lorry is loaded—and it is loaded in no time—the men have one more grim task. Each of the three hauls an inert body in Luftwaffe uniform from the plane's cargo bay and arranges it in one of the plane's seats. Still, by the time all four pile into the cab, the plane has been down for barely eight minutes. "Not bad for the first go-round," the priest remarks in German, consulting his watch. "We'll have five chances to improve our time." As the lorry reaches the gate and pulls out into the lane, an explosion tears through the custom Heinkel. None of the men turns back to watch it burn.

Maggie Brooke and her Home Guard girls were tired and dirty, but flush with the satisfaction of a job well done, when they tumbled into the Women's Auxiliary office. They'd just delivered two Messerschmitts and a Hurricane—well, anyway, the disassembled wrecks of them—to the Vauxhall factory in Luton to be made into tanks. The three Bedfordshire wrecks had taken them all day yesterday and all this morning to take apart and load up, but they brought the team's total up to twenty reclamation projects completed in as many days. Seven of those had been unglamorous farm jobs—grain silos like Lord Mitford's, broken-down combines and cultivators—and one had been an ancient newspaper press, but twelve had been downed planes. The work took their minds off the dread that the ever-increasing Luftwaffe incursions brought with them across England, the plaguing nightmare that they might wake up one morning and find themselves occupied like France. Some of those planes had been bombers—Heinkels and Stukas—and reports came in every day of attacks on airfields and factories.

It was nerve-wracking, but Maggie had to admit that she found the crash sites fascinating as well. Amazing how many downed crewmen survived to be tracked down and taken prisoner; thrilling and chilling to imagine their flights across the channel; intriguing to learn the different types, to see how different planes crashed differently, digging different scars across the fields and meadows. Too, the crash sites were often in out-of-the way, hard-to-reach places, fens and woods and back pastures Maggie would never have seen if her work hadn't taken her there. She relished the challenge of navigating the lorries into difficult places, knowing her labor was turning these smoldering tragedies into British victory. She also appreciated the opportunity, even away from her books, to analyze, to imagine: to exercise her mind. The airplanes seemed to offer opportunities for mental cultivation that grain bins just could not. And they offered her something more: a connection to her missing son. Allie was still out there somewhere, she told herself, and it was her job to take the Luftwaffe apart with a blowtorch just as it was his to take them apart with bombs.

Gladys Grimmesby's crew were just setting out on a call about a Heinkel that had been shot down not far from town. Tired though she was, Maggie felt an irresistible tug of interest. Leaving her girls to type today's report, she tagged along. Gladys was glad of her company—they had taken an instant liking to one another. A pink-and-blonde dumpling of a matron in her late 40s, Gladys had been a schoolteacher before she married, and she had missed it ever since. After both her daughters married, she had given herself over to nearly full-time reading—poetry, prose, classics and pulp with equal relish. That was until she'd joined the Home Guard Women's Auxiliary, of course. She was clever and thorough as a leader, like Maggie, of a small team of younger women—but what she really loved was any chance to ask Maggie about her work as a literary scholar. Her curiosity and admiration were tinged, Maggie sensed, by only the slightest bit of envy. "Come along, you workaholic, you," Gladys laughed. "But on the way you must promise to tell me stories about your glamorous friend, Mr. Tolkien. I've just begun reading his *Hobbit* book to the grandkids."

As the younger women piled into the back of the reclamation lorry, Maggie took the cab's passenger seat and Gladys drove. "Mr. Grimmesby never thought he'd married a lorry driver," she chuckled as the engine rumbled into life.

"It's amazing the things we dainty ladies are suddenly capable of when the war effort demands," Maggie agreed. "It's too bad we're not facing a dire military shortage of literature dons."

"Or cabinet ministers!"

"Now there's a job I'm happy to leave to the boys. Not because they're so good at it, but because I for one would rather shovel coal. But you're a braver woman than I, Gladys. Grimmesby for Parliament!"

"I'd keep that swashbuckling playboy Churchill in line, and that's a fact," Gladys said with evident satisfaction as she guided the lorry onto Henley Road, which led southeast out of town.

"I believe you would, too, and he could use it!" The lorry's cab resounded with their laughter. "Swashbuckling and statesmanship oughtn't mix. Me, though," Maggie gasped when she'd almost got her breath, "I think I'd like to buckle some swashes. There's another job I'd like to see more ladies in."

"I can just see you now," Gladys rejoined. "Brooke of Arabia. A sabre between your teeth!"

"An Isabelle Eberhardt for the new generation," sighed Maggie, her eyes distant. As so often these days, a sadness seemed to percolate below the moment's merriment. "Though I suppose we're on quite an adventure ourselves."

Gladys agreed, "These crash sites send a thrill right up my spine. We rescued a Royal Airman from the last one, did you hear?"

"You did! Who was he? Not a local boy?" Maggie asked, a little fast.

"Oh, now, love," Gladys said, patting Maggie's hand between her gear-shifts. "That boy of yours is right as rain, you'll be hearing from him before you know it. I feel it in my bones, honest." She managed, one eye still on the road, to give Maggie a sympathetic glance and a grandmotherly cluck, then went on brightly. "No, this lad was from up Leeds way. Broken leg and broken ribs, but he'll be all right. Wasn't he happy to see us! The Observer Corps called us up, and we got there before the army or anyone. Carried him out on a stretcher. Gives me a bit of a chill, though. What if that plane hadn't been one of ours? I'd hate to be first on the scene with some desperate Jerries trying to escape." She shuddered and grinned at once, like a kid listening to ghost stories at a campfire.

As Gladys consulted her hand-drawn map and turned down a hedge-lined country lane, Maggie experienced a thrill of her own. "This crash wasn't at Warborough, was it? This looks like the way to Cardinal Hinsley's country house."

"Aye, Warborough, or just outside," Gladys confirmed. "Just between a couple dairy farms, looks like. I love it down here, don't you? Have you been to see the Poem Tree at Wittenham Clumps? A great beech with verses carved in—I used to take my classes down to see it every year, way back when. They loved it. Looks like we're a bit east of there, though—between the Isis Dairy and ... Hare House, is it?"

"Poor Cardinal Hinsley! Planes going down right into his cattle pen! That's his pride and joy, you know, the dairy at Hare House; he's been expanding it to help keep the local children fed. It wasn't two months ago he showed us around the barn he was building—I guess it's done by now."

"Here we are, then," Gladys said brightly, pulling the lorry over as best she could in the narrow lane. "Good of him to crash it so close to the road, eh? Most of them give us quite a hike."

"Yes, good," Maggie murmured, opening her door with a creak and swinging down from the high cab. The hedge—scrubby oaks undergrown thickly with elderberry and brambles—would have deterred any proper prewar matron or damsel, but Maggie, Gladys, and the girls shouldered through stoutly. After their first couple of crash-site adventures, they'd abandoned their pumps and Oxfords for Wellington boots, which kept them dry and resisted brambles and nettles. Scanning the pasture, Maggie laid one hand on Gladys's arm. Pointing with her other, she said, "Better than we thought. See how the road curves round just over there? Look, we can pull the lorry right up to that gate. It'll save us hauling metal through the hedgerow."

"Well, for heaven's ... this pilot *was* a considerate one, wasn't he?" Gladys struck out across the grass towards the crash; it was still burning in spots, but the Warborough Fire Brigade was already there and hosing it down. Most of the plane was thoroughly blackened— it was in worse shape than any crash she'd seen yet—but from a hundred feet Maggie could make out the swastika on its tail. Maggie's eyes traced the short, deep gouge the crashing plane had dug across the meadow, suggesting that the landing's violence owed more to the plane's weight than to its speed, A twinge passed over her. Something here seemed off. But what?

They drew nearer the crash, rubber-smoke and ozone acrid in their noses and eyes. The fire was pretty much out now, though the Fire Brigade continued pouring water onto the steaming wreckage, cooling it so that the women could take it apart without burning themselves through their heavy work gloves. Two firemen were digging a big square pit nearby. As they moved within earshot, Gladys called out to the firemen, "No fugitives from this one, I'm guessing."

One wiry fireman with long, grandfatherly side whiskers separated from the group at the plane and stepped forward and shook Gladys's hand awkwardly. "I expect you're the, ah, the reclamation team, ma'am?" he asked, his pale watery eyes flitting nervously among the girls, a couple of whom trailed Maggie and Gladys while the others, having pulled the lorry around, briskly unloaded equipment. "We've, um. Well. It's an unpleasant subject for ladies, isn't it?"

"That's all right, sir. We're professionals, you can be frank," Gladys assured him.

"Well, then. Er. That is. We've recovered two sets of, er, remains. Ahem. That were thrown clear of the airplane, we believe by the explosion upon impact. The boys are digging a, em. And. We would expect to find two more, er, sets, once the wreckage is cool enough to examine, which ought to be shortly now. So if you ladies will just stand back, we'll ... er ... " But Maggie was already at the downed craft, her sturdy leather work gloves in place, opening its door gingerly, her face turned away to avoid steam burns. "Ma'am!" the nervous fireman called, running over to her. "Ma'am!"

Once the initial burst of steam from the door had cleared, Maggie leaned in and took stock. Her nose definitely registered the sickening-sweet aroma of charring flesh, though there was no one in the plane's navigator's seat. "With that greenhouse nose, this must be an He 111, right?" she asked the fireman, who stood behind her sputtering inarticulately. She cast a glance over her shoulder at him, then turned back to the plane. Gladys's girls were already swarming around with screwdrivers, wrenches, and pliers, removing propellers and doors and ferrying them back to the lorry. Maggie leaned back out of the plane; the air outside was cool and sweet by comparison.

"How would you know that?" the fireman finally choked out. "I really have to—"

"The Home Guard office keeps Observer Corps manuals on hand. I've been studying up," she explained simply. "Besides, I read the papers and watch the newsreels. Is that unladylike?" She strode around to the pilot's side, where young Jacqueline Leeds stood holding the detached door in her hands and wrinkling her pert nose. All the door's glass was smashed.

"The pilot's still in his seat," Jacqueline pointed out, "but I don't think he's going to give anyone any trouble. 'Cept maybe Saint Peter, if he's so lucky." She handed the door off to another girl, then turned her attention to a nearby propeller. Maggie crossed herself as she approached the pilot, who was hardly more than a charred skeleton. Still she had the sensation that something wasn't right. She let the firemen shuffle her a bit to the side so that they could lift him out and into the shallow group grave; they had to fumble a bit to get him out since he was still strapped into his seat. Maggie watched them lay him out in the hole next to the other two. Looking closer, she saw that the side of his blackened skull had a hole in the temple almost as big as her palm; the other side was mostly intact, except that the cheekbone didn't seem quite to connect at its back corner. She couldn't quite put her finger on what it made her think of.

The fire brigade were finished now, and all the plane's crew accounted for, so the men departed and the women were left alone to take care of the plane. It was well past tea-time now, but the late summer light would hold for hours yet. Cows lowed in the distance, and as the smoke dissipated, the normal smells of the summer countryside tiptoed back: hay, manure, tannic oak, wildflowers. Gladys's girls worked hard, and Maggie pitched in, using a blowtorch to carve the plane's body and chassis into manageable chunks once all the easily-disassembled parts had been removed. Starting to work on the plane's belly, she asked Gladys, "Have you done other He 111s? Is this what the crew hatches usually look like?" Gladys came over to examine the gaping hole where twin doors had been removed.

"Now you mention it ... " Gladys mused for a moment, head cocked quizzically. "They do look a little funny. Double doors? You reckon this is a newer model?"

"I don't know," Maggie confessed. "It just strikes me as ... odd. I can't quite say what I think happened here, but this whole crash seems a little ... off, somehow. Don't you think?"

"What do you mean?" Gladys looked grave, interested, though she had a grease smudge over one eye that gave her a funny puppyish look.

"Well ... that pilot, for one thing. The damage to his skull seemed strange, somehow. And the hatches being wrong. And then ... look at the tracks where the fire brigade drove out." Maggie pointed towards a double path of flattened grasses that led towards the gate outside of which their own lorry waited. "But what do you make of *those*?" Maggie's pointing finger swung a few degrees to the right. Once she'd pointed it out, Gladys couldn't believe she hadn't noticed before:

another set of tracks, these deeper and made by wider tires, also led from the crash to the gate. "Was someone else here and gone by the time we came?"

"Reckon the Army came out to check if there were any survivors to capture?"

"Well, maybe," said Maggie. "But if that were so, wouldn't they still have been here when we arrived? After all, the fire brigade hadn't found all the bodies yet when we showed up, remember?"

"Well, for heaven's ... that is a puzzle! What do you think it could mean?" Gladys's blonde eyebrows drew together; her little bow mouth pursed in thought.

"I'm sure I don't know, but we've got to report it to someone who might. Gladys, do you mind if I write up an addendum to your report? We've got to pass this information up the chain. It all just seems too irregular—it—I don't know. My gut's just telling me there's something wrong."

"Well, of course, you should write it up," agreed Gladys. "But as for something being wrong—Maggie, when this summer has anything been *right*?"

CHAPTER FIVE:
OUT OF THE WILD BLUE YONDER

I have looked upon those brilliant creatures,
And now my heart is sore.
All's changed since I, hearing at twilight,
The first time on this shore,
The bell-beat of their wings above my head,
Trod with a lighter tread.

—W. B. Yeats, from "The Wild Swans at Coole"

" ... THREE WEEKS AGO, and we haven't managed to get our superiors to pay it any mind. But it just seems too odd to ignore, wouldn't you say?" Maggie finished her tale all in a rush, then added quietly, over her shoulder, "Thank you, Zofia." She poured the tea—first Gladys Grimmesby's, then Ronald Tolkien's, and finally her own; she handed round the piping-hot scones Zofia had just brought in and beamed as her guests exclaimed over the jewel-like colors of Zofia's quince jelly and apricot jam. "She's going to make jam from our rose hips come autumn, if she can get the sugar for it. That girl is a treasure," Maggie sighed. "I'm just sorry it took a war to bring her to me."

"No doubt that's just what the Home Guard is saying about you, my dear," Mr. Tolkien said, patting Maggie's hand.

"Oh, I doubt it," she rejoined. "They keep reminding me that I'm there to reclaim scrap metal, not to investigate irregularities. Our sergeant keeps making Agatha Christie jokes."

"Oh Lord," Mr. Tolkien groaned. "These bureaucrats. *Perform your function, don't think for yourself.* It sounds as if I've dodged a bullet in not being called up by MI-5's cryptanalysis project."

"MI-5?" Gladys inquired, impressed.

"Well, Mrs. Grimmesby, you've read *The Hobbit.* You know our Mr. Tolkien is an impressive linguist—he's also, by the way, written a simply marvelous translation of *Beowulf* that we can't get him to publish yet," Maggie said, smiling warmly at her Oxford colleague as he waved his hands in a self-effacing gesture. "But I digress. When was it they called? This spring?—"

"Yes, just earlier this year," Mr. Tolkien took up the narrative. "They first called me up and asked whether I would be willing to work in the Foreign Office, you know, in the event of a national emergency." He spread his hands with an ironic half-smile, indicating the current situation. "A couple of months later, they called me in for a few days' training. Most instructive—I found it fascinating work. Brings together odd sorts, though. There was one fellow—a mathematician, very young indeed, name of Turing—" Mr. Tolkien's eyes were distant, remembering.

"Turing! I believe I've heard Allie mention that name. Did he deliver a lecture series at Cambridge last year?" Maggie inquired.

"Could be. Your Allie's quite the young physicist, isn't he? All of those chaps seem quite keen on this fellow's ideas. Intelligence from machines, you know. Which, in a way, is what cryptology's all about." He shook his head. "Anyway, my point is, it was all very interesting. But thus far I haven't heard from them again. And there you have it, ladies," he finished with a showman's smile, "the entire history of my life in espionage."

"I suppose they may call you up yet," Gladys pointed out.

"Oh, perhaps, perhaps not. We shall see. I fear they find me entirely too likely to spill national secrets to entertain charming ladies." Mr. Tolkien winked and Gladys blushed. "At any rate, it seems to me that you two are the ones with some interesting intelligence, if only you could get them to attend to it. That's the trouble with MI-5 these days—if it's not cryptology, they've no time for it. I appreciate the good old-fashioned detective spirit. How long did you say it takes you to get to a plane once it's down?"

"Ah, well," Maggie said. "We reclamation girls aren't exactly an emergency service, are we? But I do like to get there when the scene is fresh if at all I can. Just for my own intellectual satisfaction. Usually the fire brigade is there before us—the Observation Corps calls them first—and sometimes the army, checking for survivors they need to track down and—well—redeploy or arrest, depending on who they turn out to be. But all in all we're usually there within an hour and a half, and sometimes as quick as half an hour."

"And you say that now you've seen a second irregular plane?" Mr. Tolkien leaned in, intrigued.

"Yes," Maggie's eyes sparkled and her voice hushed conspiratorially. "I've been ever so eager to talk it over with Glad—with Mrs. Grimmesby, and here's our opportunity. I shall be glad of your thoughts on the matter, too, Mr. Tolkien.

"It was just yesterday morning. It hasn't been especially busy this week; I had my girls making some calls to local farmers to see if anyone had any junk we could haul away. To be honest, I was about to start on a crossword when a call came in from Stadhampton about an He 111 that had just gone down, so in the lorry we all hopped and were there about as quick as we've ever been to a scene, not more than 35 minutes, I'd say. And Gladys, it just made the hair stand up on the back of my neck—how similar it was to that other one three weeks ago.

"First of all, it was so easy to get to. You know how you take the Watlington road to get to Stadhampton? We took a little lane off that not three minutes, and there the plane was in the field, and a gate right there. Mr. Tolkien, I can't tell you how much doing it often takes to get to a crash site—they go down in ponds, and fens, and the most inconvenient spots. But this one—practically at the road, waiting for us to come and get it. Special delivery. And the extra set of lorry tracks, deeper than the fire brigade's. As if it was carrying something big and heavy that a lorry came and took away. What do you make of it?"

"What would the Germans want to smuggle *in*? Soldiers, sure, but they're not so heavy. Gold, maybe? For bribes? But that would be an awful lot of gold." Mr. Tolkien's eyebrows drew together. "Did anyone escape from the crash?"

"It didn't seem so. We expect an He 111 crew to be four men, and there were four bodies," Maggie said.

"What about the shrapnel?" Mr. Tolkien asked. "Did it look typical?"

"Shrapnel?" asked Gladys. "I'd never have thought to pay attention."

"I've been meaning to tell you about this, too, Gladys, and Mr. Tolkien, you're exactly right to ask. You see, Gladys, usually when a plane goes down, the bombs in the hold explode on impact and you'll see bits of the bomb casing—especially the fins—in the wreckage. Think about it—that's what we usually see, right?" Maggie urged.

"Now that you say so—yes, I suppose that's true," Gladys nodded.

"It occurred to me that night while I was lying in bed that I hadn't seen any sign of bombs in that bomber—neither unexploded bombs nor bomb-casing shrapnel. It seemed so odd to me that I drove back out there early the next morning to double check—and nothing. And this new crash site yesterday was just the same. In these, the fires were just burning fuel."

"Bizarre," Mr. Tolkien remarked.

"And something else," Maggie went on. "I didn't find any bits of bomb casing in that field, but I did find this." She fished in the pocket of her cardigan. "I almost missed it. Out of the corner of my eye I just caught the sun glinting on something, and I thought it might be shrapnel, so I went over to look. It was sort of halfway between the crash site and where they dug the grave, and it was caught on a clump of cow parsley. Look." Maggie produced a bit of metal on a chain, a coin or medallion, mostly blackened. The corner that was still bright carried the letters S – V – A – T. "Do those letters mean anything to either of you?"

Gladys Grimmesby and Ronald Tolkien both murmured their demurrals; there was a quiet moment when the three of them were all sunk in thought. "Did this second plane have the twin-door hatch like the other one?" Gladys asked after a pause.

"I couldn't tell," Maggie said. "The plane was too mangled. But—and this is the spookiest part—the pilot's skull injuries were identical to those on the other pilot. A big hole in the outer temple, smaller damage near the inside ear. What are the chances?"

"Good god. That sounds like the damage from a gunshot, doesn't it? Smaller entry wound, larger exit. And you said the smaller wound was on the side of these men's faces towards the *inside* of the plane?" Mr. Tolkien had been stirring his tea, and now his hand kept on stirring as if on automatic pilot while his storyteller's mind spun out scenarios.

"Mind, you'll spill," Maggie said gently, then remarked, "Perhaps we should be looking for a fifth man, after all—someone in the plane who shoots the pilot. But why? Why would they kill their own airmen?"

"*Why* is not a question often answered in war," Mr. Tolkien observed, "and yet, shooting one's own pilot in the midst of an air invasion strikes me as beyond the usual senselessness. Especially shooting him from inside a plane that's—what? Still in flight? Or crashed, burning, about to explode? It's very strange, very strange indeed. I hope you reported this crash, too, Mrs. Brooke."

"Of course I did, but it was nothing but the usual 'Mind your knitting, Mrs. Christie' from the sergeant. I hate to go over his head, but ... do you think this might merit it?"

"It might, at that. Why don't I put you in touch with my contact over at MI-5? Perhaps he can direct you to more receptive ears. It's worth a try," Mr. Tolkien said, taking another scone.

Maggie had been so absorbed in their conversation that she didn't even hear the telephone ring. But suddenly Zofia was beside her, a hand on her elbow. "Mrs. Brooke, I am sorry to intrude, but the telephone—it is a call from Scotland. Urgent."

Despite the August sunshine pouring through the high windows that lined the hospital corridor, Allister O'Hare Brooke shivered in his thick flannel bathrobe and wool socks. He'd been cold ever since he'd gotten to Glasgow, and he hadn't even been conscious for most of it. The hospital corridors *sounded* cold, with their echoing stone and tile. He held the slender young nurse's arm lightly as if escorting her into a dance, but really he wanted to clutch her to him, to have her hold him until he was finally warm. He couldn't remember her name—Sister Mary Fiona? Sister Mary Fenella?—but he knew that she was kind and smelled of soap and cakes and most of all that she was warm.

"You're remarkably steady on your feet," she said now. "Sure you haven't been practicing when my back was turned?"

He blushed, pleased at her praise despite himself. Three months ago he had been flying, and now they were proud he could walk. It was as if he'd woken up inside some sick joke. *Father was right,* he thought, and was ashamed of thinking it. His father had never wanted to be right, not about this. He breathed deep, composed himself. Took another shuffling step. Willed himself to keep his grip light on her arm, his smile light on his lips. "Where're you from, then? You don't sound Glaswegian."

"No, you're right. Holyhead. And you're from just across the sea from me, aren't you?"

"Dublin, aye." He lit up, genuinely now. "Been away from there for some years. You've a good ear on you, to catch it."

"Not so good as all that," she said, giving his hand a pat. "You can take the boy out of Dublin ... Puts me in mind of a joke. Are you up to it? Not going to break you, am I?"

"No, no, a joke'll do me good. Let's hear it."

"All right," she said, and leaned in so she could speak quietly. "An Irish boy goes into a Glasgow pub. He has a few, starts feeling homesick. Then his ear catches a bit of an accent that seems familiar. He can't be sure, but ... he thinks the three girls at the next table might be from the home country, so he saunters over. Or. Staggers, more like. They're big girls, big farm girls, you know, wide shoulders, stout. And he says, 'Pardon me, but is any of you ladies from Ireland?' 'No, they say, Wales.' Stop me if you've heard this one."

"I haven't. Go on," he said. They kept walking, slow and steady down the corridor, their heads close.

"'Wales,' these big girls say, 'Wales.' And so *he* says, 'Beggin' your pardon. Is any of you *whales* from Ireland?'" She waited a beat, then added, "And that was the last thing he remembered." She watched him closely as he laughed, then winced. Reflexively his hand went to the bandage around his head. "Now don't be messing about with that," she said, swatting his hand away gently. "Remember what the doc said, you've got to be tender with it for a while yet. I guess it was too soon for a joke, after all."

"No," he said with a weak grin, "no. It was just what I needed."

"Good," she said, guiding him around a corner, down another long sunny corridor. "The telephone's not far now—just down here. So it's Dublin you'll be calling, then?"

"No, no." His grin was rueful. "We're complicated. Or maybe not. Mother and Father both teach at Oxford. They met at Trinity, Dublin, and that's where I grew up, but it's been Oxford for a few years now. Father grew up not far from there. Wanted to get back to his roots, but all I could think of was flying. Flying, flying. And you see where it's gotten me."

"Well, I think you're very brave." She patted his hand again, and he breathed the clean vanilla scent of her. Suddenly he missed his mother horribly, viscerally, as he would have missed his lungs or his stomach. "Wounded in combat," the nurse was saying. "I'd say that makes you a hero—Oh! Don't cry." She pressed a dry square of cloth into his palm, and he raised it to his cheeks.

It took him a moment, but he composed himself. "I can't tell you how grateful I am," he said. "You've been so kind."

"Not at all," she said. "We all have our duty to do. But truly, this is my pleasure. When you came in, we didn't think you'd live—you were so burned, your head was so banged up—we didn't know who you were, and when you first woke up, you didn't know either. And now look at you! You'll be back in Oxford in no time."

"I can't go yet, though. I can't go until—"

"Hush. You're fine. I don't know that we've ever had a patient as strong as you! You'll go when the doctor tells you to go, and that's that." Her voice was emphatic. After a pause, she spoke again, more gently. "You know there aren't any guarantees. You're a miracle already—conscious, walking, joking. Even still handsome. Do you know how lucky you are, with no burns on your face?" He was blushing again, furiously. "So. As your head trauma heals, maybe your sight will come back, and maybe it won't. But where would we be without Homer and Milton? Without Leonhard Euler and Saint Lutgarde?"

He smiled a little. "Nicholas Saunderson."

"Tell me about him," she said.

"He was a friend of Isaac Newton's. A mathematician at Cambridge. Blind from childhood." He laughed. "And Antoine Ó Raifteiri. Anthony Rafferty, an Irish fiddler. My mother's mad for his poetry."

"So, there. You see," she said. "You're bound for great things, one way or the other. And there aren't enough beds in this hospital for you to hang around until you're sure. They'll be sending you home within the week, mark my words. So here we are at the telephone. Flying Officer Allister Brooke, call your mother. That's an order."

CHAPTER SIX:
HOME AGAIN

Nor law, nor duty bade me fight,
Nor public man, nor cheering crowds,
A lonely impulse of delight
Drove to this tumult in the clouds ...
—W.B. Yeats, from "An Irish Airman Foresees His Death"

FOR THE HUNDREDTH TIME that afternoon, Maggie paused by the front parlor's windows and craned her neck to look up and down the street. The smells wafting out from the kitchen were delicious: Eugenia and Malcolm had sent up some of their ration coupons ahead of time, as had Anne, so that Zofia could create a true feast for Allie's homecoming party. But today Zofia had resisted all of Maggie's anxious offers of assistance and finally had chased her away from the kitchen entirely. It was for the best: Maggie knew that she was more of a hindrance than a help in the kitchen, but she was too excited and nervous to sit still, to work, even to read. For the hundredth time that afternoon, she adjusted the arrangements of home-grown dahlias and butterfly-bush on either end of the mantelpiece, on the little end table, on the dining room table and sideboard, on the hall tree in the foyer. For the hundredth time she consulted the train schedule to be certain she would be at the platform and waiting when her son came home.

Finally she stood still, closed her eyes, breathed deeply. She performed her very best and most meditative calming ritual: "I will arise and go now, and go to Innisfree," she recited, and as she said the words she allowed them to paint a glowing picture in her mind. She imagined herself standing up and walking outside, and then magically walking towards a rowboat docked at a lakeside. In her mind's eye she saw the island growing larger as she rowed, the little wavelets on the cold Irish water. She saw herself landing, roaming the island, gathering mud and sticks for the construction project in the poem's second line: "And a small cabin build there, of clay and wattles made." She made herself imagine every action, not skip over or speed past anything: as the poem says, peace comes dropping slow. She made herself go slowly. She made herself love and paint in detail each bean-vine, each honey-bee, each cricket and linnet. The fuzz on the leaves and pods, the delicate insect legs, the quick eyes, the overlapping feathers. By the time she got to the final line, to the "deep heart's core," her heartbeats were measured, her mind still.

She had just thought of going to her study to write a bit about Yeats's prosody—about the poem's progress from that first line's crowd of unstressed syllables to the calm space around the final three stressed, booming words—when the door was opening and in tumbled rugged Malcolm and his wife Eugenia, her ample curves swathed as ever in a mumsy floral print; cheerfully sunburned Colin; and Ian, all in what felt like a rush. The house had been so quiet this summer, Maggie and Zofia both so solitary in their separate domestic spheres, and suddenly the place was filled up with the noise and warmth of family. Maggie was kissed and embraced, hats and summer jackets were arranged on the hall tree, valises deposited in bedrooms, a bottle of Malcolm's redcurrant wine presented and admired. It all went merrily and fast as a stream singing over stones. More guests arrived: Cardinal Hinsley with Sister Angela Curran at his right hand; Anne, bearing a basket of wild mushrooms; Mr. and Mrs. Williams, the parents of Harry Williams, Allie's closest chum since second form. Harry was a midshipman now in the Royal Navy. The house filled with conversation; Zofia circulated, distributing drinks, and Eugenia's girl Sylvia assisted her. Ian played the welcoming host graciously; Maggie did her best, but her heart was in her throat, and every minute or two her eyes stole towards the tambour clock on the mantelpiece. Finally it was time.

Out of long habit, Maggie slipped behind the wheel of their blue Morris 8 and Ian took the passenger's seat. Before she could start the car, Ian pressed both of her hands in his for a long moment. "It's good," he said, his eyes holding hers. His face looked more lined than at the beginning of the summer, though he was more carefully shaven today than she'd seen him in months. He wore his customary brown tweed suit with a handsome plum-colored silk bow-tie she didn't believe she'd seen before. She wondered whether it had been his father's. His big dark eyes were bright, though whether with joy or tears Maggie couldn't tell.

"It's good," she echoed. They stayed that way for another moment, and then she backed the car out of the carriage-house and onto the tree-lined avenue.

The station was crowded, but then again, no more crowded than usual. Southbound travelers waited on the platform with valises and duffels; parents, wives, husbands, and sweethearts stood by with dogs on leads or florists' bouquets to keep their waiting hands busy. On a bench, an old grandmum and a pretty young woman, heavily pregnant, sat knitting in unison. The enormous clock on the platform

indicated that—assuming the train was on time—they had two minutes to wait. As they mounted the platform stairs, Maggie noticed that
Ian's limp seemed worse. Still, his hand on her elbow tried gallantly to
offer support rather than lean on her. He held his cane smartly under
the arm that held hers—he never leaned on it when he was walking
with a lady. She patted his hand. He was a good man, a good husband.
His familiar scent—a blend of tobacco, pepper, and warm horsehair—
soothed her. "How long will we have him?" Ian asked. "Did he say?"

"He didn't," Maggie said. "He just said he was coming home to
convalesce. He didn't make it sound as if it would be long. After all,
if they're discharging him—if he can take a train all the way from
Glasgow—"

"Well, but. They're sending another young man to escort him.
Does that mean he needs assistance? Is this chap coming to push
his wheelchair? Are they afraid he's likely to faint?" Ian looked troubled, rubbed the back of his bad thigh absently. It was something he
did when it hurt him but he wasn't quite conscious of it, or when he
didn't think he was thinking of his old injury.

Maggie took his hand and said, "He told me he'd walked from his
bed to the telephone. He said it was the first time he'd been out of
bed, but that he was getting stronger every day. That was ten days
ago." Suddenly all of Maggie's resolve broke, her patient strength, and
she let out a great shuddering sob and turned her face to Ian's lapel.
"Oh, Ian. Our boy. Our little Allie. I was afraid—" She couldn't finish
the sentence aloud. Ian's arms went around her for the thirty seconds or so it took her to recover herself. Then she took out a dainty
blue eyelet handkerchief, dabbed her eyes, and blew her nose like a
ploughman. She laughed ruefully, but didn't look up. "What a mess I
am," she said to Ian's shirtfront. "I couldn't let you know how afraid
I was—I couldn't let myself—" Ian shifted his cane over so that it

could support him, then put his free hand under Maggie's chin and raised her great gray eyes to his dark ones. A few stubborn curls were escaping, as usual, from her bun, giving her a soft and girlish air despite her height, her gray, her formidable self-control.

"Of course you were terrified, my love," Ian said. "We both were." He laid a kindly hand on her cheek. "Poor Malcolm's been trying so diligently to teach me the business, but I've spent the greater part of every day on the telephone with offices, hospitals ... if you hadn't gone to Canterbury, I would have. I've been to Leeds—lots of boys were evacuated there from Offranville and Dieppe—but I couldn't have you know how sick I was, how frantic ... " He closed his eyes for a moment, covered his mouth and cleared his throat. Then he fixed her again with eyes both solemn and joyful. "But that's over now. Our son comes home today, and we'll keep him for as long as we can." Ian tucked a curl behind Maggie's ear.

He looked as if he were about to say something else, but at that moment the train's whistle blew, at a little distance but approaching fast, and soon the tracks and platform were shaking with the train's thunder. This was the moment when, up and down the tracks, those waiting divided themselves most clearly into travelers and greeters: the former bustled around madly, loading themselves up with bags and newspapers, taking leave of friends and family, checking the benches and the floor for forgotten items, while the latter stepped back a bit, drew themselves up taller, tried to be visible and to contain their peaking anticipation. Like the other greeters on the platform, Ian and Maggie scanned the windows of the train pulling in as if those smoke-streaked portals were likely to yield a hint about which car contained their precious one. They held themselves back from the mad rush as conductors opened the doors and placed stepstools strategically, as porters applied themselves to the baggage cars, and as embarking passengers drew around, jostling to be first to board (except for the few travelers who hung back to prolong their farewells: young men in uniform mostly, kissing their sweethearts goodbye or receiving the final blessings and admonitions of grave-faced parents).

Ian and Maggie held themselves aloof a bit from the confusion, letting only their eyes rush about the platform; it wasn't until the train began to pull away again, its windows now open and travelers leaning out to blow kisses or wave goodbye or just to take one long last look, and the platform cleared a little that they spotted them: two tall and slender young men in blue uniforms and caps, flying badges spreading wings across the left breast of each. One sported a sandy blond old-fashioned mustache; his fingers rested lightly on the elbow of the other, dark-haired, who wore heavy round glasses with smoked lenses. "There he—" Maggie began joyously, then broke off and looked at Ian.

"But Allie doesn't wear—" Ian was saying, and then he returned his wife's gaze. The question in her eyes was reflected in his.

Allie could hardly believe the train trip's sheer tediousness.

When he thought about it, he supposed it made sense: seven hours in a stuffy compartment with no scenery to look at and nothing to read. He had hoped that Flying Officer Bartholomew Greeley would be good traveling company, but it turned out that Officer Greeley cared for little besides polo and the genealogies of his father's polo ponies. Having undergone a series of surgeries to remove shrapnel from his shoulder and back, Officer Greeley found himself feeling remarkably well; he was looking forward to his three weeks' leave for recuperation at his parent's Oxfordshire estate largely because it would afford him an opportunity to become acquainted with his father's handsome new bay. At Allie's prompting, he conceded that it would likely be agreeable to see his fiancée, especially if she would consent to ride out with him—though he had to confess that she had been a bit reluctant to do so in the past, and that in fact on one occasion his horse had bitten her.

"Just a love nip, really—it hardly even left a mark—but she really didn't take it very well." When Allie inquired what had brought Officer Greeley and his love together, he was silent for a moment. "Well, her father and mine were school chums, weren't they?" There was another pause. "I suppose I've planned to marry her since … well, I don't know. Mother and Father always talked about it. And then when old Adolf started misbehaving and I signed up, Father suggested that the time had come to propose, so I did." Allie could hear Officer Greeley shifting in his seat. "Do you ride at all, old chap? Play any polo?" Allie confessed that although he had taken a riding lesson or two in his life, he had never played polo nor even seen it played. "Never seen it? You haven't lived, man. You must come round next week—the University club is putting on a match, despite everything—"

"I'm certain I should love to see it," Allie snapped, bitterness growing in his voice. "The sun on the ponies' flanks, the pennants, the fancy maneuvers, the team colors and all—I'm sure there's no sight like it in the world. My eyes will no doubt be dazzled." The last sentence he spat in a voice like a curse.

But Officer Greeley, when he replied, sounded mild. "Quite, old chap. Quite."

Allie made his mind up then to go to sleep, which he wasn't able to do, or to pretend to sleep, which he felt he did quite admirably, though his neck kinked and his head—unbandaged now at last—throbbed.

Not that his pretense of sleep mattered: Officer Greeley nattered on about Gerald Balding and Cowdray Park and how many hands at the withers all the way until the train pulled into the station at Oxford. Then Greeley took Allie's elbow—quite chivalrously and gently, Allie thought, the future Mrs. Greeley would have nothing to complain of there—and guided him out of the car and onto the platform.

There they stood for a minute or two, activity swirling around them. Allie could hear porters breathing hard as they heaved luggage about, feet rushing to find the proper cars to board, fabric on fabric as people embraced their hellos and goodbyes, and everywhere the shouts and murmurs of human voices, buying, selling, greeting, sending off, asking directions, praying. A dog barked, and farther off, automobile traffic ebbed and flowed through the city. The tender scent of fresh-cut peonies broke through the station's miasma of coal dust for a brief, blessed moment, and Allie wondered who had cut and gathered them, with what love, for whom. In the mad swirl of sensations that surrounded him here on this platform, Allie was grateful for Officer Greeley's protective hand on his elbow, and at the same time he hated himself, and Greeley, for that pathetic gratitude.

And then the voices and smells surrounding him were the ones as familiar as his own—his own name belled out in his parents' duet, his mother's scent of nutmeg, his father's, for some reason, like a very clean stable—*Greeley ought to like him for that,* Allie thought—and then his face was pressed against two different textures of wool tweed, warmer than the August evening air that surrounded them, and he let himself be enfolded by relief like a great blanket. It was the sensation he'd felt a thousand times as a little boy, when his adventures went on a little too long and he was frightened, but thrilled too, feeling that this time he was truly on his own, the lone hero facing untold dangers, hunger, and fatigue—until at last, now as ever, he was rescued by this pair, bundled up and brought home for warm milk and a good sound scrubbing by Mrs. Phipps.

His mother had him by both hands and his father's hand rested on his shoulder, and as their initial flurry of embraces subsided, his parents turned their attention to Officer Greeley. "Maggie Brooke," his mother said; "I'm Al—I'm Officer Brooke's mother. I hardly know how to express my gratitude to you for bringing home my son." As his father echoed her and Greeley made little self-deprecatory noises, Allie felt himself filled with a nameless fury. A moment ago he too had felt grateful for Greeley's company and steady hand, but suddenly it felt demeaning and infinitely unfair that this thundering bore, who after all had done nothing more heroic than get himself blown up and then share a train compartment with Allie, should be thanked and praised in the same terms he had heard again and again when he was brought home by a farmer or a policeman or a thrillingly smelly fishwife. Once again, he had been whisked from the role of the lone hero into that of the rescued damsel, while some minor character in his saga was heaped with heroic praise. His head, neck, and shoulder throbbed, and he could feel—to his great shame—big hot tears welling in his eyes. At least the dark glasses would hide them. "You must come raise a glass with us," his mother was saying, "we're celebrating safe homecomings tonight."

Before Greeley could get through his polite demurral, Allie growled, "Let's just go," turning curtly away before he realized that he was powerless to stalk off as he had intended. And then from the jumble of sounds and perfume he knew that Lord and Lady Greeley had appeared, and there were introductions and congratulations and thanks all around again while Allie stood with his back turned, sulking like a little boy.

"Allister, son," Ian called out to him after a few moments. "Come shake hands with Officer Greeley's parents." Allie did so, politely, ashamed to have his manners directed like a child's. He managed to get through polite thank-yous and goodbyes and then his parents guided him out of the station and to the car. They put him in the passenger's seat and his father sat in back, leaning forward between them, as his mother started the car and put it in gear. "Why didn't you tell us?" Ian asked, but Allie made no reply: he didn't know what to say. They were silent for the rest of the mercifully short car ride; Maggie let Ian and Allie out in front of the house, then pulled around to the carriage house to put the car away. Ian started to take Allie's elbow, as he would have taken Maggie's, but he thought better of it. He clapped Allie on the back, then propelled him forward with a hand between his shoulder blades. He cleared his throat, then said, "What you can't see is that there's a great banner hung across the face of the house, welcoming you home." Ian described it—light Air Force blue with the Union Jack in the canton, the R.A.F. roundel's concentric rings to the right, and between, "Welcome Home Flying Officer Allie" in foot-high dark-blue lettering. Allie's seventeen-year-old cousin Colin had spent a week on it, bursting with pride that it would be the first thing returning Allie would see. "Watch here," Ian said, "we're getting close to the front steps." Allie fumbled a little, feeling his way, but made it to the top on his own.

From there, Allie could hear jazz music playing on the gramophone and the gentle buzz of conversations inside the house. "Who's here?" he asked, then stammered, "I didn't realize—I didn't want—"

But it was too late. Ian threw open the front door, and the conversations ceased. Then he announced, "Let's welcome our hero home," and everyone applauded.

The noise of conversation resumed around the room, but tentatively, as Allie was handed round for hugs. But as he encountered each person, he could hear shock and confusion meeting forced heartiness in almost every voice. One exception was Cardinal Hinsley, who merely placed his hand on Allie's head and intoned over it, "This son of mine was dead and is alive again; he was lost and is found," provoking a chorus of reverent *amens*.

Another was his cousin Colin, whose voice was pure awe. "What's it like, flying, Allie? I mean really, what's it like?" he asked, then murmured encouragement as Allie went into a trance of beautiful memory—the freedom, the speed, clouds and sunlight and the remote toylike world below. Colin couldn't get enough. "You'll come down to Henley-on-Thames, won't you, or to Hambleden? It's never so jolly as when you're there, Allie, truly. You used to get me into such glorious trouble! No one else thought up the games you could. And now—think of the girls who'll want to chat up a real R.A.F. bomb aimer! We'll be the hit of the Henley pub. Oh, do come down and tell me everything you've done."

But too soon he was whisked away to Sister Angela, to Aunt Anne and Aunt Eugenia and to Harry's parents. He could hear the horror in their voices, and the pity, and it filled him with a rage that choked him, and a black despair too. He was an officer in the Royal Air Force, a skillful bomb aimer, a promising scientist, a young man with his whole life ahead of him—and then he imagined those years and days and hours opening blank and black and insufferable as train compartments, pitying whispers at his back and ginger fingers at his elbow, and never rowing a boat down a river or catching an updraft with a plane, never another adventure again. It was bitter as pitch and it made him want to retch and spit.

His mother took his hand and guided him to his place at the dinner table; as the other guests took theirs, he overheard Mrs. Williams whispering, " ... can hardly demand a speech from the poor fellow, can we, under the ... "

It was too much, simply too much to be borne. His hand found his teaspoon, his empty wine glass, and he tapped for their attention, though he didn't know what it was he wanted to say. The room was silent for a moment—it seemed to him that they were all holding their breath. Then it came out in a rush. "You want a speech—you all *deserve* a speech from the returning hero. The fine flying man come home to you, or most of him. What's left of him. The fine young man you were so proud to see off, or maybe who you wished you could keep home. Well, here I am. I've bombed the Nazis in Belgium. I've been to France, and I've been to the clouds! I've been a bird in flight. I didn't do it for my country. I didn't do it for my God, and I didn't do it for you. It was *dulce et decorum*, all right, but this was not"—he took his dark glasses off and held them aloft; without them, his eyes were as large and blue as ever, though fixed now on some horizon above the heads of his rapt, horrified audience, far beyond the house—"This was not *pro patria*. This was because ever since I could talk or walk, ever since I can remember, I've wanted to be out there in the world. Ever since I can remember, I've wanted to be a man. To be a man! To make my own way, to understand and to be free. And so I went out, and so I come home to you today almost whole, but in defeat. I have come home at last to submit to being a boy. A boy at best. No more running off, no more adventures. I shall sit in the parlor with my hands folded and be your good little Allie at last—" He broke off, choked and sobbing. Hands out before him, he found his own way quickly to the door. Turning, he spat, "I shan't frighten you any more, Father." His footsteps receded down the corridor; there was a muffled crash, the indistinct sound of his voice, and then his steps retreated up the stairs.

For a moment a spell of paralysis held over the room. Then Zofia, all innocence, came in with the soup and was bewildered to find the guests all standing. Sister Angela Curran had the Cardinal halfway out the door. Maggie and Ian had both started towards the stairs, but Malcolm motioned to them to wait. "I'll go talk to the lad," he said simply.

Maggie turned to Ian with a groan. "How could we have been so stupid?" she asked. "It was too much for him, it was all too much. Oh, why did we have to spring a party on him tonight?"

Ian's every muscle, meanwhile, was taut with barely-controlled rage. "How could we have known!" he bellowed. It wasn't a question. "He told us he was all right, that he was coming home. Of course we had a party. He didn't tell us, he didn't tell us a thing. What did he expect?" Then the fury went out of him and he sank back down into his chair at the dining table. He repeated his question softly, but Maggie, leaning near, her hand on his shoulder, heard him. "What did he expect?"

Upstairs, Malcolm tapped lightly at the frame of Allie's bedroom door, though it was open. Allie had flung himself facedown across the bed, but he started up at the sound and pressed his fingers into the corners of his eyes. Malcolm held out a handkerchief, then thought to say, "Here you go, son. Dry your eyes." He pressed the handkerchief into the hand Allie held out, then sat on the bed next to his nephew. They were silent together for a long moment.

"I've been terribly rude," Allie said. "I'm so ashamed. It's not their fault." Allie controlled his voice with an effort. "Only I'm so—I'm so—I don't even know." He shook his bowed head. "It's called corti- cal blindness. Maybe it's permanent, maybe it's just while my brain is swollen. But it's been months, I'm starting to lose hope. My eyes are fine, it's the nerves that connect them, do you see? Each day that goes by and I'm still blind, I've a little less hope that one day, I'll wake up and see again. We were over Sedan, in Ardennes, just south of the Belgian border. I was on my bombsight, ready. Then Göring's boys jumped us from above—the 109's cannon—they're fierce, they tore us apart. I don't really know much, I don't remember anything. When they found me I was unconscious and naked. No one can understand how I survived the crash at all. I was barely breathing. And now, when I think of it, when I think of all I'll never do again, all I'll never do at all, I still can't breathe. I feel I'll never breathe again." He buried his face in his uncle's handkerchief.

Ian's voice floated through the floorboards, muffled but audible, enraged. "He should never have gone!" Maggie's voice responded in soothing tones, her words indistinguishable. "His duty was in Cambridge, with the science men at Mond! A mind like his should never have been risked—" Maggie's quiet tones cut in again but were silenced by Ian's heavy, uneven footsteps. "The adventuring of a *boy*!" he roared, and the front door's slamming shook the house.

Malcolm put his hand on Allie's shoulder for a long moment, then pulled him in close. He held him as he hadn't held him since he'd been little. Malcolm remembered Allie blue and shivering, refusing to be finished swimming in some Scottish loch one summer, insisting that he wasn't cold. He remembered wrapping Allie in a big soft towel and holding him just this way until he was warm.

CHAPTER SEVEN:

ALLIES

And for an hour I have walked and prayed
Because of the great gloom that is in my mind.

I have walked and prayed for this young child an hour,
And heard the sea-wind scream upon the tower ...

—W.B. Yeats, from "A Prayer for My Daughter"

"SEE, NOW?" Maggie said in a teasing tone of voice. "It's glorious out." She was right: the summer heat was beginning to ease, migratory birds called restlessly to one another, and everywhere the air smelled of ripening. "The sky is a perfect blue, Allie," she narrated, "and none of the trees have started to—oh! Well. I'm a liar. I see one now with some yellow leaves—that delicate flowering thing in front of the Burkes'. But by and large they're all still green. It's a perfect day for a walk—I *am* glad you've come out at last. And I'm glad you decided to put those glasses away once and for all. You're too handsome to hide behind them." She hugged her son's arm to her, still awash in gratitude to have him back alive—but newly troubled, too. "I do wish you could find it in yourself to go easier on your father, darling. You know he loves you." Maggie guided them along the tree-lined block, then chose a roundabout, scenic route for their walk to campus.

Allie paced alongside her dutifully, but his posture was hunched and miserable. Despite his bulky Aran jumper, his beard growing in, and the creeping shagginess of his dark hair, he looked smaller to her than he had in his uniform. An old man's note of tiredness crept into his voice when he said, "Father could find it in himself to go easier on *me*." He turned his face towards her through long social habit, and but for the blankness in his blue eyes she might have thought he was searching her face. "Does he think this is how I planned for things to turn out? Does he think I did my job badly, that getting shot down was somehow my fault? Ah, you'd think he thought I got what I deserved! I'm just as glad he's down at Hambleden most of the time."

"Look out, darling, there's an uneven spot in the walk coming up here. Just ... yes, there, you've passed it. Good." She gave his arm a squeeze, then raised her hand in greeting to a neighbor. "Hello, Mrs. Brisby!" she called, and then said to Allie, "Mrs. Brisby's kneeling out front, putting in her tulip bulbs for next spring. They *were* a glory this year! I wish you could have seen them—all red and orange, like flames. And here we come now to the old Jasper place on the left. Did I tell you they've rented it out? And they cut down all that shrubbery at the corner, right down to the ground. It looks a bit bare now; I hope they'll plant some flowers." Narrating their walk helped keep her pulse calm and her breathing even. It gave her a bit of space to gather herself. Maggie restrained Allie for a moment to let a schoolboy on a red bicycle pass, then guided him across the street. "Allie. Darling," she went on in a lower voice. "You know that it's your suffering that breaks your father's heart. He couldn't be prouder of your accomplishments and your courage, you know that. It's just he wanted to keep you safe, and he can't stand the thought that you weren't safe, that you're not happy, that there's nothing he can do to fix it for you. But I'll bet he'd be thrilled if you went down to Hambleden with him. He could use a fine engineering mind like yours to help him bring the plant up to date."

"Just what I need!" Allie growled with a bitter fierceness that seemed to surprise even him. "To lock myself up in the office of a father-and-son business. To wear a suit every day and have all the lads suck up to me because I'm the boss's son. No thank you!" Allie caught his foot in a crack in the sidewalk and stumbled a little, then righted himself. "Not to mention, I'd be useless to him now. How am I going to inspect the plant? How am I going to read schematics or draw up sketches? I can't even do math anymore unless it's in my head. Useless." He trailed off into mutters.

"I expect you'd be more help to him than either of you imagines," Maggie said. "Oh, love, I wish you could see this. We're coming up to Mr. Whitby's place, and his apple tree out front is just loaded. The branches are practically breaking. The apples are still mostly green, but they're just starting to get a blush on them—oh, just lovely. Smell that!" As they drew closer, Allie found himself enveloped in the heady, rose-reminiscent aroma of ripening apples. He couldn't help but relax, breathing in their lovely scent. "Remember that apple tree we had out back in Dublin? How it never had any fruit on it?"

"And the one year it did have—the one year it had three yellow apples on it—I waited and waited and waited for them to get ripe enough to pick—and then Mrs. MacGowan's cow got loose, came in our garden and ate them all three!" Allie tried to restrain his smile as his mother burst into peals of laughter.

"Oh, my darling, you were so disappointed! I thought your little heart would break," she said, chucking him under the chin.

He shook his head in a lifetime-familiar gesture of affectionate annoyance. "I never did like that bad-tempered old cow." His face creased into a mischievous twinkle. "Nor Mr. MacGowan, neither."

"Oh, stop, you're terrible," Maggie laughed. After a pause, she added, "And here we are—Banbury Road. Once we cross we'll be at St. Hugh's. Quite a change! They've made it a wartime hospital. The grounds are still pretty, though." They crossed the street and emerged into a courtyard ringed with long, low temporary buildings. The old college buildings rose up behind them, ivy-covered and handsome, and late roses hung onto the bushes in several of the courtyard's remaining beds, interspersed with yellow autumn lilies. "Smell that," Maggie said, holding up a fallen lily appreciatively. Allie savored its wet, refreshing fragrance, then shivered a little as a cloud scudded across the sun. All around them, he could hear nurses and doctors calling to one another—sounds familiar from his hospital stay in Glasgow—but he and his mother were enveloped in an island of peace and quiet. With his feet he could feel the moss pushing up between the courtyard's bricks; in the eye of his memory he could see its intense green against the brown clayey red. Something tickled his nose; when his mother giggled, he realized she'd been teasing him with a bird feather. "A goose quill," she said, "good sized. They're starting to fly over now." She pressed it into his hand and he delicately felt with his fingers how its vanes interlocked and resisted being stroked the wrong way.

"I have to admit it's good to be outside," he said.

"Nothing like it for cheering a person up," Maggie agreed. "I've been out a lot myself, lately, and I don't think anything else would have helped so much, when—" She broke off, a tremor in her voice.

"Oh stop it, you," he said, giving her a playful punch on the shoulder. "Look." He bent down and suddenly he was standing on his hands, his boots waving skyward. "I'm not sure I've done this since I was twelve. Well. Fourteen," he gasped, taking a couple tentative steps, his balance superb. "Best stay cheerful or I'll run off and join the circus." He righted himself, stumbled dizzily, clutched the air near Maggie. She steadied him. "I'll marry the horseback ballerina, and then you really *will* never see me again." He took a deep breath, adjusted his shirt and jumper. "Seriously, though. You've abandoned Mr. Yeats, really? You're collecting scrap metal for the Home Guard instead?" He took her arm properly now, a familiar and chivalrous gesture, one he'd learned from Ian. "Doesn't sound like you, Professor Brooke." They strolled from one of St. Hugh's courtyards to another.

"I wouldn't say I've turned my back on Yeats entirely," Maggie countered with a dreamy smile Allie could hear. "In fact, lately I've been thinking again of that essay I wanted to write about Maud Gonne. Remember? A couple of years ago, I spent the summer back in Dublin, making notes in the archives, and nothing ever came of it, but I think I've finally found a way into what I might want to say. Mind, there's a step." They mounted it gracefully together.

"I think my feet remember this place," Allie remarked.

"They may, at that," Maggie agreed. They turned into the street, their faces towards home. "In fact you might be a real help to me in my Home Guard work," Maggie said. "You know a lot of the metal I collect is from crash sites, right? Downed planes from both sides. Perhaps you could help me make sense of some things that have been perplexing me." She told him about the strange Heinkel crash sites she had encountered—the odd landing gouges, the unusual crew hatch, the lack of shrapnel, the pilots who looked as if they might have been shot, the deep, mysterious lorry tracks.

"Odd for certain, I'd say." Allie agreed. "And you haven't been able to get any attention from your higher-ups?"

Maggie shook her head, then remembered to say aloud, "No."

"I wonder ... " Allie's brow furrowed and he pressed the fingers of his free hand against his eyes. "What kinds of kills did those two claim? They always claim kills, you know. Usually more than is accurate—always better to overclaim. The R.A.F. does it by squadron, but the Jerries are braggarts. Each pilot keeps his own score. Red Baron and all that, you know."

"Of course. The German aces got the Blue Max in the Great War. And I've seen the recent claims in the papers ... but those two in specific ... I'd have to look back. I should still have the papers stacked in the larder—remind me to check when we get home. See, your expertise is coming in handy already!"

"Always trust a blind man to help you read the paper," Allie said, his eyebrows quirking ironically.

"No self-deprecation, now, and no self-pity," Maggie scolded lightly. "I won't have it. And I want you to stay at the ready—the next time I'm called to a downed German plane, I'm picking you up on the way. I really do think you may be able to help me—show me what I'm missing. Direct my attention. You know?" She hugged his arm closer again; clouds were gathering, and a damp chill had come into the air.

"You can't be serious, Mother," Allie protested. "I'd really only be underfoot. Most likely I'd just end up stepping on your evidence."

"If the radio plays are to be believed, I'll be able to count on you to bring the crucial clue to light by tripping over it." Maggie chucked his chin again, and Allie snapped his teeth in her direction, only half-playfully. "Really, though, I do think your experience with planes and aerial bombs could help me tremendously. You'll know far better than I what to look for, how to interpret the scene."

"That's just the trouble, though. I can't look, I can't see the scene. How can I interpret what's all dark?" Allie hunched his shoulders against the chill, against his own sense of uselessness.

"Who is this sniveling defeatist, and what has he done with my Allie?" Maggie asked sharply. Then her voice softened and warmed.

"Use your mind's eye, my boy. You've always had a brilliant imagination. I'll tell you what I see, and you'll ask questions and tell me what you think. I'll be your eyes, and you can be my engineering teacher. If there's a German plot afoot, I know there's no one wants to discover it more than you do, Allister Brooke."

"Well … I'll do my best, I suppose. There's no harm in a fellow bumbling about and getting in his mum's way, is there?"

"That's my boy. None whatever, and I shall be glad of your company," Maggie said, then noticed a group of figures approaching them along the walk. "Goodness me. I believe that's Mrs. Fanshawe I see coming. And … can that be Major Fanshawe? But he wasn't in a wheelchair the last time I saw him. I wonder what's happened? Here they come." Maggie drew Allie a bit to the side of the walk to make room as the little band approached: Major Fanshawe in his wheelchair, dark glasses covering his eyes, with Mrs. Fanshawe behind, pushing, and his left hand on the golden flank of a magnificent, patient retriever who kept perfect pace with the chair.

"How do you do, Mrs. Brooke?" Mrs. Fanshawe hailed them. "Terrible news we're getting from London the past few days, isn't it?"

"The air raids? Terrifying," Allie agreed while Maggie shook first Mrs. Fanshawe's hand and then the Major's.

"Terrifying it's so nearby," Mrs. Fanshawe said. "And yet here we are, just down the road, and it's the beginning of a perfect autumn—seems a world away, doesn't it?"

"Not far enough," Allie said. "The radio says the French ports are bursting with barges loaded with German soldiers. Good thing His Majesty has the finest navy and air force the world over."

"And they go with my fervent prayers, I'm not ashamed to admit. But hold on a moment, young man—you're our own Allister, aren't you? Your brogue's as gorgeous as ever. But I thought you were for the

R.A F. Where's your uniform, young man?"

"Ian and I are very pleased to have Allie home with us," Maggie replied, "though I'm afraid the unfortunate reason for it is that he's been wounded in action."

"Wounded in action, you say?" inquired Major Fanshawe as his wife tutted sympathetically. "Well, my boy, you've had the reputation for a stout heart since you were a lad in short pants, and our faith in you was not misplaced. You've done your duty, and that's as much as we can ask of any man—more than is asked of most." Major Fanshawe held out a hand, and Maggie guided Allie's into it. The Major pumped Allie's hand heartily for a moment, then gave him several manly whacks on the upper arm with his other hand. "Tell us your story, then, soldier."

"I, er, well, that is," Allie stammered uneasily. "I don't remember much, to tell you the truth, sir. I was a bomb aimer out of Dieppe, and we were shot down in a firefight over Sedan. I took a nasty blow to the head; when I woke up I didn't know who I was at first. My memory has returned, but my eyesight—well, I haven't given up all hope quite yet, but ... " Allie shook his head, then remembered that Major Fanshaw could no more see him than vice versa. "Anyway, it's kind of you to ask, sir. You know I've always admired you and appreciated your sacrifice."

"Yes, yes," murmured the Major, launching into a story Allie had heard several times during his youth—although it sounded different now, somehow more vivid, or perhaps it simply landed nearer his heart. "Of course you know that I served in the Fourth Army of the British Expeditionary Forces. Yes. Well, it was the summer of 1918, and it was brutally hot in the trenches. We were dug in near Amiens. My men were restless—they'd have done anything to get back home, you know, to sit in the shade with a nice cool pint ... well, and in the dog days, General Rawlinson decided it was time to give them what they wanted. We would make one last big push, all or nothing. And, you know—it ended well for England and France, but the Hun doesn't ever make it easy on us, does he? It was about dawn on that morning, late August, and we were on the move, but a couple of my men were slowed down by minor injuries. The company medic and I had them just about set to go when that gas canister came over the top. The medic didn't make it, I'm sorry to say, but thanks to his quick thinking and selflessness the rest of us did. I lost my eyes but we managed to get the masks on the other men fast enough that they had only minor burns to their lungs. They write to me still, both of them." A smile spread across Major Fanshawe's face at this last. "They were young men at the time, of course. Your father's age—no, younger even than that. They looked up to me, and it was my responsibility to take care of them. So that's what I did."

No one said anything for a few moments. The sun broke through the cloud cover momentarily, making the trees' leaves glow. Then the dog, who had been standing patiently at Major Fanshawe's side all this time, edged forward and placed its silken crown under Allie's fingers. Allie knelt and caressed the dog's ears appreciatively. "Who's this, then?" he asked. "He's an awfully good boy."

"She," Mrs. Fanshawe replied promptly. "That's Rooney. Have you heard of the guide dog program?"

"Guide dogs," Maggie mused. "Seems like I did read something about that. They were training them to work with Great War vets, right?"

"Precisely, my dear," said Major Fanshawe. "Rooney here has been my eyes for the past year; before that, she spent a year in rigorous training, starting when she was just a bit of a pup." He held his hands out as if cradling a teacup-sized puppy. "A veterinarian over at the university runs a program training them, and they're absolutely wonderful. Not as much use to me now, though, of course. My gout just gets worse and worse. Rooney's practically human and can do nearly anything at all, but she's not much of a hand at pushing a wheelchair."

"It's a real shame," Mrs. Fanshawe added, "because she's just such a clever dog. So good at guiding. But with poor Leon's legs as they are, it looks like she'll be more of a pet."

"Unless—" Major Fanshawe struggled to straighten himself up in his chair, animated by an idea. "Young man, you've lost your sight in His Majesty's service, but you're young and bright and capable. Think of all the good you could still do if you were independent and mobile! And that's just what Rooney could do for you—you could give her back her purpose, and she could give you back yours."

"Oh, sir," Allie said, still kneeling before the dog. "I can't possibly take your dog from you. It's lovely of you to think of me, and the guide dog program sounds wonderful, but—"

"What did you study in school, young man?" Major Fanshawe demanded.

"Chemistry, mostly, sir, and physics. Aviation fuels, defense engineering. The theory, I suppose, behind the action I saw in France."

"So you've the kind of mind the military needs right now. I'm surprised they sent you to the front lines in the first place. Why, you could be developing the technology to save Britain, and Rooney can help you do it." He bowed gravely in the direction where he imagined Maggie to be. "A man's mother is a wonderful boon, but she can't go everywhere with him in life. You aren't a little boy, after all. This dog will give you back your independence, son. She'll give you back your manhood."

"Still, though, sir," Allie hesitated. "I couldn't impose on you that way. How can you bear to part with her? You said yourself that she's your eyes."

"She's only eyes for a man who can walk, son," Major Fanshawe admitted sadly. "I'm an old done man, but you—you're too young to be idle. His Majesty has need of you yet. If not for yourself, Allister, take her for England. For the decent, Hitler-hating world."

"It's a very generous offer, Major Fanshawe," Maggie said gratefully. "And it sounds as if he's really in earnest, Allie. What do you think?"

"I'm speechless," said Allie, still kneeling, his fingers wound in the dog's curling fur. "It's just so lovely of you." The dog, as if understanding their conversation, stepped forward and licked his face; Allie sputtered with delight.

"Why don't you take her with you now and get acquainted?" Mrs. Fanshawe suggested. "I'll call round tomorrow with the information about that veterinarian. You'll need to be trained to work with her, young man, just as she's been trained to work with you. But I can already see you'll get along famously." She pressed Rooney's lead into Allie's hand.

He stood and embraced her, his eyes shining, then felt for Major Fanshawe and embraced him, too. "These are dark days for you, son," Major Fanshawe whispered into Allie's ear. "When I lost my vision, I thought my life was over. Hold on. You still have work to do, and it does get easier with time."

By Friday of that week, Allie was in the thick of intensive training with Rooney, and Maggie had roughed out her essay on Yeats's influence on Maud Gonne's career and Gonne's considerable resistance to that influence. Early afternoon found her ensconced at a table in the Bodleian Library, tomes and notes scattered across its surface, her personal and already much-marked-up copy of Gonne's year-old autobiography *A Servant of the Queen* open on her knee as she leaned back, thinking. She had collected a great deal of very suggestive evidence from archives, theatre reviews, published correspondences, and Yeats's and Gonne's own writing. Still, she reflected, due diligence would probably require that she travel to Dublin and interview Gonne before all was said and done. She wondered whether Gonne might instead be persuaded to answer a series of letters. Flipping to a fresh page in her notebook, Maggie began to scrawl a series of questions for Gonne, but she paused when a shadow fell across her page.

She looked up to see a man of medium height and medium-to-slight build reading the spines and covers of the volumes on her table. Behind a little round pair of faux-tortoiseshell glasses, his large dark eyes were quick and bright; a gentle smile played about his mouth. From the frost touching his thick, dark hair, Maggie guessed he was about her age; despite the utter plainness of his dark clothing, there was something about him she found appealing, even intriguing. "A scholar of the Irish moderns, are you?" he asked affably, gesturing towards the books.

"Yeats, primarily, though just now I'm writing about Maud Gonne," Maggie replied. "Are you that way inclined yourself?"

"Sure. Strictly as an amateur, mind you—I'm no don. But I do admire the writing that's been coming from Ireland for the past few decades. Heady stuff. What do you think of James Joyce?" As he spoke, he took his hand out of his pocket and leaned casually against her table. It wasn't until Maggie let her eyes drop from his face in order to contemplate Joyce that she noticed, under his fingertips, a laminated MI-5 identification card. "Stephen Bloom," she read, along with some classification information she wasn't sure she understood. And sticking out from below his card was a note that read, "Walk with me," and below that—in smaller letters—"Be discreet."

"I loved *Dubliners*, to be sure," Maggie said; "His more recent work I suppose I have a more complex relationship with. Have you seen the novel that came out this summer?" Keeping her expression friendly and her face towards his, Maggie began gathering her things. "I was just going to a café for a cuppa—won't you join me? I'll tell you about it." She allowed Bloom to carry the library books back to the desk for her, then walked with him towards the library doors, describing as she went the associative, cyclical structure of *Finnegans Wake* and its surreal portmanteau vocabulary and suggesting some Irish traditions from which such a radical literary experiment might emerge. Bloom nodded encouragement and asked insightful questions.

Once they emerged into the pleasant early-autumn sunlight and started down Catte Street, though, their conversation changed. "So you're the poetry don who's been spinning conspiracy theories about downed German bombers, eh?" Bloom said quietly, and Maggie confirmed that it was so. "I've been assigned as your contact, available to you night and day should any further intelligence come into your possession." He withdrew a business card from the breast pocket of his somewhat shiny-elbowed black twill jacket and passed it to her; it contained his name, three telephone numbers, and nothing else, and was engraved in a nondescript typeface on medium-quality white cardstock. On the back, he penned an address in St. James's Street.

"This is my office—don't be fooled by the 'To Let' sign. I should tell you," he said, "that I've been over your reports carefully. They're quite detailed, for which you should be commended—you've quite a keen eye. Still, I haven't been able to make much headway in discerning the meaning of the anomalies you've observed. None of the German spies we've detained—and we've caught a good number—has been able to tell us anything about special Heinkels, nor could we discern any pattern of communications correlated with the dates of the crashes in question. If there is a covert German operation afoot, it is one about which Berlin and its contacts in Britain have been entirely silent." Maggie's brow furrowed, but she said nothing. "To be absolutely honest with you, Mrs. Brooke, I must confess that I have recently annoyed some of my higher-ups by insisting repeatedly that we recruit female intelligence talent. It's entirely possible that these agents felt it would be a laugh, and just what I deserved, to pair me up with—begging your pardon—a lady whose chief concern in life is poems. Be that as it may—" Bloom plowed ahead over Maggie's protests— "it's vital that we investigate your concerns with the utmost thoroughness. I can see already that you are in no way a frivolous person—that you would not have demanded the agency's attention without sturdy grounds for suspicion."

"Moreover," Maggie rejoined, "although it's true that I have no background in law enforcement or espionage, I have devoted myself to a vocation in which evidence and its proper analysis are paramount. You have already remarked upon my keen eye, and I thank you for that. An eye for detail, and for the relationship of the detail to the situation's larger meaning, is the central skill of the literary critic."

"I'm glad to see that you're no self-effacing violet," Bloom laughed, not unkindly. "Those types never get anywhere with Whitehall. And, now that you mention it, I too come from a tradition in which literary analysis is considered the highest intellectual pursuit." He produced from his watch-pocket a gorgeous antique star-of-David watch in silver. "So it was unjust of me to doubt for a moment that a scholar of poetry should be ideally suited to intelligence work. I apologize."

"Apology accepted, Mr. Bloom," said Maggie. "We women in men's fields generally have pretty tough hides, I think you'll find." She smiled one of her warm, genuine smiles—a smile like the September sunshine itself, bright and sharp yet ripening. It made the lines beside her eyes crinkle, a mark of age that somehow rendered her more, not less, handsome.

"I don't doubt it. So. What I propose for the moment is this: let's sit on that park bench over there. I have with me a copy of the *Times*, and each of us should choose our favorite section. We shall appear to all observers to be engaged in perusing and discussing the news, and in fact, you can recount your observations to me in your own words and fill me in on any particulars that might be newer than the last report I received."

As they executed Bloom's plan, Maggie appreciated the attention and thoroughness with which he questioned her about what she had seen. She related her observations as thoroughly as she could, adding questions that had occurred to her and confessing that she wasn't entirely certain what gave her such a strong feeling that those two crash sites were connected and not quite right. As they drew near the end of their conversation, Maggie said, "There's one other thing that's odd. I wouldn't have thought of it, but my son brought it to my attention. He's a bomb aimer, you know, or was—he was recently wounded in action. He thought to ask me whether the R.A.F. had reported shooting down those two planes—and it's the funniest thing. They didn't claim those two. Allie—that's my son—says it's always in a crew's interest to estimate on the high side when it comes to reporting kills. The reports come out by R.A.F. squadron but a plane on the ground or in the Channel gets counted. I looked back at the kill claims reported in the papers, just for comparison—R.A.F. boys claimed all of the other German planes I've harvested metal from. But these two—no one claimed a thing. Doesn't it strike you as odd that no one would take credit for shooting them down?"

"There's plenty here that's odd, Mrs. Brooke—that's certain. But odd's one thing and operable intelligence is another. I'll have to go back through R.A.F. records and see what I can discover, and then I'll have to see what kind of attention I can get from up the chain of command. Likely they'll tell me, 'Good job, Bloom, old boy—you've discovered a nefarious German plot to bomb England—and we'd never have known if it weren't for you.'" He rolled his eyes good-naturedly, as if to say *you know how thick bosses can be.* "But you never know what may turn out to be something, after all. So I'll give it my best research. In the meantime, do ring me if you learn anything else, or if anything occurs to you." He rose, and she followed his example. He shook her hand firmly, then held it an extra moment and said, "By the way, I really *am* a fan of Joyce. Your description of the new one was quite enticing. *Finnegans Wake,* you said? I shall have my local shop order it for me."

CHAPTER EIGHT:
DOING THE MATH

When all that story's finished, what's the news?
In luck or out the toil has left its mark ...
—W.B. Yeats, from "The Choice"

A COLD FRONT IS COMING IN, bringing a chill autumn rain with it. Hunched in the driver's seat of a refrigerated dairy lorry parked in a fallow field just outside Berrick Salome, a man dressed in clerical black checks his watch, then the flat gray sky, then his watch again. The field is the soft gray-brown of a songbird's breast, spotted with rust. In the truck's rearview mirror he can see his two employees in their dairy coveralls: smoking, one lounging against the lorry. They never lounge when they know he is watching them. But for the moment, let them: his mind is on other things. Three shipments have come in without a hitch, but the last one was shot down over the Channel, and time is short enough as it is. He knows the Reichsmarschall will accept no excuses. *Don't let any more go astray,* he silently pleads. He runs his middle finger lightly, absentmindedly down the scar that connects his eyebrow with the corner of his mouth. Against the steely backdrop of the autumn sky, the hedgerows seem to burn.

Finally, the plane comes in, short and hard. His two men get to work right away, but the scarred priest waits for the gunshot before he gets out to greet the plane's navigator and give him his dairy coverall. He is supervising the three men as they move the plane's cargo into the lorry when a man in sturdy brown canvas work pants and a well-worn brown jumper rushes up. His skin is wrinkled and tanned from a lifetime of outdoors work; under a brown corduroy cap, his thick white curls are overgrown and wispy. Sharp dark eyes peer out between his bushy white eyebrows and his bushy white beard. "You saw her too?" he calls excitedly. "A German plane! I saw her comin' down, and there she is! Did any of 'em escape?" He is still running towards the men, though he's slowing now, unsure. While his attention is on the three men in dairy coveralls, the priest melts off to the side, circles around behind the man. The dairy men have paused in their work, but at a gesture from the priest, they resume it, ignoring the newcomer. "I was repairing the fence on my south sheep pasture—" he gestures somewhere behind him— "and I come running straight away. How'd you lot get here so fast?" The farmer looks around, takes in the scene, seeming more and more perplexed. "But, but … look here. What are you lads doing?" he asks, and then the priest is behind him, black-clad arms reaching around the farmer's neck. A sudden snapping motion, and the farmer crumples to the ground.

Despite having just returned to Archbishop House from a meeting with her liaison Father DiGangi, Sister Angela Curran was restless. How many hours a day could she be expected to listen to pompous old Cardinal Hinsley's foolish prattling? It wore on a body's nerves. Still, Sister Angela reflected, the Cardinal did have his moments. It had been all she could do not to crow aloud this morning when he confided his concern for his dear friend Mrs. Brooke, that great grey myna bird. It seemed that Mrs. Brooke had gotten herself entangled with an investigation of Heinkel bombers and strange air-crash sites, and now she'd been visited by a representative of MI-5. Even while the Cardinal was devoutly hoping that his Mrs. Brooke wasn't in over her head, Sister Angela was already working on a reason why His Eminence would need to send her over to the offices of London's acting Apostolic Delegate. Reluctant as DiGangi had been upon occasion— and trying as she found his big, tragic, accusing eyes and the little framed photo of his sister that he caressed more often than he did his rosary—Sister Angela couldn't deny his skill with Latin codes, and his Vatican-credentialed couriers were given swift passage toward Rome. But the couriers did not go there. With the Reichsmarschall stationed on his personal train in northern France, the couriers could usually provide Sister Angela with a reply within seventy-two hours. She and the rest of Father DiClemente's team were given every ounce of strategic and operational support the Luftwaffe could muster. No doubt the Reichsmarschall was already considering how to vary his pattern.

Sister Angela shivered in the early October chill and shrugged into the gray cardigan she liked to wear inside Archbishop House; stepping into the corridor, she almost collided with a mousy serving girl who was carrying a hot water bottle on a silver tray. "For His Eminence?" Sister Angela asked, and the girl nodded, eyes cast down. "I'll take it," Sister Angela said, and away the little mouse scurried.

As Sister Angela entered his cozy, book-lined study, the Cardinal was just resettling his private telephone on its hook. "There you are, my dear," he said, "I'm so glad you're back. Thank you," he added, nestling the hot water bottle between his chair and his lower back.

Sister Angela tucked the now-empty silver tray under her arm and waited for him to continue. "What would I do without you, Sister Angela?" he sighed. "You're so very capable, and I'm so often in perplexities; you are my Benjamin, the support of my age." He shook his head, his eyes fixed upon the telephone on his wide mahogany desk. "Our Mrs. Brooke has just rung me up. I'm more concerned about her all the time."

Sister Angela carefully composed her features and voice into their best expression of sympathetic solicitude. "Oh?" she asked carefully, afraid that the acuity of her interest would show. *Your only concern is for the Cardinal's well-being*, she told herself.

"I've always admired Mrs. Brooke's imagination, you know, and the keenness of her insight. But we've all been under a great deal of strain lately, and Mrs. Brooke more so than most—with her mother-in-law's death, and the closing of the universities, and her son's disappearance, and then his coming home blind ... We all invent fancies sometimes, don't we, when life is too much? I pray that Mrs. Brooke doesn't lose herself ... It seems she's convinced herself," the Cardinal said, "that on the days of the crashes she's become obsessed with, some sort of special vehicle ought to have been lurking about. Something to do with tracks she saw and can't explain. She's been interviewing the farmers round about Oxfordshire about what they saw out driving on the roads on those days. And do you know what she's taken into her head?"

"I can't imagine," Sister Angela murmured as mildly as she could. She turned her cherub's face towards a warm orange sunbeam slanting in through the study window's stained-glass scene of Saint George battling the dragon. The saint, his golden armor gleaming, stood on the wild creature's back; its long neck curved around to look at him, its wings spread wide, and his spear pierced its mouth savagely. Sister

Angela couldn't help but feel a bit sorry for the magnificent, broken beast. It was just like the English, she thought, to choose this scene for their country's emblem: the magical and mysterious slaughtered to make way for the prosaic, the anticlimactic human. The sunbeams slanted in and lost themselves among the rich patterns of the study's Oriental carpets.

"She says the only thing all the witnesses agreed on was that our lorry—our dairy lorry with the cow on it—that our lorry was seen near all of her crash sites." The Cardinal shook his head again. "Well. She sounded a bit confused about it herself, and apologetic. And who knows? If there's something to all this—I don't want it thought that the Archdiocese was harboring Nazi spies! But really, I'm concerned that Mrs. Brooke is exhausted. She ought to be in Hambleden with her husband, not chasing around the countryside—ah, well. But she knows best what's right for her, I suppose." Sister Angela could see tears standing in the Archbishop's eyes and felt a pang of scornful pity. How anyone could be so moved by that prying heron of a woman was beyond Sister Angela—but she couldn't help but feel alarmed at the woman's perspicacity. "Sister Angela," the Cardinal resumed, "will you be an angel and go up to Warborough to meet with Mrs. Brooke this afternoon? She'd like to interview the dairymen and lorry drivers. You'll see she gets everything she needs, won't you?"

"Of course, Your Eminence," Sister Angela said. "Anything to be of service. There's a train in half an hour—is there anything you need before I go?"

"No, no, my dear—well—yes. Have the girl lay a fire in the grate here, won't you? It's a mite chilly." Sister Angela bowed slightly and made towards the door, her fingers tapping lightly against the silver tray she still held under her arm. She said a silent prayer of thanksgiving for the old man's pliancy—she hadn't even needed to manipulate him into sending her to Warborough, he'd done it on his own. She would have the train ride to consider her strategy for containing Mrs. Brooke's visit to the dairy that afternoon; if she arrived early enough, she might even be able to talk it over with Father DiClemente. At the thought of DiClemente's imposing tactical intelligence—and of the rugged scar that traversed his handsome cheek from brow to lip—Sister Angela felt an entirely un-nun-like blush spread across her cheek. "And Sister Angela?" the Cardinal interrupted her just as she reached the doorway; she half-turned. "Would you bring back some cream from the dairy for Sunday's luncheon? There's a good girl."

Allie's train trip from Oxford to Cambridge couldn't have been more different from his trip home from Glasgow. When he first sat down in his compartment, the window was open and he could smell the sharp tang of wet fallen leaves and a crisp hint of frost. After he closed the window, the compartment smelled companionably of leather, wool, and Rooney's silky fur. Rooney, Allie reflected, was altogether a better conversationalist than Officer Greeley and more helpful besides. He had explained to his mother that it was important to him to make this trip without her as a kind of test of his training in partnership with the dog.

Getting her to understand his voice commands had been a challenge at the beginning of their training, but now Allie felt they were passing with flying colors. The crowds and complex smells in Charing Cross Station threatened to distract Allie during their complicated train change, but Rooney was single-minded and herded her charge safely up and down stairs and past all obstacles. In the train compartments she folded herself neatly against Allie's shins, out of the way of other passengers, a warm and reassuring presence. And during the London-to-Cambridge leg of the journey, she provided a pretext for a very pleasant young woman to strike up a conversation with Allie. He enjoyed imagining what she must look like, based upon her vivacious laugh and her stories about rambling around Switzerland with her goat-herding cousins. He decided she must be short but athletically built, with blooming cheeks, a sky-blue traveling suit, and curls the color of caramel. The time flew by so quickly that he hadn't decided on a color for her eyes by the time the train pulled in at Cambridge Station.

On the platform, Allie once again enjoyed the incipient bite of the autumn air; he could smell the mums of a flower-seller who was set up nearby, and further away, the aroma of something fried. He distracted himself with snippets of the conversations of passersby during the twenty anxious seconds that passed before he felt a hearty hand on his shoulder and found himself in the brotherly embrace of his university chum Charlie Flaherty. Half a head shorter than Allie, Charlie outweighed him by at least five stone of solid muscle, most of it in his chest and shoulders. He'd been a promising young hurler back in Cork, but at Cambridge he'd become obsessed with nuclear chemistry. He and Allie had graduated together, but when Allie enlisted, Charlie returned to Cambridge for graduate study—and to assist his professors in their defense research.

"Look at you," Charlie exclaimed in his fine, whiskey-golden brogue. "I was expecting a broken man, but you're in the very pink of health. I'm glad to see it! And who's this?" he added, leaning down to give Rooney's ears a ruffle.

"This is Rooney. She's been specially trained to assist the blind— have you heard about these programs? They're quite interesting. You'd be amazed how smart she is. We've just been training together three weeks, and already she's a better guide than the great toff they sent down from Glasgow with me. *You* haven't mentioned polo ponies once on the entire trip, have you, girl?" Allie smacked the dog's flank affectionately.

Charlie chuckled, then said, "Right, then, we're off. I'm assisting a few of our old dons in the defense lab, and the work we're doing is fascinating. It's a bit hush-hush, so keep what you learn today under your hat, won't you, old boy? But I've cleared your visit—everyone here trusts you completely. This way, then—" he tugged Allie's elbow to indicate direction— "off we go!"

"Rooney, *come!*" Allie enunciated, starting after Charlie, but immediately he stumbled into his old friend, who had spun in his tracks when he heard Allie's direction to the dog.

"Can you repeat that?" Charlie could barely get the words out around his irrepressible laughter.

"I was just telling her to come along," Allie explained weakly. "Look, all right. She's an English dog. She's just spent a year or so working with an old Major, a Great War vet with about the poshest accent you've ever heard. So when I started training with her I couldn't get her to do a thing." He caressed her golden head absently as he spoke. "Sweet, affectionate dog, and she'd worked like a dream for the Major, but when I gave her commands she'd just stand and stare or cock her ear, puzzled like. So finally we realized it was the brogue. She just couldn't understand it."

"So now she has you talking like the Duke of York!" Charlie roared good-naturedly, clapping Allie on the shoulder several times. "That's good old English health care for you. 'Doctor,' you tell them, 'I can't see,' and they tell you, 'Come right in, son, we've got just the thing.' A month later, they release you—and you're still blind, but they've made you a feckin' Brit." He shook his head. "I never thought I'd live to see the day. Allister, old boy, I can see you'll be needing a couple extra rounds of Guinness and Jameson tonight." He took Allie's valise from him—he insisted—and the two young men began their walk towards the Cavendish Lab.

They found the lab abuzz with activity; men huddled around magnet coils and discharge tubes and cloud chambers; some called out and beckoned excitedly to one another, while others sat and mused at desks or in front of chalkboards. To Allie, it was a cacophony of regular beeps and ticks, irregular clangs and whirrs, footsteps, shouts, occasional laughter, the squeaking of chalk and the rustling of papers—all familiar from his days at the nearby Mond lab. The Cavendish lab smelled better, though—or perhaps, by its nature as a chemistry lab, the Mond smelled worse: sulfur, acetone, a rainbow of nauseous organics. The Cavendish, by contrast, smelled of iron, ozone, and frost, with whiffs here and there of chalk dust or engine grease. Allie kept Rooney close to heel as Charlie led them down a flight of stairs into a basement and through a maze of corridors.

He had lost count of the turnings when finally they stopped and he heard Charlie heave open a heavy steel door. The room inside must have been enormous—he could tell from the echoing quality of the footsteps, rustling, and quiet conversations he could hear. From somewhere far off, as if in the opposite corner, came the irregular clicking of a Geiger counter. In a voice hushed with respect, Charlie told Allie, "This is where Walton and Cockroft first smashed the atom—six, seven years ago. I'll introduce you around. These chaps are my bosses—I feel unworthy to fetch their coffee, really—they're geniuses. But you couldn't hope to meet a nicer bunch of blokes. Monsieur Kowarski!" Allie's hand was enfolded by an enormous hand and shaken with jovial vigor. "Lew Kowarski is part of the Curie team who fled here when Hitler occupied Paris," Charlie explained. "We have them to thank for the heavy water we're using in our experiments here. Professor Kowarski, this is my good friend Allister Brooke. He took a degree in chemistry at Caius last year and was recently wounded in action over France, so I invited him up for the grand tour. I've never seen a fellow as cheered by defense engineering as our Allie."

"It's a pleasure to meet you, sir," Allie said.

"The pleasure is all mine, I'm sure," returned Kowarski in a booming voice accented with a mixture of Russian and French. "I am grateful for your service and your sacrifice, young man—especially now that the whispers say Hitler has his hands on yellowcake from the Belgian Congo. You have heard? It is distressing news indeed—whether he plans to use it for bombs or energy, the thought of facing Nazis armed with the power of uranium—" Allie swore he could hear the man shuddering.

"Monsieur Kowarski has just published some ground-breaking research on nuclear chain reactions, which will play a central role in any nuclear bombs or energy plants the Allies might soon build," Charlie told Allie.

"I would love to tell you all about it, but I'm afraid I'm rushing off to a meeting," Kowarski apologized. "Several of the men—Nick, Allan, Sam—we have drawn up some preliminary schematics and will be discussing possible designs and trigger mechanisms for a fission bomb. Ah! If you are interested in defense engineering—perhaps you would like to join us?"

"Would I!" Allie's face was alight as if it were Christmas morning and he a little boy again. "Are you certain it's all right?"

"We would be delighted for you young fellows to sit in," Kowarski confirmed; what had at first seemed an offhand notion was warming up for him. "I think it will be useful to have some fresh eyes—erm—minds on the problem. We will explain more clearly if we have new ears in the room. You fellows can keep up, though?"

"We'll do our best, sir," Charlie promised. "And I think we can. Allie here has one of the sharpest minds you could hope to meet."

Meanwhile, Maggie Brooke was taking a trip of her own. As much as she had always dreaded visiting the Brookes' ancestral heap at Hambleden, it was past time and she could put it off no more. Perhaps, she had told herself, Ian would have dispatched some of its dreary furnishings and rat-chewn carpets. Perhaps he would have thrown open the heavy drapery, had the age-begrimed windows washed, and let some much-needed sunlight into the place. She dared not even hope that he had begun modernizing the kitchen or the plumbing. At least his dear departed mother had been forward-thinking enough to have the place wired for electric lights—though whether the dim orange glow these cast upon their generally brown and dusty surroundings represented an improvement, Maggie wasn't prepared to say. At any rate, by the time she left Oxford for Hambleden, she was thinking less about the house and more about what a comfort it would be to see Ian. She wasn't sure whether this afternoon's adventure in Warborough had been an adventure at all or a figment of her imagination, but it had left her unnerved and uncertain. She longed as almost never before for safe and familiar company.

But when Ian ushered her through the front door of his ancestral home, her heart sank and she felt herself being pulled back towards their old argument: the place looked and smelled much as it ever had, moldy and dank and outmoded.

"I've been devoting most of my time to learning the business," Ian explained apologetically, "and then there was structural work to be done on the foundation and roof. That's all done now. I've started excavating the attics—you wouldn't believe the things I've found! My grandfather's leaden toy soldiers, Mags. From the eighteen-thirties! Can you believe it? And boxes and boxes of letters and documents— those will take me ages to sort through, but you know how it thrills the historian in me." Peeking into the formal dining room as she passed it, she could see that its big oval table was covered with drifts of yellowed papers. Ian noticed her looking and continued in his apologetic tone, "I've been taking my meals in the breakfast room— it's cozier—and I've instructed Mr. Pippin that that's where we'll dine this evening. Malcolm and Eugenia will join us, and Colin— they're so looking forward to seeing you, my dear. I'm only sorry that Allie—" Here he broke off and a cloud fell over his features.

"You know how eager he was to get back to Cambridge and see how Charlie's research is getting on," Maggie said tiredly, squeezing Ian's arm as much to comfort herself as him. "I'm sure he'll come down—"

"Bollocks," Ian interjected, and Maggie gasped—it was unlike him to interrupt, let alone curse. "You know he's barely spoken with me since that wretched homecoming party. The letters I've written have gone unanswered. I can't keep him on the telephone for more than a minute at a time. He's still angry with me, and I don't under- stand what for."

"Darling, you know what an adjustment he's going through— what grief he's facing. I think he's lost hope that his eyesight might come back. And who knows, maybe that's for the best—but it can't be very cheering for a young man who's spent his whole life bent on seeing all the world's sights," Maggie said gently. "He's not himself again yet. You have to give him time. And you have to give yourself time, too."

"Myself? I've had nothing but time. Time waiting for him, wondering if he would come home, looking for him, and now time down here—I miss him, Mags, and I miss you. It's wonderful working at the family place, seeing Malcolm every day, and Colin is a joy to my heart—but the evenings here are so long, Mags. When will you come down, the two of you, for good?"

Maggie was saved from that dreaded question by a bustling at the front door that could only signal the arrival of Malcolm and his family. She placed a firm kiss on her husband's cheek and promised, "To be continued." They reached the dim, drab drawing room just as Mr. Pippin was settling Malcolm and Eugenia on an uncomfortable sofa Maggie judged had been there since early in Victoria's reign. She couldn't have said what color the damask upholstery had originally been, but now it hinted at a shadowy pattern of cabbage roses in shades of brown on brown. Maggie momentarily reflected that those dowdy cabbage roses went perfectly with Eugenia's frock, but then she felt ashamed for thinking such uncharitable thoughts. As Ian and Maggie entered the room, Malcolm and Eugenia sprang up to greet them, apparently grateful for the reprieve this offered their backsides.

"We've brought you a basket of pears from our tree—it's been a bumper crop this year, and they're absolutely delicious," Malcolm announced proudly, gesturing towards a large wicker basket on a side table. "Sweet enough to make you forget about the sugar rationing, hey?"

At the same time, Eugenia caught both of Maggie's hands in her own and kissed both her cheeks. In a quieter voice than her husband's, she said to Maggie, "I must beg you to excuse Colin. I let Mr. Pippin know just now. The moment he heard Allie wouldn't be here tonight, he began insisting that he had a date and that we would be ruining his life forever if we forbade him to keep it." She rolled her eyes, but her little smile was indulgent. "There's a band in town that all the young people are atwitter about. Americans, in fact. Playing a night in Hambleden, of all places, in between their big city gigs. I hope you can forgive him—I told him it was terribly rude to disappoint you."

"We understand perfectly, dear. As you can see, we've been no more successful at corralling our own young man—we know what it's like," Maggie said sympathetically, and then, in a louder voice, she addressed the room: "Ah—here's Mr. Pippin—it must be time for us to sit down."

The supper was simple and rustic, but delicious, using their small pork allotment to accent beautiful homegrown pumpkins, marrows, and root vegetables. Maggie had to concede that her mother-in-law's old cook, Mrs. Umphlett, knew what she was about. Not, she thought loyally, that Zofia wouldn't be just as skillful when she came into her own. The girl was clever and diligent, learning every day. Still, there was something to be said for a cook like Mrs. Umphlett, who remembered what British cuisine had been before the Great War.

Maggie's culinary reverie was interrupted by the awareness of a pause in general conversation, and she realized that everyone was waiting for her to say something. "I'm sorry, I must have been distracted," she said with some embarrassment. "Could you repeat the question?"

"Maggie, my dear girl, you're dreamier by the day. Quite the absent-minded don!" Malcolm teased her, and she joined in the general laugher—it was true. "I was just remarking that Ian tells me you've uncovered a little mystery on your metal-reclamation sites. I was wondering if there were any new developments in your espionage career?"

This time Maggie refused to let herself be teased. "As a matter of fact, there are some developments," she said, "but I must swear you all to secrecy before I divulge them." What could it hurt, she reasoned, to tell her family about her visit from the exciting, if paranoid, Stephen Bloom? As she related her story, she could see a new respect come into Malcolm's eyes. For all Malcolm's good nature, Maggie knew that he, like most men, subscribed to Samuel Johnson's view of women who thought and wrote: like a dog's walking on his hind legs, they reasoned, women's thinking was not done well, but they were surprised to find it done at all. Used as she was to such, the temptation to boast and be taken seriously was simply too strong—particularly after her experience this afternoon, which she still did not trust herself to talk about. "Mr. Bloom has been making inquiries, and as far as we can tell, these odd crash sites are entirely a local phenomenon—he hasn't been able to discover anything similar going on anywhere outside the Oxford area. And not even the whole Oxford area, I might add! The unusual bombers seem to crash only to the east and south of Oxford—almost as if they weren't targeting Oxford at all, but were outliers from attacks on London. But I'm getting ahead of myself— I haven't told you. I've started thinking about my investigation in a whole different way. It was Allie who helped me see it. I'd been thinking, you see, only about the evidence I saw at the actual crash sites— that was what seemed off to me, you see, and that's what immediately connects the four strange sites I've discovered."

"Four?" Ian put in. "You've only told me about three."

"That's right! I haven't had the chance to tell you about the new one this week. Allie went with me to examine the site. He brought Rooney with him—that dog is a miracle on four legs, I tell you. She's given him back so much of his independence—I doubt he even would have gone down to Cambridge if it weren't for her. There's something to this guide dog program. Every blind person ought to have one.

"But I was telling you about how Allie has changed my investigation. You see, I started off only paying attention to the anomalies

I found at the sites—on the ground, so to speak. But Allie asked me about kill claims—you know, about who took credit in the papers for shooting these planes down. The R.A.F. squadrons make their claims and Whitehall sorts it all out—Allie says for each kill there are usually multiple claims. But do you know, in all three cases—and in this new one, too, so in all *four*—no unit claimed the kill. No one took credit for shooting these planes down. And Allie says that's simply unheard of."

"That *is* very odd, isn't it?" Malcolm mused, and Ian nodded. "And it's so like our Allie to get you to change your perspective, look at the thing from another angle. Bravo to him!"

"He's always made us very proud," Maggie said, beaming at Ian, who smiled back at her ruefully. "I think in this case, it was very much an historian's instinct—the kind of thing he'd have learned from his father." Everyone looked appreciatively at Ian, who blushed a bit; his expression of pleasure lost some of its strained quality and relaxed into genuineness. "Allie's good advice has prompted me to think about other ways of using the papers to fit my strange sites into the bigger picture. It's a bit like literary criticism, isn't it? I look at all of the details and ask, *What story is being told here?* But of course, it's harder to see the whole story, isn't it, when you're—so to speak— a character inside the thing as it's unfolding. At any rate, I started poring over the past few months' papers, and not just local ones, ones for the whole country. To see if I could discover any patterns.

"And, well! It turns out that each of the unusual crash sites corresponds with a day of heavy bombing over the west and northwest of London. No odd crash sites on days when the bombing focused on any other part of London; no odd crash sites on days when the main action was over Birmingham or Milton Keynes or Dover. And! I'm most excited to add—on only *one* day when west London and south

Oxford were heavily targeted did I *not* discover an unusual crash site. There must have been one that day that I somehow didn't see or hear about—I've been talking with my Home Guard colleagues and trying to discover it, but I fear I'll never know whether there was an odd crash that day. It is, after all, the Women's Auxiliary's main task to disassemble the evidence."

She shrugged, her eyebrows pulled together in consternation, then brightened as another thought came back to her. "Here, too, though, Allie helped me change my thinking around. Heavens, you'd think *he* was the humanities scholar, the way he can turn an abstract question around to see it from a different angle ... In a sense, my observation that odd crash sites correspond to days when the Germans were heavily targeting areas near us seems logical, unsurprising, right? Of course more German planes means more chances to shoot them down. But our clever boy asked me this: what if we're looking at the thing all backwards? What if the heavy bombing on those days is precisely a *cover* that Göring has devised to distract us from the *real* mission of sending in these strange bombers, which crash without being shot down? It's almost as if their mission is to smuggle something in ... but if that's the case, then *what could their secret cargo be?*" She paused a moment to let that sink in. "And think about this," she went on. "The strange crash sites have no kill claims by the R.A.F. Did Göring not take that into account? Sort of the 'Law of Unintended Consequences' in reverse. Something he should have thought of that would not happen has in fact ... not happened. And for Göring, the leader of the Flying Circus in 1918, not to factor in claims for aerial victories—it just doesn't add up." Maggie took a moment to catch her breath. "It's all very speculative, I admit. But it does have me thinking hard ... " She shook her head, but at the same time, her thin cheeks were flushed with excitement. With her wide, clear eyes and flyaway curls, she had the air of a girl half her age, gray hair and crows' feet or no.

"Well, it certainly suits you, my dear," Malcolm said.

Eugenia spoke over him. "I don't know how you do it, Maggie. You're so clever! And I can see where Allie gets his taste for adventure. But aren't you afraid?"

Maggie drew her eyebrows together in an expression of almost-genuine puzzlement. "Afraid?" she asked. "Of what?"

"Well, first of all, there's the metal reclamation itself. Isn't it awfully heavy labor for ladies? And at our age!" Maggie started to respond, but Eugenia went right on. "And then, getting mixed up with spies and whatnot—oh, Maggie, aren't you afraid you'll wind up in some prison? Or be assassinated? I'm just—it's just—I admire you so, Maggie, you always do such wonderful things—but I *do* hope you're being awfully careful. For all of our sakes."

Maggie's first impulse would normally have been to laugh, and she almost did, though part of her felt suddenly that Eugenia was wiser than she knew. The faces around the table were sober. Mr. Pippin was clearing away the dishes in preparation for the pudding. Nodding her head soberly, Maggie replied, "Thank you, Eugenia. Your concern means a great deal to me, and I—well, I suppose as you describe it, the work I'm doing sounds so romantic and dashing. But I assure you, it's much more mundane than that. I really can't imagine that I'm in any danger. I mean, really, who am I? I'm nobody, just a potty lady down at the library studying newspapers. I barely have anyone's ear. And then, at the sites—" now she did force herself to laugh, having nearly convinced herself that she was safely insignificant—"don't you worry, I only supervise. I let the strong young girls do all the heavy lifting."

There was an awkward moment when Eugenia continued to look severe and disapproving, but good old Malcolm dived in to save the situation. "Well, speaking of espionage," he twinkled, his eyes mischievous, "remember back in May when the reports came that the King of Belgium warned his people over the radio that German paratroopers dressed as priests and nuns were landing behind their lines? Remember all the hysteria here over that? German paratroopers behind every tree? Well. I heard a Nazi paratrooper landed on the twelfth hole at Lytham St Anne's. One old gent mistook him for a white-tailed sea eagle. He forgot they've been extinct since 1918. His son knew better and pulled out the Enfield his dad kept in his golf bag just in case, but their caddy wouldn't let him shoot. The Nazi was beyond the red stakes, you see—he was out of bounds."

"The version I heard," Maggie put in gratefully as they all chuckled, "was that the paratrooper landed in a water hazard. The caddy wouldn't let them shoot for fear they'd hit a frog. After all, the Frogs are our allies." Cheerful groans all around.

Malcolm had succeeded in lightening the mood around the table, and the conversation turned to speculation about how Colin's dance was going. Mrs. Umphlett had thought to garnish the pudding with slivers of Malcolm's pears, and everyone agreed that they were just the thing. The evening ended with sherry and laughter and promises of a supper in Henley-on-Thames before long.

But as they leaned in the doorway waving goodbye to Malcolm and Eugenia's retreating tail-lamps, Ian put his arm around Maggie's shoulders and sighed, "Can't you and Allie move down? It could always be like this."

Maggie sagged. "That's just the trouble, Ian. This is lovely from time to time, but—always? My work is in Oxford. They need me. The Home Guard now, and after the war—well, I'm too young to retire.

I've another book in me—one more at least. And my students—
I'm not finished, don't you see?"

"But darling," Ian objected, trailing after her as she stalked inside, leaving Mr. Pippin to shut the door, "there's so much for you to
do *here*, too. You saw what a mess I'm in with these documents, and
Eugenia's desperate for some intelligent company, and anyway this
old place is such a lovely spot to *write*—"

"To write! *Lovely!*" Maggie snorted. She couldn't help herself.
"This drafty old pile! Ian, it's a miracle you haven't caught your death
of bronchitis, or ... or bloody *typhus* in this moldering wreck! It's as
dark and damp as a cellar, top to bottom! And ... and ... the scratch-
ings you hear here at night ... I'm certain it's crawling with vermin,
has been for years. How can you bear it?"

"Margaret! This is my home you're talking about, the place where
I grew up. How can you be so beastly?" Ian's face was contorted in
pain.

"That's just it. It's your childhood home—when you look around
all you see is your mum and dad and your happy childhood, and that's
lovely for you—but when *I* look around, I see this place as it is. Look,
Ian, look!" She pointed at the mildew stains on the walls and ceilings of the entryway; sweeping up the front stairs, she pointed to the
tobacco-colored rug on the landing, transparent with age and wear,
and to the moth-eaten velvet drapes. "When's the last time these curtains were opened? When's the last time there was any sunshine in
this place? I mean, probably it *was* a lovely house, and perhaps it could
be again—but as it is—and anyway—would you really ask me to give
up the Home Guard, and my investigation, and my research and my
students, all to come play assistant and housewife and companion to
Eugenia? Do you take my work seriously at all?" And as Ian pulled her
to him, murmuring apologies, Maggie dissolved into sobs.

Sister Angela Curran, too, was disturbed tonight as she recalled the events of the afternoon in Warborough. She had been unable to coordinate with Father DiClemente before Mrs. Brooke arrived to inspect the Hare House dairy, but as she led Mrs. Brooke around the grounds, it became increasingly clear to her that DiClemente was observing them and acting as her invisible assistant in deception. For instance, Sister Angela experienced a thrill of anxiety as she led Mrs. Brooke—chattering inanely all the while—into the cavernous dairy barn, but she needn't have. The enormous cellar trapdoors and any telltale lorry tracks were obscured by a sweet, soft, ankle-deep carpet of hay. Pointing out for Mrs. Brooke's benefit the milking stalls and the stacks of clean, empty canisters waiting to be filled, Sister Angela inwardly marveled at how DiClemente had been able to spread the hay so quickly and make it look so natural—as if it had always been there.

She cast her eye around for DiClemente as she introduced Mrs. Brooke one by one to the dairy hands. Gamely they answered the old stork's questions and showed her the dairy trucks. Sister Angela was proud and relieved by the disarming air of candor with which they gave their innocuous answers. DiClemente was nowhere to be seen. Sister Angela tried to feel only professional admiration for his cleverness and discretion, not disappointment at missing a chance to encounter him.

But DiClemente did not disappoint her. As she was accepting Mrs. Brooke's effusive thanks and goodbyes, he emerged from Hare House in his clerical black, his cheeks youthfully flushed and his salt-and-pepper curls charmingly tousled. The scar that slashed one cheek only added to his handsomeness, she thought. "Sister Angela!" he cried jovially. "I'm so pleased to see you! I spent all morning down at the chapel rehearsing Bach's Toccata and Fugue in D—they have such a charming little organ down there. Do tell me you'll come and listen to my efforts before you're off to London again." He clasped Sister Angela's hand in an unaccustomedly intimate display of friendship, and she couldn't help blushing.

"A priest who plays the organ!" exclaimed Mrs. Brooke superfluously, but Father DiClemente threw his head back and laughed as if she had made a brilliant witticism. The afternoon light glittered on his perfect canines as he extended his hand to Mrs. Brooke.

"Father DiClemente is a man of many surprising talents," Sister Angela observed. "We have him on loan from the Vatican, and he's been mentoring the young priest here in the village. Father DiClemente, may I present Margaret Brooke." Mrs. Brooke took the priest's hand and shook.

"Perhaps you will come and give me your opinion, too, Mrs. Brooke? It will be an impromptu recital, and you my most honored critics," DiClemente suggested with an expansive affability Sister Angela had rarely seen him use. He seemed able to turn it on and off like a light switch—and just now, his charisma was incandescent.

"Really, I ought to be going ... " Mrs. Brooke began. Father DiClemente looked up at her under his eyelashes in a pantomime of puppyish disappointment; Sister Angela felt he was really laying it on a bit too thick. "I can only stay a short while," Mrs. Brooke continued, "but I *do* have a special weakness for Bach, and it's so rarely that a European priest invites one to an impromptu private recital, so ... you've convinced me."

"Che Bello!" exclaimed the priest, and gave a little hop of delight. It was all Sister Angela could do not to roll her eyes. He took each of the women by an arm, and the three of them set off on the short, pleasant walk to the chapel of St. Genesis. The chapel was an ancient one of gray stone, springing up tall and narrow from the little churchyard with its leaning monuments. Inside, it was a quaint miniature of a cathedral, complete with a small organ loft, crowded with graceful, curving ranks of wooden and metal pipes, overlooking the pews from the rear. Father DiClemente mounted the steep and narrow stairs to the loft while the women stood below, near the altar rail; with little preamble, the priest began to play, choosing a simple *organo pleno* registration that allowed the expressivity of his playing to shine. The restrained and elegant beauty with which he rendered the famous opening phrases all but took Sister Angela's breath away, and looking at Mrs. Brooke, she could see that even that ridiculous woman was similarly affected.

Abruptly the organ's liquid trills broke off. "Sister Angela," Father DiClemente called down, "Would you be so kind as to come and turn my pages for me?" Sister Angela hurried to comply. In the cramped organ loft there was no space for her to stand, so she sat on the bench beside him, her feet carefully tucked away from the pedals. She shot DiClemente a questioning glance, but couldn't be certain he had seen. "I apologize for the interruption, Mrs. Brooke!" he called in his merriest voice and began to play again.

As soon as he felt certain their companion was swept up in musical rapture, DiClemente leaned—playing all the while—towards Sister Angela and murmured, "You're doing well. Keep following my lead. The perceptive Mrs. Brooke is about to have an unfortunate accident, and you and I will be its witnesses." Sister Angela gave the barest suggestion of a nod as the fugue approached its climax, then tumbled like a stream towards its resolution. There was a moment of utter stillness, and then Mrs. Brooke burst forth in enraptured applause. DiClemente gave Sister Angela a furtive nudge that sent her scurrying back down the organ loft stairs, but just before she turned away from him, he casually fingered his clerical collar and mouthed the words, "Don't worry. Jesuit." He pointed subtly towards her. "Nun. We are beyond reproach." His smile was modest but obvious. Turning on his organ bench, he beamed down at Mrs. Brooke. "How felicitous," he remarked loudly enough for her to hear, "to have met a fellow devotee of Bach!"

"I simply adore him," Mrs. Brooke sighed. "I'm a modernist in all other things, but Cardinal Hinsley—and even Sister Angela here—can tell you that I'm simply helpless in the face of baroque music, especially the sacred works."

"So the Toccata and Fugue is not your favorite Bach piece?" DiClemente asked from his perch.

"The way you play it, it may well become so," Mrs. Brooke gushed. "But the piece that's always touched me most deeply is the Ave Maria."

"A favorite of mine, as well," he declared. "It's always made me wish I were a singer, but that, alas, is not among my skills." He paused for a moment. "But Sister Angela has the voice of an angel. Sister Angela, is Bach's Ave Maria in your repertoire?"

"It's been some months since I sang it," Sister Angela hedged, "but yes, I know it." She wasn't certain how flattered she felt to be called upon to contribute her singing to Mrs. Brooke's tragic accident, and too, she felt impatient. What exactly was DiClemente's plan?

"Wonderful! Now, listen, my dears. I want Mrs. Brooke to be able to enjoy the best possible acoustical experience with which our charming little surroundings can provide her." He raised his hands to indicate the chapel around them and made a wry, self-deprecating face. "Sister Angela, stand just there, under the highest point in the ceiling. That's it—no, take another step backwards—yes, perfect. That will project your voice to maximum advantage. And Mrs. Brooke, you must come up into the loft with me—it's the best seat in the house."

Mrs. Brooke gamely complied, commenting on the stairs' precipitousness. When she reached their head, DiClemente said, "Brava. That's the spot—no—don't move. That vantage point will give you the perfect balance of Sister Angela's voice and the organ's reeds." DiClemente launched into a simple but enchanting version of the accompaniment, and soon Sister Angela was lost in the gorgeous counterpoint it offered to her melody. So spellbound was she by her musical collaboration with DiClemente she nearly forgot their other, more sinister collusion; as she offered up her final notes, she closed her eyes for a long moment, then opened them. In one horrifying glance she saw both that Father DiClemente's hand was on the back of Mrs. Brooke's neck, preparing to give her a brutal shove, and that the three of them were not alone in the chapel. A village lady—no doubt a matron of the altar guild—stood next to Sister Angela, a brass vase brimming with autumn flowers in each hand, the glow of aesthetic pleasure illuminating her face, which was upturned, fixed on DiClemente and Mrs. Brooke. The old bag had no idea, Sister Angela realized, that she was about to witness a murder—but it would dawn on her quickly enough.

What to do? How to alert DiClemente before all was lost? There was no time. Sister Angela did the only thing she could think of to do to draw his attention to the woman's presence. Just as Mrs. Brooke stumbled on the top step, Sister Angela began clapping loudly, wildly applauding her own performance.

Thank God for DiClemente's quick reflexes and sharp mind. He didn't even need to cast a glance her way to understand what Sister Angela's signal meant. Just as Mrs. Brooke lost her footing, she found DiClemente's hand under her elbow, bearing her up, as his hand on the back of her neck steadied her. "Watch out, my dear," he said in a voice full of concern. "These stairs are dangerous."

THE POLISH FILM

The night can sweat in terror as before
We pieced our thoughts into philosophy,
And planned to bring the world under a rule,
Who are but weasels fighting in a hole.

—W.B. Yeats, from "Nineteen Hundred and Nineteen"

WHEN FRAULEIN SCHROEDER *ushered the Reichsmarschall into his private study, the Führer was deep in concentration over a tactical map of Europe; he was using a set of color-coded grease pencils to make marks upon it, and with each mark he made, he gave a satisfied little grunt. The Reichsmarschall stood patiently in the doorway. He knew better than to interrupt the Führer in his task. The Reichsmarschall regarded the room: though smaller and less formal—book-lined, carpeted, painted Prussian blue and richly trimmed with fine woodwork—the Führer's private study was as imposing in its own way as his marble-lined office. For one thing, though smaller than the main office, the study was still a room of formidable size, with high ceilings, furnishings on a monumental scale, and a curious paucity of comfortable seating. Shelves and cases displayed an impressive array of German weapons, ranging from the ancient through the antique to the ultramodern and the frankly experimental. Hunting trophies crowded the upper walls, near the ceiling. Against the far wall a motion picture projector had been set up in anticipation of the test film* the Führer had specified that the Reichsmarschall should bring to this meeting. Near the Führer's desk, two enormous bookshelves had been moved aside to accommodate plastering and painting equipment; it was evident that the workers repairing this area were having some difficultly in precisely matching the room's deep Prussian blue.

The Reichsmarschall stroked his ivory baton with its golden eagles and black-enameled crosses. He had tucked the reel of test film awkwardly under his left arm so that this reassuring badge of his office could, as usual, occupy his hands. He took a deep breath and enjoyed the luxurious weight of his heavy autumn uniform. He took the opportunity to bask in the golden beams that filtered into the study's windows through the fiery lindens beyond. Northern France—where he had come from just this morning and would return tomorrow—was lovely in its own angular Frankish way, but nothing could match Berlin for pomp or stateliness. The Reichsmarschall envisioned with pleasure the formal dinner he would share tonight with Emmy, the picture of domestic bliss they would make as they looked in on little Edda dreaming in her crib. He took mental stock of the comforts he would enjoy after today's maintenance and resupply of his personal train car. He tried not to think of the syringe whose siren song was already calling to him. There would be time, he told himself, and willed his face to relax into a smile.

"What are you grinning about, you incompetent peacock?" the Führer demanded, interrupting his thoughts. "You're as bad as this painter who can't patch a simple bullet hole in my wall," he continued, gesturing towards the work the Reichsmarschall had noticed. "I should line the two of you up and execute you, one two, just like I did that sniveling general. Oh, yes, that's right," he went on in a calm voice edged with icy menace as the blood drained from the Reichsmarschall's face. "I've begun taking personal action when my … people … fail me. It brings me closer to the action, you see. I am still a soldier. I have not forgotten the hazards of combat. I have not forgotten its horrors. To stay connected I need blood on my hands, you see—hot, physical, messy. And *yet I maintain my standards. It is our gift as the master race to be precise. It is our gift to plan with care and to brook no excuses.*

"And yet, Hermann, you are failing me. Not only have you not invaded England, your Luftwaffe has not even disabled the Royal Air Force. And this despite the clear superiority of our Messerschmitt over their ridiculous Spitfire. Although you said it would never happen, their Bomber Command bombs this city—my city, Hermann—from six hundred miles away. That's four times the distance our Luftwaffe covers when it makes its raids on London. It is disgraceful! Where are our answers to the American B-17 or to this new Lancaster we hear about? Why is our rocket program not the terror of the world? You think I have gone soft, but I am telling you that my patience is running very short!" The Führer slammed his pencil down onto his desk with an anticlimactic little click. His scowl deepened.

"I assure you, mein Führer, questioning your commitment is the furthest thing from my mind," the Reichsmarschall said, cursing himself for being so promptly placed on the defensive. "I oversaw Operation Sea Lion personally, and my disappointment with its failure matches your own. True, the time to invade has come and gone, but we will continue to bomb London and other strategic locations with all our might. In the meantime, we can comfort ourselves that Project Über is in place to assure our victory in England, come what may. I have with me—"

"Ah yes, your Überweapon. Is it not true that you have had some difficulties on that front as well? Be candid with me, Reichsmarschall." It was eerie how still the Führer could be, even when he was talking—a Thuringian lynx choosing just the right moment to reveal itself to its prey. The Reichsmarschall felt the muscles around his throat contract, and he fought the strong urge to squirm.

Instead he tightened his grip on his baton, whose weight spoke to his Führer's great trust and confidence in the Reichsmarschall and of the essential and prominent role he was playing in the Reich's glorious mission.

The film reel cut into his armpit even through his heavy uniform, but that re-minder of his meticulous preparation bolstered his courage. The Reichsmar-schall swallowed hard and said, "I acknowledge that one of the six originally scheduled special bombers was shot down over the Channel, but I am pleased to report that it and its cargo were promptly replaced—Über is barely behind schedule. I am particularly proud of this achievement given the amendments we were forced to make to the final two bombers in response to intelligence that a nosy local woman was asking inconvenient questions about our land-ing sites. And I am even more proud of the evidence I bring you—"

"Wait, wait. A nosy Englishwoman? Amendments? This I have not heard about. Dazzle me with the tale of your improvisation, Hermann."

The Reichsmarschall was relieved that the Führer appeared to be enjoy-ing himself—even if he himself was not. Better laughed with than laughed at, of course—but one couldn't have everything. And an amused Führer was less likely to start playing firing squad. "Apparently she is a lady of letters. A scholar of poetry, there in Oxford. Now she is a supervisor in the Home Guard. They are reclaiming downed aircraft for scrap metal, and she happened to see two of our landing sites and to notice certain ... irregularities. She has a very sharp eye."

"Do go on."

"The good news that our liaison in the London nuncio's office reports is that this lady don is frustrated with how little notice she has been able to get from Britain's official intelligence community. MI-5 is all bluster and blunderers, you know. But I was disturbed by how much she perceived: the special doors on the disguised cargo planes, the lack of bomb shrapnel at the crash sites, the lack of damage to the planes' exteriors, the deep tire marks left by the transport truck—even the particular injuries sustained by the pilots. I took immediate action to alter the door design to attract less notice and to include boxes of bomb parts to be scattered when the planes exploded. I also reconfigured the explosives to make the damage they do look more like

damage inflicted by a Spitfire during a dogfight. Oberstleutnant Cordes-mann and I feel confident that this will be enough to deter our literary heroine from causing us any further mischief."

The Führer's lip curled in a sneer, and the Reichsmarschall felt a moment of relief at having deflected scorn from himself onto his dainty British antagonist. It was short-lived, however. The Führer asked, "And the tire tracks?"

"That was a tricky problem, mein Führer. With my team of engineers, I was able to design a track-free vehicle to load such a heavy device onto the transport truck—but there was no way for Cordesmann's team to construct it from materials available in the field. To make the vehicle available would have required a separate special-bomber delivery, and my team and I decided that the precaution was, in this instance, not worth the added time and risk. The other precautions we have taken ought to be enough to throw our gentle English rose off the scent. By adhering as closely as possible to our original timetable, I am pleased to report that by the end of the week, the six bomb components all will be in place, simply awaiting mein Führer's order to be completed with the delivery of the Teutonium core. I have with me today the film we discussed of the test detonation, and I hope that mein Führer will be as encouraged as I am by the evidence of this weapon's awesome power."

Delighted to be allowed to finish introducing the film he carried, the Reichsmarschall paused to breathe and gauge his Führer's response. The Führer, for his part, waited a beat and then gestured impatiently towards the projector at the far end of the room. "Well, man, get on with it," he snapped. Startled out of his momentary pleasure, the Reichsmarschall hurried towards the film equipment. He settled his baton carefully on the table next to the projector, double-checking to make sure it would not roll onto the floor, then withdrew the film reel from beneath his arm and removed it from its protective case. He took a deep breath and mentally reviewed the lesson his aide had given him in threading the film through the machine—all he needed was to be humiliated in front of the Führer by a technical glitch. He forced himself to work at a deliberate pace and to make sure that the film was right-side-up. When he was nearly ready, the Führer barked, "Well? Time is of the essence, Reichsmarschall."

"Nearly ready, mein Führer," the Reichsmarschall responded, switching the lamp on and adjusting the knobs with pleasure at this demonstration of his modern skill. He recrossed the room and lowered the study's main light. "May I move mein Führer's chair nearer to the screen?" he asked courteously, and the Führer allowed himself to be shepherded to an ideal vantage point. The Reichsmarschall flipped one final switch, and the screen against the wall came to life with flickering shadows. The only sound was the low and rapid ticking of film traveling through the apparatus. The Reichsmarschall fiddled with a knob, and a test pattern coalesced on the screen, then rolled away into bright whiteness and a new batch of shadows.

After a moment these shadows too resolved themselves, this time into the image of a cheerful young Heer corpsman pointing to a newspaper. The camera zoomed in on the newspaper's headline—Völkischer Beobachter, October 17, 1940—and then out a bit as the corpsman dropped the newspaper to reveal a hand-lettered placard reading Przerośl, Poland—Pop. 4,163— Viewing Station 10,000 Yards from Detonation Site. *The camera swung to a wide vista of haystack-dotted fields and hedgerows that lost leaves with each breeze. The sun shone and a couple of puffy clouds dotted the sky. It was an idyllic, bucolic scene. A gray blur entered the field of view at the lower right; the camera refocused without moving, so the countryside scene became blurred while a common tin alarm clock came into sharp focus. Its hands showed 7:59. The camera watched its second hand sweep past the six, past the nine, and towards home ... but precisely at 8:00 the picture abruptly dissolved into static, which then rolled into bright whiteness for a second or two.*

Then a second corpsman appeared, a round-faced kid, grinning. After verifying the date with his copy of Völkischer Beobachter, *he showed a placard announcing his position as Suwałki, 15 Miles from Przerośl. Again the camera swung to a sunny bucolic scene, but a different one—no hay-stacks, a distant church spire off to the left. Again the clock was introduced in the lower right of the frame; at 8:00 precisely, the ground seemed suddenly to drop away, then to reappear a moment later. The world spun crazily for a second and then came to rest; the frame appeared to show the rugged tire of a Stoewer PKW, sideways, on the ground to the right. Everything remained still for ten seconds, twenty, thirty; then the tire receded, the ground swung down, and the picture rolled back to bright white.*

Almost immediately, a third, jug-eared corpsman appeared, mugging into the camera at close range, then backing into the middle ground. This one revealed his vantage point to be Augustów, 35 miles from Przerośl. For the countdown to 8:00, the camera swung to a third sunny countryside scene: off to the right, in the distance, a barn could be seen, and to the left a small road wound towards the center point of the treeline on the horizon. At precisely 8:00, a bright flash momentarily washed out the scene, and then a towering cloud erupted from the horizon. As they watched, the camera zoomed out slightly and swung somewhat upwards to track its progress; its center seemed to spew smoke faster than its edges, causing its top to bulge into a shape like a hot-air balloon or a child's drawing of a tree. The explosion looked much the same in a fourth segment filmed 60 miles from Przerośl in Grajewo.

In the film's final segment, the round-faced corpsman reappeared, unshaven, his former grin nowhere in evidence. He displayed a copy of Völkischer Beobachter *from October 18, 1940, and the camera panned around a small rural airfield whose sign identified it as Suwałki, then zeroed in on the only aircraft apparent at the field, a sleek camouflaged Junkers Ju 86 with a swastika on its tail. A Luftwaffe pilot sat in the cockpit, and the corpsman climbed grimly into the radio operator's seat. There was a bumpy transition as the camera was handed off to him. The plane took off simply and cleanly, and the camera surveyed the partly cloudy sky, the countryside below—fields, forests, lakes—and the small town of Suwałki disappearing behind it. Zooming in on* a compass showed the flight's direction as north-northwest.

The plane flew low; scattered buildings—farmhouses mostly, and the occasional shrine or country church—were visible on the ground. The first few the film showed appeared intact, but as the journey continued, buildings on the ground appeared more and more damaged; increasingly, trees were flattened as by a storm. Ruined buildings grew denser as the flight continued; finally, the plane banked around a wide area of ground that appeared scorched. Rubble was apparent on the ground, and here and there a chimney or wall stood, but no buildings remained intact. Fires burned in patches across the devastated landscape. The camera panned across the area to give a sense of its size, but from the air distances were difficult to judge. Still, based on the sizes of the farmhouses early in the film, the Reichsmarschall estimated that the diameter of the area of total destruction was a few blocks—and Przerośl was a small place. Had been a small place—now it was nothing, a scorch mark on the map. The plane turned back to the south, and the picture rolled back to white for the last time.

The Reichsmarschall paused for a beat before reaching to switch off the projector, and then another beat before he crossed the room and turned the overhead lights back on. The Führer sat silent and perfectly still; the Reichsmarschall silently congratulated himself on the impression his test film had made. "This was a small device, mein Führer," he said quietly. "Compared with the thousand-pound blockbuster we will assemble in London, this was like a hand grenade. And yet this film represents concrete proof that we can show to the world: our weapon exists. It is operational. And we can show its effects up close—no murky images of London shot from Calais. We can send copies of this film to the Americans on the day we bomb London." The Reichsmarschall eased his baton off the projector table and into the crook of his right elbow, where it punctuated his potency.

"November 20," murmured the Führer.

"Pardon me?" the Reichsmarschall asked.

"November 20," the Führer repeated at closer to his normal volume. "It is an American holiday. Joseph Kennedy has already sent his family back to America to keep them safe from our bombs; on November 20 he will join them at their family's compound at Hyannis Port. That is the day we will strike London, and on that day we will deliver this film to Kennedy at Hyannis Port. He and Roosevelt will be desperate to make sure that Washington isn't next; coupled with the news from London, this film will send them begging to sign a non-aggression treaty. Who is our chargé in Washington now? Hans Thomsen, no? We will dispatch this film immediately to Thomsen and instruct him to deliver it personally to Hyannis Port on that morning. It is," the Führer said, making eye contact with the Reichsmarschall and allowing his expression to become frankly warm, "most persuasive. Your team in Poland is to be congratulated."

"You are kind, mein Führer," the Reichsmarschall replied with a slight bow. "I must confess that I am proud of their efforts. To my mind it is the Über combination of Nazi scientific brilliance and German precision engineering. I thank you on their behalf."

"I have only one question about the test's execution: why Przerośl?"

"It is remote, mein Führer, of little strategic significance, and at a safe distance from the Reich," the Reichsmarschall explained. "And although its population is small, it was once larger—it presented the infrastructural target of a village of twice its current size. And then, too, a large proportion of its population are Jewish. So of the list of potential villages my team proposed, I selected it as ideal."

"Very good," the Führer mused. "But weren't you concerned that its location so near the Soviet frontier might prematurely reveal our capabilities to Moscow? Our alliance with them is fragile enough, and, what, a year old?"

"It is a danger that crossed my mind, mein Führer," the Reichsmarschall conceded, "but weighed against other factors, I decided that the risk was low. After all, I asked myself: even if Soviet troops were to witness the blast—

would those clods understand the significance of what they were seeing?" The Reichsmarschall waited until the Führer gave a low chuckle, then joined in.

The Führer's mirth was brief. His face once again a mask, he warned the Reichsmarschall, "Fair enough. But Hermann, I have never been more serious in my life: you must not fail me. The Allies must not learn of this weapon's existence without the terror of witnessing its deployment against a major target." The Führer stood and, with a courtly gesture, escorted the taller man towards the study's door. "Your Über has my blessing to proceed to completion—but please understand that should it fail, the strategic implications will be disastrous. As will," he concluded quietly, "the implications for you, my dear friend."

The Reichsmarschall breathed deeply, broadening his shoulders and urging his spine to its fullest height. "Your personal concern for me touches me more deeply than I can say, mein Führer," he said. "But please be reassured. You have given me the Reich's best men, and they will not fail us. Über will bring glory—historic glory—to us all." The two men paused for a moment, their eyes locked upon one another's, sharing a confident smile. "I shall set to work immediately. Do you have any final questions?"

The Führer chuckled again and said, "Only one. How many kilograms are in a megaton?"

CHAPTER NINE:
LOOSE LIPS SINK SHIPS

O God,
Release my mother's soul from its dream!
Mankind can do no more. Appease
The misery of the living and the remorse of the dead.

—W.B. Yeats, from "Purgatory"

" … AND THAT IS WHY," intoned Cardinal Hinsley, "my homily today paid such special attention to the reading from Paul's letter to the Ephesians. 'Our struggle is not against enemies of blood and flesh,' Paul writes, 'but against the rulers and the authorities, against the cosmic powers of this present darkness; therefore take up the whole armor of God.' It's as if Paul could see directly into our hearts, now, as the middle of the twentieth century approaches." From the row of windows at the side of the Archbishop House's luncheon room, the golden sunlight of a crisp mid-autumn noon cast bright rectangles across the floor and table; behind the Cardinal, two deeply-colored stained-glass arches glowed.

As Sister Angela Curran observed with approbation the care the waiters took in serving the luncheon's main course—venison stewed with apples and parsnips, from a deer presented to the Bishop by a parishioner just yesterday afternoon—she tried, she really did, to attend to the Cardinal's wisdom. Heaven knew she needed some sort of armor as she did her work here in London, for her the heart of darkness. And yet she couldn't help but be distracted: by the wan face, diagonally across the table from her, of Father Roberto DiGangi, acting Papal Nuncio to London, who grew thinner and more ashen week by week; by the uncharacteristic drawn silence of Margaret Brooke, who sat next to him with dark rings under her eyes, her usual birdlike quickness replaced by a waxen hush. Really, Sister Angela would have thought that a quiet Mrs. Brooke would have been a relief; she was surprised by how it worried her. For one thing, she couldn't say for sure if Mrs. Brooke realized the near brush she had had the last time she and Sister Angela had met. Certainly the woman had made hasty excuses and fled the chapel, but perhaps it was really true that she was running late for a family function. Sister Angela couldn't say for sure whether Mrs. Brooke had begun to distrust her. She couldn't say for sure how much Mrs. Brooke knew about all sorts of things, and how was Sister Angela to pump more information from a silent source?

Sister Angela's attention came back to the conversation when Mr. Bullock, the Abbey's handsome, accomplished organist, asked, "Is it true, then, that Hitler is suppressing the Holy Roman Church within his territories? But I thought that he *was* a Catholic."

"I am afraid it is true," Father DiGangi murmured with his lilting accent. "Adolf Hitler was raised Catholic, but he certainly does not practice now. He is no friend of the Church." DiGangi spoke with his eyes lowered; when he had finished, he let his gaze flutter around the table, but he pointedly avoided looking at Sister Angela. She didn't think anyone else noticed, but she made a mental note to speak with him.

She was grateful, for once, to the Cardinal's pompous nephew Dr. Tibbets for lightening the mood by chiming in, "Well, if he's not for the Church, then Hitler can't be the genius at stirring the masses that they claim he is. I can't imagine anything more stirring than Mr. Bullock's postlude today."

"You are too kind, Dr. Tibbets," Mr. Bullock said, and conversation—as they say—turned general.

Sister Angela took the opportunity to address Mrs. Brooke. "It was such a lovely surprise to see you in Warborough a couple of weeks ago, Mrs. Brooke. I do so love sharing good music with others who appreciate it. And then ee are awfully proud of our diary, though I was sorry you didn't find what you were looking for when you visited. Any new discoveries since then?"

Mrs. Brooke blinked her big eyes a couple of times before answering. "I'm afraid it was a dead end, Sister Angela," she said. "Still, I appreciate your help." She smiled tiredly.

"Are you quite all right, Mrs. Brooke?" Sister Angela inquired. "You seem ... not altogether yourself."

Again, Mrs. Brooke looked blank for a moment before answering. "Thank you, dear. I'm just fatigued, though, really. You know my husband has taken over his mother's old house at Hambleden, and the place ... well, it needs so much. For example, I've finally convinced Ian to have it fumigated next week. It's all been a bit draining, frankly; were the place mine, I'd have disposed of it by now. But it was Ian's mother's place, and I think loving it is his way of honoring her memory. So." Here Mrs. Brooke took in a deep breath and regained a bit of her customary perkiness. "This, too, shall pass—and really, my problems are small, aren't they?" She beamed up the table at the two Howard ladies, the Duchess of Norfolk and her daughter Lady Davidson. "Tell us, how is Arundel faring?"

The Duchess, an ample but impeccably dressed woman whose accent retained the faintest trace of her Scottish upbringing, said, "Arundel is perfectly lovely at this time of year. Really, I must urge all of you to make the trip sometime. And I'm pleased to say that—although, of course, we all miss our men who are gone to fight—Arundel has suffered very little as a result of the Luftwaffe's … *incursions*. To the extent that Lady Davidson and I agreed between ourselves that we ought to spend some time in our London house and see what we can do to bolster morale here."

"Quite admirable," the Cardinal remarked.

"Meanwhile, both my son—The Earl Marshal—and my son-in-law Lieutenant Colonel Davidson are doing their bit to protect the homeland from invasion," the Duchess went on. "We couldn't be prouder of them."

"Tell me," Mrs. Tibbets put in, addressing Lady Davidson. "Am I correct in supposing that Lady Manci Howard is your sister-in-law?" The Cardinal shot Mrs. Tibbets a dark look, and Sister Angela would have sworn that Dr. Tibbets kicked his wife under the table. For her part, the Duchess flushed a deep red.

"Certainly not," Lady Davidson managed in a strangled voice. Her mouth—habitually downturned anyway—threatened to creep at both corners down off her chin.

Regaining her composure, the Duchess turned kindly, if a little stiffly, to Mrs. Tibbetts. "I suppose it's an honest mistake, my dear, but that creature is married to our distant cousin Mowbray Howard, Earl of Effingham. That branch of the family," she sniffed, "went back to the Church of England in the eighteenth century. I suppose not everyone had the … resources … to hold the recusant line. At any rate, one must feel rather sorry for poor Mowbray. He's not a bad boy at all. In fact—and this is rather interesting, rather dashing—his regiment has just been renamed the Third Maritime Regiment. An *army* regiment, you understand—but working *at sea*. It seems they're helping to protect supply convoys from the Luftwaffe and these awful new ... what do you call them? U-boats. Thrilling stuff. Anyway, there poor Mowbray is, soaking and shivering somewhere on a boat to protect his country, while this Manci Gertler, this Hungarian tart, traipses up and down London, fraternizing with God knows whom ... I hear she's seen with all sorts of Continental types. Well. I've said more than I ought. But really, can one help being concerned for one's relations, however distant?" The large morsel of buttered bread that the Duchess popped into her mouth no doubt signified the depth of her concern.

Sister Angela made a note to herself to learn more about this Manci Gertler Howard individual. Although she was nearly certain that the woman was in no way connected with any of Göring's agents here in London, such colorful characters made for excellent scapegoats and red herrings should the water get too hot. Sister Angela would ask Father DiClemente about her. Meanwhile, Mrs. Tibbets made her apologies to the Howard ladies as if it hadn't been evident to everyone at the table that she was drinking up every drop of the gossip the Duchess had let spill. After all, they hadn't even sat down to table yet before Mrs. Tibbets had made Lady Davidson confess that the Earl Marshal's wife Lavinia was not with them today because she had declined to convert to Catholicism. The woman's thirst for scandal was shameless. Sister Angela decided she must remember to sit closer to her from now on.

As Father DiGangi came to the Howard ladies' rescue by engaging them lightly on the topic of Mediterranean travel, Dr. Tibbets turned to Mrs. Brooke and asked, "Did I hear you say that you plan to fumigate your late mother-in-law's house? I hope that your family have made plans to be away for several days. The poisons have a tendency to linger and can be especially noxious during the cooler months, when our lungs are more delicate."

"Yes," Mrs. Brooke replied, "Ian's brother Malcolm has been most hospitable. He has a lovely place in Henley-on-Thames and his son has been begging Allie for a visit for weeks, so we'll all go down on Wednesday and stay as long as we need. I really can't tell you how grateful we are to him."

Henley-on-Thames on Wednesday. Sister Angela reminded herself to remember—Father DiClemente, fuming once they were alone together, had reiterated that he must know *everything* she knew about Mrs. Brooke's movements. Finishing her parsnips, Sister Angela hoped that Father DiClemente wouldn't be angry that she had gleaned so little. Mrs. Brooke, as she had told him, was usually so forthcoming. She didn't have long to ruminate on it, though—in removing the meal, one of the waiters managed to drop the Duchess's plate on the floor. Sister Angela would never have believed that servants could be such a handful.

Not for nothing was Maggie Brooke exhausted at Sunday Mass and at the Cardinal's luncheon afterwards. Her Saturday had been entirely too adventuresome and had stretched entirely too late into the night. In fact, although she had very much looked forward to bringing Allie and introducing him to the Cardinal's circle, that Sunday morning she couldn't bring herself to wake him in time to catch the seven o'clock to London. Rooney had barely lifted her head off her paws when Maggie looked in on them at dawn, and Allie hadn't even stirred under his blankets.

Her Saturday afternoon had begun in a way that was representative of her new routine: she and Gladys Grimmesby took their tea together in the Ladies' Auxiliary office, munching their egg salad sandwiches and compiling their weekly reports beneath that impressive bank of war propaganda posters. Just that afternoon, in fact, they'd put up a new one: blue water on the bottom, the silhouette of a sinking destroyer against a red sky on top. In large letters it proclaimed, "Loose Lips Might Sink Ships." Maggie still preferred the "Bring in Your Junk" poster, but this one did have a nice graphic boldness to it, she decided as she sipped her Darjeeling.

In fact, Maggie's official weekly report had been finished and turned in hours ago; she was keeping Gladys company now partly because she liked the woman, but also partly in order to fulfill her new routine of cross-referencing areas of heavy bombing, kills claimed, and crash sites reclaimed by the Home Guard. Air attacks outside of London proper had been even fewer this week than last. There had been one day of heavy bombing to the west and northwest of London, but the few crash sites she had visited or read about in others' reports had been kills claimed by R.A.F. units. If there was an irregular bomber crash among this week's reports, it must be Gladys's. Much as she had been enjoying their chat about the books Gladys had been reading—*Treasure Island* to the grandkids, John Donne's Holy Sonnets on her own—Maggie brought the conversation around to the point: "Listen, Gladys, you remember those odd crash sites I was looking into? With the unusual doors, and the different pattern of damage to the planes, and such as that? Are you sure you didn't see a site like that on your travels this week?"

Gladys rested her plump pink chin on one finger, adding one more dimple to her already dimpled face. "I'm glad you asked me. As a matter of fact, I've been meaning to talk with you about it. There was a site that—well, it had me a bit confused."

"Confused?" Maggie prompted.

"Yes. Well. It was on Wednesday morning, and we got called out to a site just a couple miles south of town. I remember you just missed the call—your crew had just left for that scrap automobile yard up in Yarnton that kept you busy 'til yesterday. Well anyway, we got there pretty fast, and I noticed the heavy lorry tracks to the site and thought to myself, *this is another one for Maggie.* And it was an He 111, just like those others. But then, strangest thing. I started looking for the other signs we'd talked about—the lack of bomb shrapnel, the pilot with a possible bullet wound behind his ear, the different doors—and I didn't see any of it. Just the heavy tracks, that was all. The crew was all dead, nobody got out—just like the others as well. An old gent from the Observer Corps arrived just after us. He saw it on fire from about five miles away. One engine was pouring smoke he said."

"That *is* a bit confusing. Hmm. Wednesday morning, you say? That's the day I marked as likely. And just south of town?" Maggie consulted the notes she had made from news reports of kill claims. "That *is* a crash no unit took credit for! So it must be one of my irregular crashes. But the doors weren't unusual, you say? And it looked like it had been shot down with bombs on board that blew up after crashing, and burned the whole crew?"

"Yes, exactly. What do you make of it, Maggie?"

"I confess I'm perplexed," Maggie said, and paused for a moment to think. Then she asked, "Do you think you could drive me out to the site? I'd like to see it for myself."

"Well, you know, love, there's not much there to see," Gladys pointed out. "We carried off pretty much the whole plane for reclamation, and the bigger pieces of shrapnel too, and the Fire Brigade boys buried the bodies, poor souls. They were terribly burned. And by the time we were all done with it, I'm sure we'd made more tire tracks than—but, well. If you'd like to see it, of course I'll show you."

The drive down didn't take long, but the autumn sun was already below the tops of the hawthorn hedgerows when they arrived at the field. As Gladys had said, it was a mess of criss-crossing tire tracks, but one set were still noticeably deeper than the others, and Gladys confirmed that those were the tracks that were already on the scene before the Fire Brigade arrived. She pointed out the corner of the field where a mound of fresh-turned dirt marked the German airmen's shallow communal grave. With a sudden intake of breath, Gladys said, "Oh, Maggie! One other thing. Remember the necklace you found at that first odd crash site?"

Maggie nodded, reached her hand into her pocket, and ran her thumb over that blackened disc, its one bright corner reading S-V-A-T, whatever that meant. She remembered the lumps of melted metal around the necks of others since then—not dog tags, but something personal, heavier. "Of course. Why?"

"This one was wearing a necklace too. Something around his neck. I didn't get close enough to take a real gander, you know, I just noticed—when they were carrying him away—it dangling, like," Gladys said, her voice strained. Maggie knew that seeing these bodies wore on Gladys, made the Germans too real for her. Once they'd been just faceless villains, but more recently—"They look just like our boys," she'd whispered to Maggie tearfully.

Scattered about, and ground into the earth by the tracks of vehicles and boots, Maggie could see the same small debris she saw regularly, at normal crash sites—the kind of bomb-casing shrapnel so noticeably absent at the crash sites that had caught her attention. Here and there, bits of broken glass glittered in the slanting light of the sunset. Like the other unusual crash sites, this one seemed oddly convenient to a road. But what did it all add up to? Shaking her head, Maggie had to admit to herself that she couldn't say. "Thank you, Gladys," she said. "Let's go home."

The little Oxford house was cheerfully lit and seemed all the more cozy and welcoming after the recent excursions to Ian's mother's dank and drafty place in Hambleden, which somehow contrived to feel both cramped and too big at the same time, with its winding corridors and profusion of tiny, high-ceilinged rooms overstuffed with furniture. Here lamplight combined with the light of a merry fire to lend the broad windows a hospitable orange flicker. Maggie let herself in, waved to Gladys as she pulled away, and was hanging up her coat when Zofia rushed out from the kitchen to help her. "I am sorry," Zofia fretted, "I am back in kitchen and did not hear when you arrive."

"Don't worry, dear, I'm managing just fine," Maggie reassured her. "How was your Sabbath?"

"Very nice, thank you," Zofia said as Maggie peeked deeper into the house. The kitchen table had tea things on it, and she could see Rooney's tail thumping against the door frame. Following her glance, Zofia explained, "Mr. Allie decided he want to take the tea in kitchen with me. I hope is all right?" When Maggie nodded, Zofia added, "Is nice to have company. Mr. Allie is very interesting, very intelligent!"

"I couldn't agree more," Maggie said. "Don't let me interrupt you, then." Zofia retreated to finish her meal, and Maggie started towards her study—but stopped and turned towards the telephone nook in the corridor. There she had left the card of her MI-5 contact, Stephen Bloom; she read out to the operator the first of the three telephone numbers printed upon it. Bloom picked up almost immediately.

"Good evening, Stephen Bloom speaking," he said. "How may I assist you?"

"Mr. Bloom, it's Margaret Brooke from Oxford," Maggie said. "I hope I'm finding you well?"

"Quite well, thank you, madam," he said pleasantly. "May I caution you that one never knows who is listening in on a telephone conversation?"

"Er ... oh dear," Maggie stammered. The truth was she'd never thought about it. "Thank you. Yes. Well, em ... do you remember the pattern we discussed when we met before?"

"Perfectly. And I've read your subsequent reports. Has something new happened?"

"Well," Maggie hemmed, "I'm not sure. That is to say, there's been a crash that fits the pattern in some regards, but not in others."

Mr. Bloom was silent for a moment, and then said, "I see. I shall have to come and speak with you in person. Would tomorrow be all right?"

"I shall be in London tomorrow morning anyway," Maggie said. "May I call at your office just after nine?"

"Splendid," Mr. Bloom agreed, and then he asked, "Have you collected all of the available evidence regarding this anomalous incident?"

"What do you mean?" Maggie asked.

"I just mean ... before we talk, it would be helpful if you could do as exhaustive as possible an examination of the physical evidence available to you. I'm sure you've been very thorough, but—"

"Quite. I understand. And I have been conscientious, but ... " Maggie's voice trailed off as she thought about that necklace Gladys had seen on Wednesday's pilot.

"What is it, Mrs. Brooke?" Mr. Bloom asked.

"Well, er ... to what lengths ought I to go in order to make my investigation complete?"

"Mrs. Brooke," Mr. Bloom said, his voice grave. "I believe that you know as well as anyone how high the stakes are—isn't that why you persisted until you brought this matter to my attention? It is your duty to be as thorough as possible. You may be saving lives."

Maggie took a deep breath. "I—I understand," she said. She started to ring off, then changed her mind. "Mr. Bloom, do the letters S-V-A-T mean anything to you?"

"S-V-A-T," he repeated thoughtfully. "Where did you run across them?"

She thought for a moment about how much would be safe to say, then risked, "I saw them on a medal around the neck of a foreign pilot. I don't think they were the complete inscription, but that's all I saw."

Mr. Bloom paused for a moment, and then said, "I'll have to check, but ... I believe the Czech word for saint is S-V-A-T-Y. Could it have been a saint's medallion? Like a Saint Christopher or something?"

"Yes, I rather think it could. Thank you, Mr. Bloom. I look forward to speaking with you in the morning."

"As do I. For one thing, I've begun reading *Finnegans Wake* and I'm afraid I can't make heads nor tails of it," Mr. Bloom said with a laugh. "I hope you can set me straight, Mrs. Brooke. Good night."

As Maggie replaced the receiver in its cradle, Allie stuck his head around the corner, for all the world as if he were looking to see if she were there. A half-second later Rooney's head came round the corner too, and she gave a short bark. "Mother?" Allie said. "Is everything all right?"

And that is how Maggie found herself in a field south of Oxford in the darkest hours of Saturday night, supervising her son in digging up the Heinkel crewmen's shallow grave. "I have an awful feeling it's desecration of the dead," Maggie had confided to Allie during their whispered conversation.

"Don't worry, Mother. We'll be very respectful," Allie had countered. "And your MI-5 contact was right—we may be saving lives. Think of it as a forensic exhumation."

The late-October night was chilly, and their task was a grisly one. Maggie couldn't help but be reminded of her childhood in America, and the gleefully spooky late-October traditions she had observed there: the hawthorns' branches pointed at the moon like skeletal fingers, and occasional gusts of wind made the few larger trees creak like ghostly knee joints. Unfortunately, this grimness was not ritual but real. Maggie held the electric torch steady and directed Allie: move back a step, move back another step, now over to the right, and to the right again. Rooney ran joyously back and forth along the expanse of the moonlit field once Allie gave her the command that let her know she was off duty. After a half-hour of Allie digging, though, Rooney joined him in the pit. "Maybe we should let Rooney take over now," Maggie said. "They're not likely buried much deeper than this, and her soft paws are less likely than that spade to damage them."

Not five minutes later Rooney alerted them with a whine that she had found something: Maggie shone the torch down and shuddered to see that, around the middle of the far side of the pit, the dog had uncovered a hand. Maggie crossed herself and then, ignoring Allie's protests, jumped down into the grave. Through a combination of directing Rooney and hand-digging herself, she began uncovering the crewmen's faces and shoulders. She tried not to think about the faint smell they were already beginning to emit, nor about how horribly they were damaged. The third man's uniform shoulder bore the strap of a lieutenant, which Maggie had learned indicated he was the pilot. Feeling gingerly around his charred neck she found a chain; giving it a gentle tug, she unearthed a medal about the size of a shilling. By torchlight she could see that it was blackened and that its left edge had melted into a lump. Polishing it with her pocket handkerchief, though, she was able to make out the ends of two words: along the top edge, *-A-T-Y*, and along the bottom, *-C-L-A-V.*

Could that be Czech? She couldn't say, but felt confident that Mr. Bloom would know. But why would a Czech pilot be flying a German mission over England? She knew that the Czechoslovak government was operating in exile in London, so she couldn't imagine it would happen except under duress. A chill crept up her spine—could it be a coincidence that none of the Czech pilots had survived his special mission? Crossing herself again, she unclasped the medal from around the airman's neck. "I'll say a special prayer in mass tomorrow for your soul," she promised the man, and put the medal carefully into her coat pocket with the first one. Then, clambering back out of the shallow pit, she said to Allie, "All right, son. Let's start filling it back in."

CHAPTER TEN:

RATS

The cold, wet winds ever blowing,
And the shadowy hazel grove
Where mouse-grey waters are flowing
Threaten the head that I love.

—W.B. Yeats, from "The Pity of Love"

WEDNESDAY MORNING DAWNED in the watercolor splendor of damp English autumn. Workaday sounds were hushed by the whisper of drizzle, and despite the sky's gray-blue, the trees of Oxford were luminous as stained glass. Maggie was still enjoying tea and the morning paper in her window-lined study—that hour of peace she claimed as her early-riser's prerogative, savoring the quiet before the house arose and stumbled to the breakfast table—when she was startled by the tinkling of the telephone. She folded her paper and stood, listening as Zofia's footsteps approached, paused at the telephone nook, and approached again. Likely Ian was calling to ask her to bring some item or other for him on their trip to Henley this afternoon.

Sure enough, Zofia called out, with a light rap on Maggie's open study door, "Mr. Brooke for you, Mrs. Brooke."

"Thank you, Zofia," Maggie said, passing her in the doorway, hearing the gentle clinking as Zofia gathered up the teacup and saucer from her desk. She lifted the receiver and said in a joking tone, "Margaret O'Hare's delivery service. What may I bring you, Mr. Brooke?"

"Nothing at all, I'm afraid," Ian's voice responded. "Malcolm has just rung me up, and it looks like we'll have to put off our holiday in Hambleden. Colin has measles."

"How dreadful!"

"Quite," Ian said. "It seems he's been feeling low for a few days, but only this morning has the rash made his diagnosis undeniable. Eugenia has her hands full with him, and, to tell you the truth—I don't believe I've ever had measles myself, so I confess I'm just as happy to stay away. It sounds like he's awfully disappointed, poor chap, but I told Malcolm we'll just postpone things a week or two. I hope this doesn't inconvenience you awfully, my dear?"

"I suspect that this case of measles is a plot contrived by the rats in your mother's cellar. Anything to buy some more time." Ian didn't laugh, so Maggie said, "I'm sorry, darling, that was a terrible joke. Does Eugenia need anything? Is there anything at all I can do?"

"No, dear, I think it's just a matter of time and rest. I imagine that by the weekend Colin will be on the mend. And your joke—I don't suppose it was *so* bad. Mrs. Umphlett made a most unpleasant discovery in the potato bin last week. I won't elaborate except to say that as usual, my dear, you were absolutely correct to say the house needs fumigating."

"Poor Mrs. Umphlett!" Maggie laughed. "Oh dear me. I can just imagine the look on her face." After a pause, she added, "Well, but, you must already have packed up and cleaned things out for the fumigation. Are you going to be all right down there?"

"Things are a bit at sixes and sevens," Ian admitted. "I had Mrs. Umphlett empty out the pantry, and then I sent her off for ten days at her sister's in Guernsey. She left yesterday morning, and Mr. Pippin has gone to see his daughter in Cumbria. So I shall be roughing it here on my own—but I think I can manage. There's a shop in town does a lovely kidney pie."

"*Please* tell me you're joking," Maggie said. "That is one dish my American palate will never accommodate. But seriously, Ian, do come home, you'll be more comfortable. Or we can come down there and rough it with you."

"You tempt me, my love, but business goes on," Ian said. "Perhaps I'll come up to Oxford at the weekend. For the moment I can't get away, but I wouldn't ask you to come down to this place without even any Mrs. Umphlett to make it appealing. No, you stay there, darling. Why don't you ring up Jack Lewis for some literary talk?"

"Oh, Jack and Ronald, Ronald and Jack," Maggie groaned, vexed. "They're having another of their Inklings functions tonight. You're a man, perhaps you understand these things, so tell me. If they're truly a literary club, then *what* can they be doing that's so scandalous as to preclude the presence of ladies?"

"Oh, I'm sure the doings of grand literary fellows are beyond me," Ian teased. "Probably they're smoking cigars and reading out only the naughty bits of the classics." He chuckled, then added, "It's only their excluding you that makes their little club exclusive, dear. They're just boys in a treehouse. Don't give them the satisfaction."

"I'm sure you're right, darling. Thank you. Do try to stay comfortable down there, and promise me that before we speak again you'll have eaten *something* green."

"I'm sure I'll eat many green things, my dear," Ian assured her. "After all I can't speak for the age of that shop's kidney pies."

The Home Guard Women's Auxiliary ladies were surprised when, despite having put in for a week off, Maggie turned up at the office that morning barely later than her usual hour. And, as always, they were delighted that she had brought Allie and Rooney with her. Allie took a seat at one of the room's large tables, and the girls vied for the seats closest to him. His gently flirtatious banter was particularly welcome just now. Metals reclamation had been slow: farmers were too busy with the harvest to sort out and dispose of junk, and for the past two weeks or more, the German air attacks had focused almost exclusively on central London, so local crash sites were thin on the ground. The girls had been filling their time by knitting socks and scarves for servicemen, but it was dull work compared with their adventures of the summer.

The girls' surprise at her arrival was nothing, though, compared with Maggie's surprise when, not half an hour later, a knock came on the office door and Stephen Bloom poked his head in. "Professor Brooke!" he said. "Just the person I was hoping to see. Might we continue our conversation?" With a little gesture he indicated that she should follow him, so Maggie gratefully set down her half-finished army-green sock and followed him down the corridor to an unoccupied office. "I'm glad I caught you," he said as she settled herself in a chair. "Your supervisor tells me you put in for the week off, but came in today anyway. I hope all is well?"

"Yes, thank you, just a change of plans due to an illness in the family," Maggie said. "What can I do for you, Mr. Bloom?"

"Mostly I just wanted to fill you in. I've shared all of your reports up my chain of command—they certainly seem of interest from my point of view. The anomalies and coincidences do seem to form a pattern. But my superiors at MI-5 tell me that none of our information adds up to any credible threat in their eyes." He raised his eyebrows and pursed his lips in an if-you-say-so expression. "There's no confirmation, no corroboration. Furthermore, Whitehall has now confirmed that the Nazi invasion attempt is off. Of course, this is wonderful news; as Britons we should be cheering in the streets. The German invasion fleet that has been docked at Normandy is shutting down its operations."

"I'm certainly delighted not to be invaded by the Germans, Mr. Bloom, but I must make two objections. First, let me remind you that I am an American citizen and my son is Irish, by law and by my plan. Much though we love Britain, we are not Britons but volunteers— though I think my son's sacrifice gives you an idea of how far we would go to protect England and defeat Hitler. Second and more to the point, this talk of 'no corroboration' confuses me. What about the consistent pattern we saw of downed planes that went unclaimed as kills? Didn't you tell me on Sunday morning that R.A.F. records had confirmed that all of those crashes were unclaimed, and didn't you agree with my son that unclaimed kills are unheard of? Don't you suspect that the R.A.F did not in fact shoot these planes down? And if they didn't—then who did?" Maggie tried not to feel flustered, but had always found herself upset by the freedom of those in power to ignore evidence and logic.

"I'm afraid I don't really understand any better than you do, Mrs. Brooke," he explained apologetically. "You and I can rest in the knowledge that we did our research, we did our homework. We presented the strongest case we could to MI-5, and they're choosing not to act on it. The best I can tell you is that often, the men up the chain are guided by information that you and I aren't privy to." He paused and watched her struggle to retain her composure. "Mrs. Brooke, do you ever read any German literature? Are you familiar with *Das Schloss*?" When her face remained blank, he said, "I don't believe it would be wrong of you, even given present world circumstances, to read Herr Kafka's work. He's important, as important as our Joyce, and I'm sure Hitler considers him subversive." Mr. Bloom smiled. "But it *would* be unpatriotic of me to say that reading his work might give you a sense of what it's like working for government. So." He stood, then shook Maggie's hand when she rose. "Let's both stay in touch should anything change. And thank you, Mrs. Bloom, for your attention and your intelligence. I mean that in the sense of brain power. England could use more like you." He went out and left her still searching for what to say or ask.

Maggie was troubled for the rest of the day as she knitted, despite Allie's and the girls' cheerful chatter and Gladys's untrained but intelligent literary questions. She was troubled at dinner, despite the elegant clear borscht, rich mushroom pierogis, and braised rabbit that Zofia had prepared in response to Allie's curiosity about the life she had left behind in Poland. And her trouble turned to horror the next morning before dawn when she collected the newspaper from her front steps. On the front page, a headline announced: Village of Henley-on-Thames Devastated by German Bombs. The article described aerial bombers converging from the east and north and reported that the sleepy village had been virtually obliterated. It described survivors' shock and horror as well as the confusion of the authorities, who insisted that the village had been of little tactical significance and housed no military or industrial infrastructure.

Maggie raced to the telephone and tried to reach Ian, then Malcolm, and then Ian again, but there was no answer at either home and it was far too early to expect anyone at the business, though of course she rang that number too. Consulting her wristwatch, she debated the wisdom of ringing Anne in Canterbury. She decided that it was too early, recited an Our Father and a Hail Mary to steady her nerves, then began on "The Lake Isle of Innisfree," but by the time she got to the part about the bee-loud glade she found herself in the corridor with the receiver in her hand. At Anne's, Mrs. Lanspeary answered groggily but insisted that Maggie had not awakened her. She reported that Miss Brooke was still abed and had not heard from either of her brothers overnight. She offered to fetch Anne to the telephone, but Maggie demurred: "Let her sleep for the moment, poor old thing. But do let her know that I rang, and I'm beside myself. And tell her that I'm at the ready the moment we have any news, or should she need anything at all."

By the time she rang off, fingers of rosy light were creeping along the corridor from the dawn that was breaking across the windows of Maggie's study. The soft clattering of drawers and dishes reached her from the kitchen, followed not long after by aromas of toast and tea. Zofia brought her tray, as usual this fall, to her study, and before she finished them, the telephone rang. It took all her self-restraint to allow Zofia to answer it. "Mr. Brooke for you," Zofia reported, and Maggie thought those words had never sounded so sweet.

"I'm ringing from London," Ian said, hoarse with fatigue and grief. "Maggie, I—I can't even think how to tell you. Something awful has happened."

By midmorning, Sister Angela Curran was greeting Maggie, Allie, and Rooney at the door of Archbishop House. "Cardinal Hinsley will join us for luncheon, and he'll welcome you himself then," she said, "but I know he'll tell you to think of Archbishop House as your home for as long as you need to be in London. Let us know anything we can do to assist you during this terrible time." She pressed Maggie's hand between both of her own. Maggie couldn't put her finger on what it was about Sister Angela's demeanor that always gave her the air of an actress reading from a script. It wasn't that she seemed insincere, quite, Maggie didn't think—just, there was something a little wooden around her wide pale eyes, something a little flat behind her warm Drogheda brogue. "Your husband is waiting for you in the library. I'll take you to him. Just leave your bags with George." She indicated the footman with a vague gesture, then waited a moment for Maggie and Allie to shuck their coats and hats before she led them to Ian and discreetly withdrew.

Ian's face was puffy, his eyes ringed and bloodshot; his clothes were rumpled and stained, and smelled faintly acrid. He fairly leapt from his chair when he saw them, reaching to enfold them both in his arms with the air of a drowning man clutching a buoy. Then he collapsed back onto the settee where he'd been waiting, pulling Allie down with him, his arm still around his son's shoulders. Rooney tucked herself neatly beside Allie's feet. Maggie fumbled behind herself and pulled up a nearby ottoman so that she could sit without withdrawing her hand from Ian's grasp. She leaned in as he began to speak in a low, dazed voice.

"It was around eleven last night. I'd gone to bed early, but the planes woke me. They came in low and flew right over Hambleden on their way to Henley. It sounded like being run over by a locomotive. I have to confess that for a moment—for a moment—" he choked on his own horror, then took a breath and steadied himself. "For a moment it took me right back to that trench in Picardy." He freed his arm from around Allie long enough to rub his bad thigh; then he took Allie's hand and squeezed it hard. "I made a dash for the cellar, of course. Mr. Pippin fixed us up a shelter down there when the Germans started raiding last summer—some chairs and supplies and a radio. Just in case, you understand. But I thought—" He shook his head. "I ran down there, and as soon as it occurred to me I turned on Mr. Pippin's little radio. At first there wasn't any news, but the music was a relief, you know, and then there *was* some news. And I knew I had to get over to Henley right away, to lend a hand if I could, and to make sure Malcolm—to see—" He choked again, shook his head, found his way back to his story.

"I caught a ride down with the fire brigade boys. And when we pulled into Henley, well—you couldn't even recognize it. There wasn't any Henley there. It really was like Picardy again. There were fires everywhere for them to put out, but as soon as I got my bearings, I ran of course to Malcolm's. Only. Malcolm's house—it just wasn't there anymore. It was—there was—the new wing was still standing, and on fire. But otherwise, just piles of stone and debris. And then I heard him screaming. Or not screaming—moaning, more like. Towards the back of the house. I had to dig to find him. He didn't know what was going on, he was in a daze at first. Shock, the medics said. But once I got him out, he was more or less all right. He said—he said he'd been sleeping in the cellar. He wasn't feeling well, and the light was hurting his eyes. So Eugenia had set him up a cot down in the cellar. And it—and it saved his life." Sobs overcame him.

Maggie gave him a moment, then said gently, "This is Colin you mean. Colin is more or less all right."

"Yes," Ian said, finding control of his voice. "They've got him over in the hospital. We can see him after lunch, they said. He had some cuts and bruises and he was favoring one leg. When I first saw him I thought he was burned, but then I remembered the measles." He gave a short laugh, and Maggie released his hand so he could get out his handkerchief and wipe his eyes.

"But Malcolm and Eugenia ... " Allie said in a tone somewhere between statement and question.

A little more air seemed to go out of Ian; his moment of lightness fled. "Malcolm and Eugenia are—they—" He couldn't finish the sentence, only shook his head, but Allie understood even without seeing. He put both arms around his father. In a strangled voice, Ian said, "He was the best little brother a chap could have had."

After a moment, Allie said, "And I know he would have said you were the best big brother. I know that—despite everything this year, despite our disagreements—I know you're the best father." Tears ran freely down his cheeks and onto Ian's ruined gray tweed jacket. "Poor Colin. What he must be going through. I don't know what I'd do if I lost you."

Ian held Allie tighter, then leaned back so that he could look his son in the eye—an automatic gesture of sincerity, even if Allie couldn't see—though did his pupil dilate in response? Ian had the unspoken, almost unarticulated feeling that he and his son were truly looking at one another. "I thought I *had* lost you this year, son. And if it had been true, I think it would have killed me. I know you feel I try to hold you back. I hope you can forgive me. I know I oughtn't do it. The truth is, you're so precious to me that I get frightened."

In her heart, Maggie was repenting, too. She was sorry about how little of herself she had offered to Eugenia, who had always been so friendly and kind. But more than that, she was wondering whether Malcolm's and Eugenia's blood—the blood of all the dead of Henley— might be on her hands. Henley was just such an unlikely target for a Luftwaffe attack. As hard as she had worked to get MI-5's attention— was it possible that she had gotten someone else's attention, too? She thought about the changed patterns at that last special crash site. Had someone found out that she was onto them? She wondered how many people she had told that she would be in Henley on Wednesday night. Was it possible that the Nazis were trying to kill her—not just as a resident of Britain, but as an individual threat to their plans? She tried to dismiss her worries as delusions of grandeur, but the part of her mind that churned out hunches and intuitions—the same part that couldn't let go of the oddity of those Heinkel crash sites—that part of her mind was certain that something about the bombing of Henley was just not right.

Chilled to the core, Maggie chose Ian and Allie's reconciliation as a perfect moment to withdraw discreetly and put in a call to MI-5. She had slipped Stephen Bloom's card into her skirt pocket before leaving the house in Oxford, and as she stepped out of the library and into the corridor, she withdrew it. "Pardon me," she asked a passing footman. "Do you know where I might place a telephone call?" Obligingly, he led her to Cardinal Hinsley's private study, settled her next to the telephone, and shut the door for her. As before, Mr. Bloom answered promptly at the first of the three numbers printed on his card.

Maggie got right to the point. "No doubt you know about the German aerial bombing of Henley-on-Thames last night. Mr. Bloom, I have the most horrible feeling that those bombs might have been intended for me."

"For you? Personally?" Mr. Bloom asked. "What makes you say so?"

"I am certain that the bomber crashes we've been discussing are somehow evidence of a plot, and I am beginning to believe that the Germans know I know. Why else would they have begun to vary their patterns after I brought them to your attention? I don't know how they know, but I'm almost certain that they do. And if they know that, they could just as easily know that I was planning to be in Henley-on-Thames last night. As I told you yesterday morning, the only reason I didn't was because of a last-minute illness in the family."

"Mrs. Brooke," Mr. Bloom said. "You know I am an admirer and supporter of your intellect and that I'm convinced by the evidence you've shown me of a German smuggling plot using those supposed crashes. But now you're telling me that Hitler organized a whole bombing raid and wiped a village off the map *just for you*? I hope you don't mind my pointing out that it sounds a bit ... " He broke off, searching for a way to convey his meaning without offending his informant.

"A bit paranoid?" Maggie supplied. "Please tell me that I'm only being paranoid." She couldn't seem to lower her hackles, and she recalled again the priest's hand on the back of her neck in that organ loft in Warborough.

"Frankly? Yes, Mrs. Brooke, you're being paranoid. Listen. Air raids go astray or confuse their targets from time to time—it does happen, especially on a night as overcast as last night. My superiors are telling me that no new threat arising from the Battle of Britain— that is, from the general bombing that the country suffered this summer and autumn—no new threat arising from that bombing is likely. The weather over the Channel has turned bad, and for the next four months it'll only get worse. The Nazis have changed their strategy. They're not trying to invade us. They're concentrating on wiping out

London directly. So a couple squadrons went off course and bombed the wrong spot. That's war. But to think that Göring is pursuing a personal vendetta against you? Mrs. Brooke, listen to yourself."

"Mr. Bloom, I *am* listening to myself, and I know how it sounds," Maggie faltered. "I hardly believe it myself—and yet ... let's look at the facts. The Luftwaffe has some of the most sophisticated navigational equipment the world has ever seen, if the newspapers can be believed. And if they can be believed, then Henley was attacked by squadrons coming from *two different directions*, which suggests to me—if I may be so bold—that the bombing of Henley was no mistake. Does Henley has some military or manufacturing importance that the newspapers haven't told us about? Is there something else about Henley that makes it a Luftwaffe target?"

"Not that I am aware of," Bloom admitted.

"In that case," Maggie said, haltingly, her voice dropping nearly to a whisper, "In that case, our only lead in understanding Henley's destruction is a certain foolish woman who's been crying to the heavens that the Luftwaffe is engaged in some sort of secret operation. Except that if that woman is really so foolish as all of that ... then why bomb—and not just that—why *saturation* bomb Henley?"

As she followed the thread of her argument, Maggie's voice regained some of its accustomed confidence. "I bring all of this to your attention, Mr. Bloom, not because I think *I* am anyone of particular importance, not to aggrandize myself, but because England is my adopted home and has been good to me, and I would like to keep it safe. And if that is your aim, too, Mr. Bloom, then I suggest that London be on full alert. In fact I suggest that London and all of the area between it and Oxford be on full alert. My brother-in-law and sister-in-law are dead, Mr. Bloom, and my nephew is suddenly orphaned. I know that wars are fully of tragedy, but I also believe it is the responsibility of people of good faith to avert all the tragedy they can. Can MI-5 show me some good faith, Mr. Bloom?"

There was a pause during which Maggie discovered that there were tears running down her cheeks and her nose was threatening to run. She reached for her pocket handkerchief, but discovered that in the morning's rush and confusion she had come away without one. "Oh, bother," she muttered, delicately dabbing at her face with her blouse sleeve.

"Mrs. Brooke," Mr. Bloom said delicately. "I am sorry. I haven't treated you very sensitively, and I apologize. As I said yesterday morning, I agree with you that the crash sites indicate that some sort of German covert operation is afoot. Even my superiors, I'm starting to see, concede that. It's just that none of us can fathom the aim or discover the details. Sometimes I worry that the greatest downfall of men in the intelligence community is our great fear of discovering that we are foolish. Mrs. Brooke, it may be that we have simply been afraid to admit that Göring is making fools of us.

"So I'll tell you what. First of all, I promise, going forward, to take your concerns for your family's safety much more seriously. Second, I shall continue diligently attempting to work this puzzle that the Luftwaffe has set for us. And finally, I shall make it a personal priority to increase the number of sentries in Oxfordshire and west of London, starting today. You have my word on that. Is there anything else I can do to help you right now?"

"No. If you can do those three things—I mean *really* do them, in good faith—then I'm satisfied," Maggie said, then added, "for now."

"All right. Then please stay in touch should any further information come to your attention. And please know that you and your family have my heartfelt sympathies at this terrible time," Mr. Bloom said. He added, just before he rang off, "Thank you, Mrs. Brooke."

CHAPTER ELEVEN:

THE CORE

A shape with lion body and the head of a man,
A gaze blank and pitiless as the sun ...
—W.B. Yeats, from "The Second Coming"

NOVEMBER IS MORE THAN HALF-SPENT, and a waning gibbous moon presides over a chill Wednesday evening. The Nazi military zone on the coast of Brittany is lit up like a carnival, though, as it has been night after night throughout the summer and fall. The air is as sharp and effervescent as a Norman cider. Twenty English-speaking Brandenburgers are loading a leaden cube five feet on a side, into a stripped-down Heinkel He 111 and making last-minute adjustments to the rockets that will assist the overloaded plane in its launch. The hydraulic hoist strains under its load. The Reichsmarschall hovers nearby, inspecting, hefting his ivory baton, making everyone nervous. The Reichsmarschall is heard to mutter that at least tonight's mission doesn't require the participation of any verminous Slavs. The Brandenburgers complete their preparations, don their paratrooper equipment, and strap themselves into the accompanying troop plane's custom-designed hold: tonight they will parachute into Oxfordshire. In another context, it would be a gorgeous sight to behold—twenty parachutes like dandelion seeds broadcasting themselves across the countryside. One can only assume, though, that should any Englishman observe the Brandenburgers' descent tonight, he will be terrified.

Before the troop plane's hatch is closed, the Reichsmarschall stands stiffly before it and addresses the men. They make themselves uncomfortable craning their necks, and many of them still cannot see the Reichsmarschall, but the alternative would be his addressing them while stooped inside the cramped hold with them. So crane their necks they must. "Soldiers," he addresses them. "What you do tonight, you do for the Fatherland and to the glory of the German people forever. Should you fail, we are ruined utterly. Do not disappoint yourselves. The Überweapon is in your hands. Heil Hitler!" He salutes and they salute back, and in a confusion of fire and G-forces the two planes are aloft. Below them, the English Channel swallows light as if it, too, were made of lead.

Like the He 111s that have preceded it, this one and its troop-bearing companion fly amid a formation of standard He 111s and Junkers Jus that will participate in tonight's heavy bombing raid on London. The night is clear. Somewhere far below, England sleeps: mothers and children, bankers and street sweepers, sheep and sheep-dogs. Sixteen-year-old Colin Brooke, recently recovered from the measles, sleeps fitfully at his Aunt Anne's home in Canterbury, his dreams alternating between sweet and terrifying. In Hambleden, Mrs. Umphlett snores in her cozy den behind the kitchen while Mr. Tibbetts dreams of trout-fishing in his room under the eaves. In Henley-on-Thames, the silver moonlight picks out scenes of desolation and ruin. In London, in a tiny basement office in St. James's Street, Stephen Bloom studies dossiers and maps, creating an elaborate graph of tick marks and figures in his notebook. He double- and triple-checks his data, then his data's sources. He wonders whether he will come to regret having signed the Secrets Act, which obliges him to keep in strictest confidence what he has learned about the code-breaking project going forward at Bletchley Park. Periodically he caresses with his thumb an antique pocket watch embossed with the Star of David.

Cardinal Hinsley is uneasily watching this night, too, though he can't say why. In his richly-appointed chamber at Archbishop House, he kneels and tells his rosary over and over. And in Oxford, while Allister Brooke dreams of all the sights of China and Argentina, of richest reds, vibrant greens, and blues so profound they're inky, of ruined temples, intricate carvings, and sunlight on the glossy black hair of women, and while Ian Brooke sighs in his sleep, his arm flung out across his wife's pillow, a lamp burns in Margaret Brooke's study. She has set aside her chapter—nearly complete—on Maud Gonne and taken up a literary journal. The name of a young poet she likes, W. H. Auden, has caught her eye, and she reads a poem that ends with a blessing perfect for this troubled world:

> Noons of dryness find you fed
> By the involuntary powers,
> Nights of insult let you pass
> Watched by every human love.

She has heard that Mr. Auden has recently moved to America, and she smiles at the backwards symmetry with her own life. Wiping a tear from her cheek, she decides that she is certain she detects an echo of Yeats in this poem.

The village of Warborough, too, is sleeping, and exhausted from her day's tasks at Hare House, Sister Angela Curran sleeps with it. At the other end of the house, Father Roberto DiGangi sleeps as well, troubled by dreams in which he searches desperately for his sister. But the Hare House dairy is buzzing with hushed activity. The dairy's longtime employees are all at home in bed, but the six new men who have trickled in during recent weeks are hard at work, supervised by the handsome priest with the scar down one side of his face. Tonight these men are not dressed as dairymen, though, nor does their Oberstleutnant wear clerical black. Tonight they wear stiff new uniforms in the khakis and browns of the British Army, and the military transport lorry they are preparing—one whose impressive size dwarfs the refrigerated Hare House Dairy lorry parked next to it—is similarly marked as Army property. These men speak German to one another in private, but when they are on Hare House grounds they are careful—even now—to use only their impeccable English. When they are satisfied that all is ready, five of the men leap into the lorry's vast cargo area. The sixth takes the wheel, and the Oberstleutnant-priest rides beside him. In the dark, the lorry noses out past Hare House's gate of archiepiscopal crosses. Its headlamps are not lit until it is half a mile from Hare House, around a bend and out of sight.

The lorry drives north and west, not very far, to a lonely lane between two pastures. The men don't have long to wait at this rendezvous point: before half an hour is up, a Heinkel He 111 appears from the North, flying low, its lights extinguished. A repeating pattern of sparks glows around the port engine, and a long plume of smoke trails behind, but this plane doesn't crash. It makes its landing neatly at the far end of one of the pastures, on the bank of a cow pond, its approach illuminated by the lorry's headlamps. The twenty Brandenburgers are on the ground nearly as one, and rolling their chutes faster than would have been believed possible, all run towards the He 111. The lorry, too, pulls in to meet the plane; under the Oberstleutnant's watchful eye, the twenty-six well-trained men make short work of transferring their five-ton leaden cargo. When the He 111 is empty, ten men guide it down the cow pond's bank. They watch it disappear beneath the cold black water. The pond isn't deep; eventually, the Heinkel will be discovered. But by then it won't matter: Operation Über will be complete.

The men load themselves into the lorry as efficiently as they loaded the enormous lead box. The lorry will return to Hare House by a different route than it arrived: its heavy cargo makes choosing paved streets over dirt lanes prudent. It is now that they encounter an unexpected obstacle: a Home Guard checkpoint that wasn't there yesterday. Security in this area, Oberstleutnant Cordesmann confesses to himself, has become increasingly uncomfortable of late. The meddling literary woman about whom Sister Angela Curran warned him must have found an ear. His consolation is that these sentries can't possibly know what it is they are looking for, even now that they are looking. As the lorry slows to a stop, he takes control of the situation.

"Good evening, sir," he says, saluting the sentry in the British fashion.

The sentry salutes him back. "Officer," he says. His checkpoint is quite basic: two floodlights, two men, a few sawhorse-style barriers, chairs under a tent for warmth, a field telephone.

"This is a test run of an experimental vehicle rated for up to eight tons," the Oberstleutnant tells the sentry. "We're using a dead weight to determine the vehicle's practical hauling capacity, and I've added my platoon for extra weight."

The sentry's face is blank. He looks at the clipboard he carries, then back at the Oberstleutnant, and his blank expression does not change. The Oberstleutnant fingers the Walther PPK in his pocket with a thrill of adrenaline, but then the sentry says, "All right then.

We'll just take a look, then off you pop." The Oberstleutnant relaxes a fraction.

From the back, the sentry's partner calls out, "Frank, will you bring the crowbar? I want to check inside the box." The sentry Frank fixes the Oberstleutnant with a firm *stay-right-there* look, ducks into the tent, then emerges crowbar in hand and joins his partner at the lorry's back door. The Oberstleutnant waits a beat, counting upon Frank to become fully engaged in the task, then slips out from behind the wheel, draws his pistol, and follows Frank on velvet feet. His unfamiliar British Army uniform feels stiff, tight in odd places, but still he moves quietly enough.

Around back, plump Frank and his wiry geriatric partner are heaving for all they're worth on the crowbar. For a moment it seems the leaden lid will shift—the edge seems to rise a quarter inch—but then the two sentries lose their grip and pause to catch their wheezing breaths. Wiping sweat from his brow, Frank looks troubled. "Why've you got a lid on the box if it's just dead weight?"

The Oberstleutnant's response is as prompt as if this were a signal. Frank pitches forward as a rose of blood appears between his shoulder blades; the Walther is quiet, less a *bang* than a *pop*. The other sentry falls to an echoing *pop* from another German pistol. The men leave the bodies where they've fallen—in the lorry with the box; the Oberstleutnant regains his seat, and the rest of the road to Hare House is clear. The sky is lightening almost imperceptibly in the east as the men stow the two Home Guard bodies in the Hare House dairy and begin loading, two per stolen British Army lorry, the six heavy but now oddly delicate apparati that have been secreted there. Each of these strange objects resembles a partly-disassembled giant steel box, some of its sides folded back to reveal cocoonlike enclosures from which wires and electrodes sprout. The folded sides' inner faces are concave. Oberstleutnant Cordesmann watches the men's work with satisfaction, then checks his watch. Five o'clock. Ten hours now before detonation. At his family's compound in unimaginable Massachusetts, the American ambassador's family should be getting tucked into bed. There's one more task the Oberstleutnant must see to personally before the journey to London, and it's a task he faintly regrets. Glancing once more to see that his men are working smoothly, Oberstleutnant Cordesmann—Father Antonio DiClemente—turns towards Hare House proper. It's dark; the household is still sleeping. Silently the Oberstleutnant lets himself in at the kitchen door.

CHAPTER TWELVE:
THE TOOTH

Had I but wakened from sleep
And called her name, she had heard,
It may be, and had not stirred,
That now, it may be, has found
The horn's sweet note and the tooth of the hound.
—W.B. Yeats, from "Two Songs of a Fool"

THURSDAY MORNING DAWNED bright and frosty. Revising her Maud Gonne chapter as the sun's first rays reached her study windows, Maggie Brooke reflected that at home in America today, families would be gathered for turkey dinners. By eight o'clock, though, the time for reflection was done; Maggie and her Home Guard girls were warming up the metals-reclamation lorry in preparation for their eight-thirty appointment with Sister Angela Curran. Cardinal Hinsley had promised them some old ladders and buckets, outdated beekeeping equipment, and other such scrap from his estate in Warborough and Sister Angela had promised to meet them at Hare House and oversee the reclamation. In observance of her home country's holiday, Maggie reminded herself to be grateful for the useful work, for the great, lumbering lorry that had hauled so many tons over the past few months, for the cheerful, hardworking girls, lovely this morning with their frosty breath and cold-reddened cheeks, and for Zofia's promise that dinner tonight would somehow involve pumpkin.

Between Oxford and Warborough, frost sparkled on the stubbly fields and mostly-bare hedgerows. Crows quorked to one another across the lanes down which the lorry rattled. As they turned in beneath the archiepiscopal crosses of its gate, Hare House's white-washed stones gleamed tidy and inviting in the autumn sun. The maid who shepherded them all inside, though, and handed round steaming mugs of tea, was anxious and flustered. "I just don't understand it, mum," she said to Maggie. "I know Sister Angela was planning to meet you; she gave me instructions last night. But this morning, she's nowhere to be found. She didn't come down to breakfast, and she left her bed unmade—not like her, mum, not like her at all. And the clergyman who came up from London with her—Father DiGangi, was it?—no one can find Father DiGangi, either. I thought maybe they'd gone out for a devotional morning walk, but it's been three hours now since we first missed them. We get up pretty early 'round here, you know. I've asked the beekeepers and the dairymen to keep an eye out, but the truth is I'm worried."

Maggie was worried too. Her girls made short work of the heaps of scrap Cardinal Hinsley's employees had gathered; this job was much easier than what they had become accustomed to. Still, while Maggie's hands were busy loading up dented wheelbarrows and corroded tin roofing—and while she sat idle in the lorry's passenger seat on the ride back to the Home Guard office—Maggie fretted. She kept turning and turning Sister Angela's disappearance over in her mind, and that of Father DiGangi as well. Maggie didn't know the man personally—they had met once or twice—but she knew he was an important man, the Pope's acting Nuncio in London. What was he doing out in Warborough? Was it reassuring or alarming that the two of them had gone missing together? Could they have gotten lost or hurt somewhere on the Hare House grounds during an early-morning stroll? Maggie reflected on the sparks of interest Sister Angela had shown in her stories about crash-site reclamation. When Maggie rang Mr. Bloom from Hare House two weeks ago, had she heard the "click" of an eavesdropper on her line? Surely Sister Angela couldn't be mixed up in whatever plot was afoot?

Maggie's unease grew more and more persistent. As soon as she regained the office, she drew out Stephen Bloom's card and rang him. He answered on the third or fourth ring, and Maggie said, surprised, "Why Mr. Bloom! You sound out of breath."

"Sorry, Mrs. Brooke," he replied, recognizing her voice. "I'd just stepped away from my desk for a moment. How may I assist you?"

"I'm not sure," Maggie confessed. "Really, I'm just going from my gut in calling you. But I wanted you to be informed of anything that might have any bearing whatever on our investigation."

"Go on."

"Where to begin? I don't know if you know that Cardinal Hinsley, the Archbishop of Westminster—that's a Catholic archdiocese, you know—has a country estate not far from Oxford," Maggie began, hoping that if she gave Sister Angela's disappearance some context she might be able to pin down why it worried her so much.

"Hare House in Warborough, I believe. Is that correct?"

"Yes, that's it," Maggie assented. "Yesterday, Cardinal Hinsley's private secretary, a nun named Sister Angela Curran, traveled to Hare House from London. The acting Papal Nuncio—that is, the Pope's representative in London—went with her. Father DiGangi, an Italian. And now it seems they've disappeared." Maggie filled in the details of her conversation that morning with the Hare House maid.

"And you're certain they haven't returned in the interim?" Mr. Bloom inquired.

"I asked the maid to ring me here at the Home Guard office right away if they were located," Maggie explained, "and she hasn't done, so it seems they haven't."

"I see," he said, and paused for a moment. "Mrs. Brooke, I think your gut had the right idea in calling me. It does look awfully odd for two of the key players to go missing on the morning of a meeting planned among national civic and religious leaders."

"I beg your pardon?" Maggie asked, perplexed.

"Yes—I selected the security detail myself, as it happens. Sister Angela Curran is a young woman with big ideas, it seems. She organized this meeting—a summit of sorts—herself. Cardinal Hinsley and Father DiGangi, Archbishop Lang of Canterbury, Churchill and King George—they're set to discuss arrangements for refugees to Britain and to hear the Pope's proposed encyclical on the vital religious and moral importance of toppling the Nazi regime. According to Sister Angela, the Pope is anxious to get London's views before he issues it—and why did it never occur to me until this very moment to ask why Cardinal Hinsley's personal secretary is speaking for the Pope?" Mr. Bloom was silent for a moment, during which Maggie imagined him castigating himself for his credulity. "At any rate," he resumed, "it's quite a do. Strange that they should have left town just before it—haven't they preparations to make? And now they've vanished. It smells altogether odd. What does Cardinal Hinsley say about it?"

"Oh!" Maggie cried. "To tell the truth, it hadn't occurred to me to speak with the Cardinal. He's in London, you know—he often sends Sister Angela to Warborough to oversee things for him. He says it's like being in two places at once."

"All right. Let's do this: you ring the Cardinal and see whether he's heard from Sister Angela. If there's a legitimate reason for her to go AWOL, he's the one who'll know it. Meanwhile I'll have a poke around from my end and see what I can turn up. Call me if you learn anything more."

"I will," she agreed, then asked, "Mr. Bloom? Do we suspect that they're spies? Or victims of a crime?"

"It's too early to know, Mrs. Brooke," he said. "But you'll find that in the espionage game, people often become both."

Cardinal Hinsley, summoned to the telephone by a nun Maggie did not know, was eager to bless Maggie on the day her native country was devoted to giving thanks. At first she tried to interrupt him, but finally she realized she would have to submit to his florid benediction before he would be of any use to her. In a turn for which Maggie truly *was* thankful, the Cardinal ended his speech by asking whether Sister Angela had provided Maggie's Home Guard girls with everything they needed that morning.

"That's just what I'm calling you about, Your Eminence. Sister Angela was not there, and the household staff tell me that she's gone missing," Maggie explained.

"But she's not missing at all! Though we do miss her here," the Cardinal rejoined. "She's taken Father DiGangi to Hare House for a day of breathing country air. The poor man is quite overworked, and the bombs and sirens set his nerves on edge so. You have only to call for her at Hare House, Mrs. Brooke."

"But that's just it, Your Eminence. I called round to Hare House this morning, and Sister Angela *was not there*. In fact, Father DiGangi was not there either. Their beds had been slept in, but before the household staff rose this morning, Sister Angela and Father DiGangi were *gone*."

"Gone?" the Cardinal asked. "But that's *most* alarming. Sister Angela is due back here by lunchtime. We have so many things to do—"

"So you haven't any idea where she might have gone?" Mrs. Brooke inquired.

"Not the slightest, my dear," Cardinal Hinsley admitted. "I am quite perplexed. She knows how very much we have to do to prepare for the religious summit King George has convened this evening. In fact, I tried to dissuade her from going at all. The Hare House staff can manage the scrap metal reclamation just fine without you, I told her, but you know how she likes to make certain everything is just so. 'I'll be there and back before you know it,' she told me yesterday evening when she left. And now she's disappeared? This is most unlike Sister Angela. I depend upon her entirely, you know, and never has she let me down."

"How would her absence affect this evening's summit?" Maggie asked.

"Well, my dear, I really don't see how I should manage—Sister Angela is my good right arm. I imagine that for others the upsetting absence would be Father DiGangi, as he is scheduled to deliver a message from His Holiness the Pope. Without that, the proceedings lose their focus somewhat. I imagine that the King would be most displeased—he set the agenda personally."

"The King arranged this meeting, you say?" Maggie asked, frowning into the handset.

"Why, certainly. At least—as I understand it. I leave the scheduling of my engagements entirely to Sister Angela, and she briefs me each Saturday for the coming week and each evening for the coming day," the Cardinal explained. "Sister Angela told me that the King had invited us."

"I see," Maggie said, though the truth was that she didn't see at all. Why would Sister Angela arrange a meeting among such august men, then disappear? Why would she mislead the Cardinal about who had called the meeting? She hoped Stephen Bloom would understand better than she did. She wished the Cardinal a happy Thanksgiving, promised to contact him should she learn anything, and rang off. Then she telephoned Stephen Bloom.

This time Mr. Bloom picked it up promptly. Maggie told him that Cardinal Hinsley was as much in the dark as they were about Sister Angela's whereabouts, then asked, "But why do you suppose it is that the Cardinal understood that King George had called this evening's meeting? What would Sister Angela gain by lying about that?"

"Mrs. Brooke," Mr. Bloom said after a moment, "I believe that is the crucial clue. I could be wrong, but it sounds to me as if Sister Angela may have been gathering important men in London for some unstated purpose. If that is the case—and if her disappearance is indeed linked with the crashes of the unusual bombers—then she may have been gathering targets. Had she simply disappeared, I would not be concerned. But now that we know that she also lied to Cardinal Hinsley about her role in convening the summit, I begin to fear it is possible that the plot you have uncovered is moving into a new and critical phase."

"How can I help?" asked Maggie simply.

"It is now—" Stephen Bloom consulted his pocket watch— "nine forty-five in the morning. Meet me at Hare House at half eleven."

Stephen Bloom was as prompt in his arrival at Warborough as he generally was in answering his telephone; Maggie was waiting for him with some bemusement in her blue Morris 8, pulled to the side of the lane just out of sight of Hare House's gates. "I still feel," she remarked just before Mr. Bloom's black Morgan 4-4 came into view, "that I could have handled things perfectly well on my own."

"I'm certain you could, my dear—you are a marvel," Ian replied. "Still, it seems to me that the situation might become dangerous rather quickly, if your intuitions are correct. What sort of man would allow his wife to face danger alone, without his support?"

"Besides, Mum," Allie piped up from the back seat, "Why should you have all the fun?" Rooney punctuated his question with an emphatic snort, and they all laughed. Their tone was light-hearted now, but Allie was deadly serious about protecting his mother—and his adopted country, should the situation call for it. Just in case, he had donned his R.A.F. uniform for the occasion—the first time he had had it on since Sedan—and he looked every inch the soldier, dashing and authoritative. With a start, Maggie realized there was a lump under the right-hand side of Ian's coat—his gesture towards dressing the military part, as well. His military pistol must have been twenty-five years old.

"I hear you," Maggie relented, pulling back into the lane to follow Bloom onto the Hare House grounds. "Still, I don't want to overwhelm the Hare House staff with an entire party of inquisitors. Can I appeal to you to stay in the car? You can come looking for me if I don't return within half an hour."

"Fair enough," conceded Ian. "But thirty minutes only. A minute more, and we'll be on your trail with our magnifying glasses out. We've got our hound with us, you know."

"It's a deal," Maggie said, setting the emergency brake and switching off the ignition. "Back in a jiff." She opened the car door and was off.

Stephen Bloom shook Maggie's hand in silence, one eyebrow cocked to ask if there were any further news. She shook her head, and together they mounted Hare House's tidy steps and rang the bell. The same maid appeared at the door who had spoken with Maggie that morning.

"Hello, Doris. I've taken the liberty of contacting the authorities about Sister Angela and Father DiGangi," Maggie explained, "and they've sent Mr. Stephen Bloom to investigate."

The maid Doris glanced Mr. Bloom over. She looked faintly puzzled, but if Mr. Bloom's lack of police uniform troubled her, she said nothing. Maggie smoothed the lapels of her own Home Guard uniform as if in compensation. At Mr. Bloom's prompting, Doris confirmed the time of Sister Angela and Father DiGangi's arrival at Hare House and of their last contact with the household staff. "What would you say the relationship is like between Sister Curran and Father DiGangi?" Bloom asked.

"Oh, just ... professional, I reckon you'd call it?" she said. "All business. Polite, but I wouldn't say they was friends. He's an important man in the Church, you know, but he seems sad, tired-like. So she brought him here for a day or two of fresh air and looking after. That sort of thing's her job."

"So Sister Curran was looking after Father DiGangi?" Mr. Bloom probed.

"Well, not personally. That was up to us. Frankly, Sister Angela's not so much the nurturing type," Doris explained. "She's the one who sees what needs doing, and who sees it gets done. But that don't mean she does it herself, sir, if you see what I mean."

Mr. Bloom raised his eyebrows. "I take it Sister Curran is not popular among the household staff?"

Doris colored and stammered, "Not—not as such, sir, I don't suppose. She has a bit of an air about her, you know, a bit of Miss High-and-Mighty. Still, I don't think there's anyone here with anything *particular* against her, if you see what I mean. No bosom friends on the staff, but I shouldn't think anyone would want to hurt her."

"And Father DiGangi?" Mr. Bloom inquired.

"The other day was our first time meeting him, sir," Doris pointed out. "He seems sad, like I said, and tired—but kind. Grateful. He talks to the staff not like we're servants, but as people. He's quiet, and seems faraway sometimes—but my impression is that he's a gentle soul, sir. With a troubled heart, maybe."

Doris led her two visitors first to Father DiGangi's bedroom, and then to Sister Angela's. "When Sister Angela is here," she explained, "she generally comes down for breakfast just after sunrise. My understanding is that she rises earlier and prays in her room 'til sunup. When six o'clock this morning came and no one had seen her, I thought I'd just pop in and make sure she wasn't poorly. I haven't touched anything in here—it's just as I found it."

Like Father DiGangi's bedroom, Sister Angela's was spare and tidy with the exception of the unmade bed. White muslin curtains glowed with the sunlight beyond; the room contained a narrow iron bed, a straight chair, a wooden side table bearing a small reading lamp, a Bible, and a ten-inch iron crucifix, and a suitcase stand on which lay a black valise, closed. Opening the valise revealed a carefully-folded habit, a small toiletry set, and a set of modest women's underthings. Behind the door, the wall bore a row of four hooks, all empty. From the articles left behind and the articles conspicuously missing, Mr. Bloom surmised that both of them had left their rooms willingly but in a hurry, throwing coats and shoes on over their nightclothes. No other clues announced themselves to him. "Where might she have gone, Doris? When she was in Warborough but not inside the house, where did she frequently spend time?"

"There were two places I thought of right off," Doris said. "I sent our Jim down to St. Genesis—that's the Catholic chapel in town, you know—but it was closed up tight, no sign of her, and when young Jim woke the priest up to ask after her, the poor fellow wasn't half shocked! I believe he thought we were accusing him of something improper. At any rate, he hadn't seen her."

"We'll have to speak with him. And the other place?" Mr. Bloom encouraged.

"The dairy here on the estate. The Cardinal expanded it over the summer, you know, and has been hiring new dairymen all fall. Sister Angela oversaw everything herself and has taken a tremendous interest in it. She's always going down there to inspect."

"Can you direct us towards the dairy, Doris?" Mr. Bloom asked.

"I know the way," Maggie said.

The walk from the house to the dairy was a pleasant one, if chilly; outside the house's low stone fence, cows munched contentedly on either side of the path, occasionally lowing. Inside the barn, the air was warmer and sweet, redolent of hay and of the structure's new wood and fresh paint. "Hello," Maggie called out as they entered the barn through its back doors, which faced the house. On her previous visits, a handful of dairymen had always been in the barn—cleaning, making repairs, processing and storing new milk. Today, though, the place was deserted. "Hello?" Maggie called again. She and Mr. Bloom exchanged looks.

At the barn's enormous front doors—broad and tall enough for lorries and similarly large equipment to pass through—were scuffs and muddy tracks that indicated the recent passing of several vehicles. The tracks led from the barn's door towards a pair of enormous trapdoors in the floor of the barn's broad central area. "Looks like a dairy cellar," Mr. Bloom said. "Let's see what's down there." Working together, they managed to heave one of the gigantic traps open. Beneath it, a wide paved ramp led down into darkness. Mr. Bloom produced an electric torch from one of his coat pockets, and then a second torch, which he passed to Maggie. "You never know when you might need a spare," he said with a shrug. Their searching beams revealed a cavernous basement space lined with gleaming milk canisters and stacked crates of cheese and butter as well as hay bales and ranks of sacks of oats.

The cellar's smooth, clean concrete floor revealed no vehicle tracks, but deep in the blackness Mr. Bloom and Maggie found six arrangements of empty wooden pallets, standing as if in readiness to store six heavy pieces of equipment—or as if such equipment had recently been removed. Above each pallet hung an electric winch; connecting the six pallets was a network of faint, shiny scratches or scuffs on the concrete, as if heavy metal objects had been dragged or rolled on sharp metal wheels among the pallets repeatedly. "Could this be where they were storing whatever was coming in on those planes?" Maggie asked, her voice full of awe. Mr. Bloom was silent, though. Maggie turned towards him and saw that his torch beam and attention were caught on something else. Against one wall was a workbench with a complete set of tools—voltage meters, power drills, and electric saws stood out. Huge batteries connected to the electric supply lay beneath the bench. At the far corner of the cellar, next to a dozen very large empty barrels labeled *Vorsicht! Sprengstoff!*, there appeared to be a heap of jumbled dark and white cloth. Its untidiness was screamingly out of place in this orderly storehouse. Wordlessly Maggie and Mr. Bloom approached the heap, but at about ten feet from it, Maggie came to a ghastly realization and gave a gasp. She crossed herself, breathed deeply, crossed herself again.

Maintaining a professional stoicism, Mr. Bloom knelt down and grasped the upper half of the heap by its shoulders. Gently he rolled Sister Angela Curran's body onto its back and examined her quickly, thoroughly, and with as much respect as the circumstances permitted. It appeared that she had been shot at close range behind her ear. As Bloom had predicted, she was dressed in her night things—a long white flannel gown—with a long black wool coat thrown over it. Her coat pockets were empty. Despite never having warmed to Sister Angela, Maggie felt a pang in her maternal heart when she saw that the young woman was wearing black Oxfords with no stockings. Her poor naked ankles looked chafed and cold, and there were streaks of blood in her pale curls. Mr. Bloom gave Maggie a questioning look; she nodded to indicate that this was indeed the missing woman.

The rest of the sad heap proved, indeed, to contain the remains of Father Roberto DiGangi, his long white flannel gown comically similar to Sister Angela's—Maggie was ashamed of her moment of amusement and assigned herself a silent Hail Mary as penance. Less comic was the similarity of their injuries: Father DiGangi, too, had been shot behind the ear. Maggie thought of the poor, mangled skulls of the Czech pilots at the crash sites. She didn't feel vindicated—she felt dizzy and sick. When Mr. Bloom gingerly rolled DiGangi's body away to search his coat pockets, Maggie saw that beneath his were two more bodies—those of a pair of middle-aged uniformed Home Guardsman, one slight, the other rotund. These had been shot more sloppily—huge blood stains bloomed on their trunks. Maggie closed her eyes and said another silent Hail Mary—this one not for penance, but for succor.

When she opened them again, Bloom had found something—an envelope with the words "Private and Confidential—Diplomatic

Correspondence" stamped on the front. It was sealed with an embossed decal. Inside was a folded piece of paper bearing a watermark. Bloom unfolded it, smoothed it against his thigh. Maggie crouched nearby and held her torch beam steady on the page. She could see that it was thickly typed, but upside down and in this light, she could make out none of the words. "It seems to be in Latin," Mr. Bloom said, and held his torch behind it to examine the watermark. "Papal," he explained, showing Maggie the crossed keys surmounted by a mitre.

"Church business?" Maggie suggested. "Or the encyclical he was to discuss at tonight's summit?"

"I don't think so," said Mr. Bloom in a puzzled voice. "This document ... it doesn't make any sense. It reads like a page of Joyce, or like modern poetry ... or like code." The memory of his recent private briefing on the cryptanalysis project at Bletchley Park broke on him like an icy wave. He had been duped. He looked up and into Maggie's eyes. He trusted her completely, and yet if he violated the Secrets Act—even with her—he would be guilty of treason. Probably he had said too much already. "I feel such a fool," he said. "Of course DiGangi had full use of Monseigneur Godfrey's diplomatic pouch. And do you know there's only one office in London transmitting regular long-wave radio broadcasts in Latin?"

"The Papal Nuncio's office," Maggie guessed, and Bloom nodded.

"If we wondered how the Nazis might know what you were doing, I'd say we've a good idea now," said Mr. Bloom grimly. "We haven't any time to waste. We'll ask Doris to ring for the coroner and the police, but you and I have more pressing business. From the looks of those tracks, a number of lorries left here this morning. The road that leaves that door exits the property without coming in view of the house, correct?" Maggie nodded, and Mr. Bloom went on. "We've got to find out where they were going."

Standing, the two of them raced out of the cellar, out of the barn and towards the house. Maggie struggled to keep up—she was impressed at the speed the unassuming Mr. Bloom could muster. He had removed his hat to keep from losing it, and he held it in his hand as he ran. Maggie's hat was affixed to her hair with pins, but she could feel them loosening, so she ran with one hand pressed awkwardly to her head. She blessed the heavens for her choice this morning of Oxfords over pumps. As they hove into view of the house, Mr. Bloom nearly collided bodily with Ian, who was limping gingerly towards the house from the Morris. "I was just coming to look for you," he said to Maggie, and then to Mr. Bloom, "Ian Brooke." Ian reached for Mr. Bloom's hand as Maggie mounted the stairs and rang for Doris. Bloom noted the pistol at Ian's hip; its vintage and origin were obvious to his trained eye. He felt within himself a budding regard for this man.

"Stephen Bloom, but I'm afraid there's no time for formalities," Mr. Bloom said, gripping the hand Ian extended to him. "But I'd be grateful for your assistance. You have a car, yes?" Ian nodded. "Then be a good chap and drive slowly from here towards Warborough. Ask anyone you see whether they noticed any unusual traffic this morning from the direction of Hare House. Mrs. Brooke and I will drive away from town and do the same. We'll meet back here in—" he consulted his watch— "thirty minutes and compare notes. Can you help us?" And when Ian nodded, Mr. Bloom clapped him on the back and said, "Good man."

CHAPTER THIRTEEN:
DETONATION DAY

What rough beast, its hour come round at last,
Slouches towards Bethlehem to be born?

—W.B. Yeats, from "The Second Coming"

THE DAY IS COLD AND BRIGHT, the sun at its zenith. Using his walkie-talkie, Oberstleutnant Cordesmann checks in with his air-support crew of Me 109s. They reassure him that the first two checkpoints he and his convoy will encounter as they drive towards London on the Abingdon Road have been cleared. From the air the convoy of four enormous British Army lorries looks like a string of toys spread across a carpet. Even at this distance, the man-high English lettering marking each lorry as belonging to a "Special Biological Warfare Unit" is visible. So is the emblem on each back cab door. At their listening station at the Benson R.A.F. field, two German-speaking Flying Officers catch a snatch of the convoy's short-wave check-in and look at one another in confusion. "What'd he say?" one asks, and the other says, "It *sounds* like German, but I can't make out any of the words." Their conversation is abruptly cut short by klaxons alerting the base to an air attack on London to their south. Pilots, navigators, and gunners race to their planes and ground staff turn their attention to supporting the flyers.

Meanwhile an Me 109 pilot making a routine all-clear check slips up and reports in standard German. "Highest Alemannic, you imbecile," the Oberstleutnant hisses in the obscure dialect, his face flushing red around the white slash of scar that runs from his eye to the corner of his mouth. In Highest Alemannic, the pilot apologizes. Then he returns his attention to scanning the road ahead of the convoy for potential pitfalls.

In central London, sirens blare and civilians race for bomb shelters: doctors and nurses shepherd patients into hospital basements; retirees hobble down stairs as quickly as they can; policemen and omnibus conductors direct confused shoppers towards public shelters. Here a young mother frantically gathers her children; there another says a silent prayer of gratitude that hers are safe in the country. Scarcely are the streets clear when the bombs begin to fall. Buildings shake with the force of the explosions. Spitfires and Hurricanes appear, herding the German bombers away from the most populous and historic areas. An He 111 is shot down, diving into the side of a tenement building like a knife to the abdomen.

The road from Oxford to London is broad, in good repair, and relatively free of traffic today. The Messerschmitts take care of Home Guard checkpoints from the air; on the ground, pedestrians and motor traffic alike take one look at the legendary "Special Biological Warfare Unit" and the ominous British Army-issue gas masks worn by the lorry drivers and they steer clear. The Oberstleutnant and his commando team are ahead of schedule; they will easily make London and assemble their weapon in time for detonation at three o'clock in the afternoon. In Hyannis Port, Ambassador Joe Kennedy will hear the news over his family's Thanksgiving Day breakfast. The Oberstleutnant smiles at the thought. The convoy is making good time, despite driving cautiously to protect the delicate machinery they carry. Except for the commando who is driving the Oberstleutnant, the men smile and joke with one another, anxious about their vital mission, yet enjoying the pleasant countryside bathed in autumn sunshine. The man driving Oberstleutnant Cordesmann enjoys the sunshine, too, but he knows better than to show it. In front of their superiors, the men are all business.

Reaching the western outskirts of London, the convoy slows. There are more checkpoints in the city than in the countryside, and the Messerschmitts can't always get clear shots, but the Biological Warfare Unit disguise does its job. Sentries wave the lorries through, pressing handkerchiefs to their noses and suppressing psychosomatic coughs. At the Oberstleutnant's direction, the Ju 88s and He 111s move their action east, away from the convoy's destination. It would be too sad an irony if Operation Über failed due to friendly fire. The convoy skirts Hyde Park, then Green Park, and the Oberstleutnant briefly fantasizes about a change of venue to Buckingham Palace. On their right-hand side, the lorries pass the tasteful townhouses of Belgravia, then bear left as the century-old chimneys of Victoria Station come into view. Just a few turnings more brings the convoy within sight of its target: Westminster Abbey.

In preparation for the evening's religious summit, Westminster Abbey is closed to the public (who are at any rate huddled just now in bunkers and shelters across the city). Two dozen Royal Marines, deployed to secure the area in advance of the meeting, patrol the premises. The convoy's lead lorry speeds towards the north transept door and parks with one great tire on the sidewalk; Oberstleutnant Cordesmann springs from the passenger door, unfastens his gas mask, and in a authoritative voice demands to confer with the site's ranking officer. The Royal Marines scurry for a minute or two, then produce him.

The Oberstleutnant salutes the Marine in British fashion, then says, "Sir, I'm sorry, but there is no time for formalities. I have received a report that an unexploded biological bomb struck this building during today's hostilities. My unit is trained to deal with this situation. We have with us a great deal of sophisticated equipment, as you can see." He motions towards his convoy. "We need your men to secure the perimeter, then stay out of our way while we defuse the bomb and contain the threat. There isn't a moment to waste."

The officer facing Oberstleutnant Cordesmann cannot yet be thirty years old. He has no radio or walkie-talkie on him. If the low rank designated by the insignia on the Oberstleutnant's stolen British uniform fazes him, he does not show it. Rather, he allows the older man's sense of urgency to pervade him. He salutes the Oberstleutnant again, then turns to his men and begins barking orders. Before he dashes around the building's corner and out of sight, he turns back to the Oberstleutnant once more and says, "Anything you need, just let us know. We're here to help."

CHAPTER FOURTEEN:

THE CHASE

For everybody knows or else should know
That if nothing drastic is done
Aeroplane and Zeppelin will come out,
Pitch like King Billy bomb-balls in
Until the town lie beaten flat.

—W.B. Yeats, from "Lapis Lazuli"

THE DAY WAS COLD AND BRIGHT, the Abingdon Road broad and empty. Stephen Bloom's Morgan 4-4, on the other hand, was somewhat overwarm, noisy, and comically overcrowded—Mr. Bloom, Maggie Brooke, her husband Ian, their son Allie, and his guide dog Rooney all had smashed themselves into the little sports car. The four-passenger edition was new, its rear seats comfortable only to youngsters. But it was that or nothing: the staid Morris 8 couldn't possibly hope to catch up with the convoy of Army trucks that had been sighted leaving Hare House and heading towards London just an hour ago, whereas even overloaded, the Morgan was muscular and fleet. Allie allowed Rooney to put her head out the car's small rear window—she enjoyed the breeze as her ears flapped beside her head.

At Mr. Bloom's direction, Maggie reached into the glove box and drew out a small radio. She activated it as Mr. Bloom instructed, then held it towards his lips. "Lieutenant Davies," he hailed, "Lieutenant Davies."

After a moment of staticky crackling, a hearty voice boomed from the small box, "This is Lieutenant Davies."

"Stephen Bloom reporting, sir," Bloom enunciated into the radio. "Following the Abingdon Road from Oxford, headed towards London in pursuit of a suspicious convoy of large, heavy-laden transport vehicles. The vehicles appear to belong to the British Army, but I suspect they are instead operated by Germans. They may be carrying biological weapons. Or huge conventional ones—we found evidence at Hare House to suggest that Germans had smuggled in a massive amount of high explosives."

"Roger, Bloom. Will investigate," thundered Davies through the static. "Keep me posted. Over and out."

A Home Guard sentry post appeared in the distance ahead. Mr. Bloom said, "Everyone hang on. We'll try to maintain reasonable speed through here, but we may need to brake suddenly." But as the post drew closer, the party could see that the sawhorse-style traffic barriers had been moved aside and that no one was stirring in or around the post. The Morgan zoomed through the post; looking back, did Maggie glimpse a boot and uniformed leg lying prone on the ground behind the sentry tent? She couldn't say for sure.

"Have just passed the Home Guard checkpoint below Watlington," Bloom radioed with Maggie's help. "No personnel appear to be on duty. Repeat, Watlington checkpoint deserted. Lieutenant Davies, I hope the sentries have not come to grief."

Ten seconds of crackling ensued, and then Davies's jovial voice assaulted them again. "Have been unable to contact *any* sentries along the Abingdon Road. Repeat, *no* Home Guard checkpoints responding. Convoy sighted near Beaconsfield. Relaying your information to the Royal Marines. Over and out."

"*Now* they call the Royal Marines," Maggie fumed. "Now that it may be too late. If the Marines had been paying attention to crash sites in Oxfordshire the past six months, we wouldn't be chasing a convoy of lorries into the capital city right now." She flushed with fury, then looked away from Mr. Bloom. "Then again, I was suspicious about Hare House Dairy not two months ago. I went there to investigate, even. How could I have missed that cellar? I was so *close*. If I'd had any support at all—" A tear sparkled in her eye, but did not fall. "Do you suppose I could have saved that poor girl?"

"I feel relatively certain," Mr. Bloom said drily, "that *that poor girl* was a spy in the service of Hitler. But you're right, Mrs. Brooke, we should have supported you sooner. If only we'd paid better attention to the Nuncio's Latin radio transmissions—"

"Oh, *blast* the radio transmissions," Maggie exploded, "they were the *least* of our clues. Unless—" A memory was dawning on Maggie, and a thoroughly infuriating realization.

Davies's thunderous voice broke in again. "Royal Marines are converging on the West of London," he reported ear-splittingly.

"Can't we turn that thing down?" Ian asked in an aside from the back seat, but Bloom just winced and shook his head.

"Churchill has been alerted and is standing by," Davies bellowed. "Convoy has been sighted near Gerrards Cross. Over and out."

"Good," Ian observed, "that means we're catching up to them."

"How come they keep just *sighting* the convoy," Allie groaned, "and not *stopping* it?"

"I'm afraid information travels faster than munitions or men, my boy," Ian observed.

"Oh, I know, Dad. It's just galling, is all," Allie said.

"Galling is right," Bloom agreed. "Notice Davies promised me Royal Marines, but he didn't say anything about *how many*. Typical." Then he added, hurriedly, "Not of Davies, it's not his fault. It's just hard to get any support from up the chain, unless—"

"Unless it's codes. Is that it, Mr. Bloom?" asked Maggie sharply. *That's the trouble with MI-5 these days*, Mr. Tolkien had said, *if it's not cryptology, they've no time for it.* "They wouldn't give me the time of day because none of my information came through their cryptanalysis project? I could see it—even *you* sprang into action—I mean got really serious—when you saw those Latin documents. The whole ministry's got code fever, and you're not immune. Just picture it: Göring blithely passing notes to his people via a diplomatic pouch while all of Whitehall sits at attention for a radio message that never comes."

"I'm sorry, Mrs. Brooke," Bloom said quietly and carefully, his eyes on the road. "This is a topic I'm not at liberty to discuss." But his face was troubled, and when he glanced over and caught Maggie's eye, his look was as good as an admission.

Maggie thumbed the radio off. "Mr. Bloom," she said, "codebreaking is well and good, and I can see how it might save many thousands of lives. But do you really mean to tell me that the British intelligence community has become fixated on cryptology to the point of ignoring physical evidence? Even at risk of the lives of British citizens and residents? I have a rather personal stake in this, remember. Göring has tried to kill me personally. So I ask you: when Hitler invaded Belgium, did we wait for cryptological corroboration of the event before we declared war on Germany?" When Bloom remained studiously silent, Maggie rolled her eyes and muttered, "Oh, for heaven's sake."

She thumbed the radio back on. "—Palace," Davies shouted. "Repeat, convoy sighted just south of Buckingham Palace. Respond,

Bloom, for God's sake." So focused had she been on her discussion with Bloom, Maggie had missed the moment when they arrived in London.

"CSI," Maggie said, "that's what we'll call it." The three men in the car just looked at her and didn't respond. "CSI will be the new name and designation of my unit when we are done here and get the respect we deserve from Whitehall. Our own unit, insignia, the whole bit. We women ... Allie, too ... are smart, tireless, and dedicated. We will be a real force in counter-espionage."

The three men looked at each other with blank faces. Allie spoke first. "Mum," he asked, "What does 'CSI' stand for?"

"Crash Site Investigations, of course," Maggie intoned with an air of confidence.

"But what makes you think such a unit is needed further?" asked Ian. "You've uncovered the plot."

"What makes you think it isn't?" Maggie replied.

"We're nearly there," Bloom told the radio. "We've practically caught them. Where are my Marines?" The streets were all but deserted—the day's heavy bombing had seen to that—but military personnel were no more in evidence than civilians.

"Oh, god," said Ian. "You don't think they're targeting Buckingham, do you? The blow to morale—"

"Convoy has passed Buckingham palace and is continuing along Birdcage Walk towards the Thames," Davies's voice drowned him out.

Allie's brow knitted. "That sounds like they're targeting Parliam—"

"The platoon of Royal Marines securing Westminster Abbey have just reported admitting a convoy of Special Biological Warfare Unit vehicles to the Abbey premises," Davies thundered. "Please advise."

"Arrest all personnel on those lorries," Bloom sputtered. "We'll be there in five minutes! For god's sake don't let them unload those vehicles!" The Morgan had been racing at top speed all the way from Warborough, but Maggie would have sworn Bloom put on a little extra gas now. The four of them leaned forward as if urging on a racehorse; Rooney gave a single encouraging bark. Maggie said a silent prayer for courage, and another for the patience not to strangle any agents of MI-5.

But when they arrived, breathlessly, at the Abbey, it was clear that all Bloom's instructions had come too late. The Royal Marines there were just breaking their perimeter and moving inside to confront the disguised Germans, but many of them seemed confused. Outside the north transept door, four enormous army lorries marked "Special Biological Warfare Unit" stood deserted and empty. One young man accosted them. "Madam," he said with a salute, "and sirs. We are containing a possible biological threat at this site and must ask you to remain outside our perimeter for your own safety."

"Best double-check with your commanding officer, my boy," Bloom responded, flashing his credentials. "I am Stephen Bloom, an agent of MI-5, and these are my associates. I'm afraid your platoon has been duped. The men who arrived in these lorries are German agents bent on deploying a weapon of unknown type, and it's up to us to stop them." Indeed, as he spoke, a Marine commanding officer was shouting orders and Royal Marines were changing direction and racing back towards the Abbey. "You are a—" Bloom studied the young man's insignia for a moment— "You are a Lance Corporal, yes? What's your name, Lance Corporal?"

"Lance Corporal Andrew Clayworth, sir," the young Marine said with another salute.

"Lance Corporal Clayworth, this is Flying Officer Allister Brooke of the Royal Air Force," Bloom said, indicating Allie. "He's the nearest thing to a munitions expert we have on hand at the moment.

Unfortunately, he's recently been blinded in action. I need you to go around to the southern transept door and accompany Flying Officer Brooke into the Abbey. Quietly so as not to attract undue attention, you must describe to him, in as great detail as possible, anything and everything that might help him determine what sort of weapon we are facing. Can you do that?"

"Yes sir," said Lance Corporal Clayworth with yet another salute. Turning to Allie, he said, "Follow me, Officer Brooke." The two young men rushed together along the side of the great cathedral, Lance Corporal Clayworth at first watching out solicitously for Allie's footing, then realizing that Rooney kept him from tripping on stairs or walking into walls. Clayworth let out a low whistle. "Smart dog you've got there," he remarked.

"Rooney's a miracle," Allie agreed, "and yet she's not much good at telling Germans from Brits or describing machinery. 'Red wire, blue wire' is not her forte—I shall depend upon you for that."

"Yes sir," Clayworth assented and led the way into the Abbey's south transept, his service weapon drawn. The entrance gave into Poets' Corner; it took Clayworth's eyes a moment to adjust to the low light inside the cathedral, but after a moment he was able to make out candlelight glinting on the gravestones of Tennyson and Browning. A great flurry of activity—clanking and banging, brief exchanges in German, and the whine of electric winches—was audible from here, echoing hollowly through the vast stone nave, but the south transept was blessedly deserted. Clayworth backed Allie into a shadowy nook between two memorial busts. "Stay here a moment, and be very still," he instructed, and then Allie was alone among the chilly stones. The cathedral smelled of burning candles and of centuries of incense. Rooney pressed herself against Allie's shins, and he tangled his fingers in the lush fur of her neck. Cautiously, with his other hand, he explored the statue to his right. Its marble was smooth and—though certainly not warm—not as cold as he had expected. He had looked at the statues in Poets' Corner dozens of times over the years, but he couldn't remember ever having touched one before. He smiled to himself—if he'd been younger when they'd come to Oxford from Dublin, he probably would have scampered all over Shakespeare's and Chaucer's shoulders, to his parents' mingled horror and secret delight.

Under the fingers of his left hand, Rooney's muscles tensed. Allie held his breath and strained his senses. Was there a faint shuffling of many feet in the north transept? Allie thought so, but they were *very* quiet. Closer to him, Clayworth's return was announced less by footsteps than by the whisper of his uniform's fabrics as he moved. "They're mostly in the nave proper," he whispered, "and they're quite absorbed in their task. Add to that they're making plenty of racket. So keep mum and stick close, and we shouldn't have much trouble, sir." He placed Allie's hand on his shoulder and, keeping low, the two of them moved swiftly north into the Abbey. Allie could feel the changing air currents on his skin as they emerged from the south transept into the long south aisle, and again as they moved forward and ducked into the choir. Allie remembered this structure as something like a cabin of intricately carved wood openwork standing in the Abbey's center, with the two transepts radiating north and south, the apse behind its gothic brass screen to the east, and the great open space of the nave, sometimes filled with folding wooden chairs but more often simply bare, to the west. Once inside the choir, the two young men crawled on their hands and knees to its western edge and concealed themselves among the wooden choir pews. With his seat on an embroidered kneeler and Rooney's warm body leaning against his, Allie found himself surprisingly comfortable.

Clayworth had no such luxury, but propped himself with one knee on a pew and his eye pressed against the wooden openwork in order to see as much as possible of the action in the nave without being seen himself. "They've built a gigantic metal ... thing," Clayworth whispered. "Like a box the size of a room, or like an upside-down ziggurat. It's maybe ... ten feet tall, and its walls are angled—the top is a bigger rectangle than the bottom. I'd say the top, the big part, is thirty feet or so by ten, and the base, the footprint, is a bit smaller than that—maybe twenty by eight." He paused and took a breath. "It's mad, these guys have been here less than ten minutes. How did they ... these guys. They move like an auto-racing crew, I mean, synchronized, fast. They're like a machine themselves, it's poetry to watch."

Another pause. The air smelled of ozone. Allie played the scene out in his head in as much detail as he could. "What are they doing now?" he asked after a moment.

"Well, it looks like ... " Clayworth struggled to understand the scene well enough to put it into words. "They're on top of the box. They're pulling parts up from—it looks like the box must have a hollow center, or something smaller inside. They're pulling panels up from inside. The panels stand up another couple feet from the top of the box, and they're—it looks like—welding them in place. Does that make any sense? They're—"

Whatever else Clayworth would have said was lost in a sudden clamor of shouting and gunfire. Allie could hear English voices coming from two directions—immediately north of him, just outside the choir, and west, where the Abbey's great ceremonial entry lay beyond the end of the nave.

Stephen Bloom and Ian Brooke had been unified and adamant in their insistence that Mrs. Brooke remain outside the Abbey when the Royal Marine platoon stormed it, but Maggie possessed a lifetime's experience in nodding, smiling, and then doing what men had told her she mustn't. The Marines had split themselves into two groups, one group entering from the north while the other group circled around to enter the Abbey from the west. Bloom and Ian joined the latter group, so it was relatively simple for Maggie, once the other group's attention was committed to the task in hand, simply to follow the men in through the north transept door. She winced at the thunder of gunfire echoing through the Abbey's enormous stone space—it was nearly as loud as Lieutenant Davies's voice had been. Slipping between a wall and a life-sized marble of the Blessed Virgin Mary that stood conveniently at the corner, she peeked out at the firefight under way in the nave.

Men in Royal Marine and British Army uniforms had spread out and taken cover behind the forest of columns, statuary, and woodwork, firing off rounds in syncopated bursts. The Germans in their stolen British Army gear had mostly been forced to abandon their work on the bomb as they were steadily beaten back by volleys of gunfire. Several nevertheless remained at the foot of the metal doors, welding equipment in hand, dark goggles firmly in place. Despite the bullets screaming past them, they did not budge. Their task must be of extreme urgency to sell their lives in such a calm and measured manner, thought Maggie. She watched one German go down, then another and another. She reminded herself that they were her murderous enemies, but in their British uniforms, she couldn't help but see how much they resembled Allie's and even Colin's classmates.

The hammering of her pulse in her ears threatened to drown out the sound of gunfire. As a contingent of Germans came pounding up the aisle towards her hiding place, though, a terrified Maggie shrank into a puddle of shadow and prayed for invisibility—and it seemed her prayers were answered. As the Germans arrayed themselves against the wall of the sanctuary, they had eyes only for their Royal Marine adversaries across the cavernous room. She could have tapped these four men on their shoulders, so close they had positioned themselves to her, and for the first time in her life she ardently wished for a gun.

She needn't have, though. Almost before she completed her wish, the foremost of the four Germans toppled over, a red-black stain spreading down his shirtfront from the throat. The other three drew closer, scanning the area, taking shots. In a moment, another of them was facedown over the first. Looking up, she could see Ian's right hand and service weapon retreating behind the cover of the far corner of the choir. Her heart constricted.

The two remaining Germans in front of her now emptied their magazines at that corner of the choir, disintegrating the gorgeous old wood in a shower of splinters. She hoped that she had only imagined Ian's voice emitting a strangled cry. The Germans' sudden focus on Ian paid off for the Marines, though, as the two Germans were picked off by bullets that came whizzing from another corner. Maggie kept her eyes trained on the choir's ruined corner, praying that she would see Ian emerge unharmed. Throughout the Abbey, the shooting had slowed from a continuous roar to individual *bangs* and *pops*. Maggie still could hear shouting in English and German, though, and a confusion of running boots. "*Schnell, schnell!*" she thought she heard, and then a garble ending with "*der Gefahrenzone zu sein.*" She searched her mind, but she simply knew too little German to make sense of it. And anyway she was distracted: Ian raced in a flash, faster than she would have thought him capable of, from behind the choir into Poets' Corner. A flood of relief washed over her, then a hitch came into her breath: the left shoulder and upper arm of Ian's blue-gray tweed jacket had been soaked with blood.

A few minutes into the pandemonium of gunfire that had broken out, Clayworth leaned down and whispered to Allie, "They seem to have abandoned their machine; the ones who stayed on top are dead, or close to it. Do you want to take a look?" Allie nodded and Clayworth once again placed the other man's hand on his shoulder. Together, the two crept silently to the choir's door, then down the south aisle towards the metal behemoth, Lance Corporal Clayworth keeping a sharp eye out in front of and behind them for the enemy. But the Germans were absorbed entirely in fighting Royal Marines, giving Clayworth and Allie the chance to creep along to the far face of the machine. Once behind its cover, Clayworth began trying to describe what he saw. "Right," he said. "There's a ladder leaning here—this must be how the Nazis climbed to the top to weld those panels."

"Are there any features on the outer walls of the box? Any markings or wiring?" Allie asked.

"Nothing on the three sides we've seen—the east, south, and west-facing sides," Clayworth reported. "They're all completely smooth steel, slanting—as you can feel—outwards from the base to that big overhanging top. Shall I take a look at the north-facing side?"

"Please," Allie assented simply. The roar of gunfire swallowed the subtler, closer sounds of Clayworth's quick movements; Allie hardly realized the Royal Marine had left his side before he returned.

"There's something here," Clayworth said. "Come tell me what it means." Allie followed him—Rooney guiding him over the fallen body of a German soldier—and noticed how the soundscape changed as he rounded the corner. From this angle, the hubbub sounded sharper, less rounded—likely more direct transmission to his ears, Allie reasoned, and fewer reflected sounds. "There's a kind of panel with a series of six lights," Clayworth relayed, "two of them yellow, four green. And there's a dial here—it looks like a clock. A clock running backwards. Right now it reads twenty minutes to one—or, since it's running backwards, forty minutes to noon."

Allie pictured it as clearly as he could in his mind's eye, forcing himself to concentrate on his mental diagram rather than the gunshots, bootsteps, and shouts that filled the air around them—was that his father he heard give a brief scream?—and on the scents of gunpowder and blood in the air, overpowering the candlewax and even the incense. He took a deep breath and told himself that nothing existed in the world but Clayworth's voice. "If I understand correctly what you're telling me," he said, "it sounds as if whatever machine this is, it's a couple of steps away from fully operational."

The fighting had moved to the far end of the sanctuary, so Maggie screwed up her courage and, in hopes of a better view of the action, stepped out from behind the Blessed Virgin—and directly into the path of a handsome, compact, apple-cheeked man in a British Army uniform. To Maggie's relief, he seemed to be nursing an injured right hand under his left arm and held no visible weapon, but she quickly realized that she knew this man from somewhere. The silvery vertical lines of scar tissue that cut through his eyebrow and the corner of his mouth on one side wrinkled as a slow smile spread across his face: he recognized her, too. "Well, Mrs. Brooke," he said in English that was strange only in its absolute textbook perfection. "I have often been the cat, but never the mouse." Adrenaline rushing through her, she lunged at him, throwing her arms around his neck and attempting to wrestle him to the ground, but he shrugged her aside easily and she sprawled to the floor. In a loud voice, he called out to his men again in German, repeating the phrases Maggie had heard him use a minute or two ago. Then he turned his attention back to her. "*Auf Wiedersehen* for now, Mrs. Brooke," he said with a wink, and before she could rise he had vanished out the north transept door. Scrambling to her feet, Maggie followed, but when she opened the door, he was nowhere in sight.

Where had she seen him before? Maggie asked herself, and then, along with a wave of nausea, she remembered the feeling of a murderous hand on the back of her neck as she stood in the organ loft at the Chapel of St. Genesis, the final notes of the Ave Maria still ringing in her ears. She remembered the chill that had run down her spine when Father DiClemente had warned her that the stairs were dangerous, the chill that kept coming back no matter how often she told herself his words and touch had been innocuous. Maggie Brooke cursed herself for a fool.

"Those panels sticking up from the top of the box—they're not the same kind of metal as the rest of the machine," Clayworth reported, rejoining Allie and Rooney at the foot of the ladder.

"What do you mean?" Allie asked.

"Well, they're not steel, sir," Clayworth reported, sounding a bit confused. "They're a different metal—darker, but with a kind of pale powdery surface—a softer, heavier metal than steel. If I had to guess, I'd say they're lead."

"Lead!" Allie repeated, a sick possibility awakening in the back of his mind. "And you told me that the Nazis were lifting these panels and then welding them in place, right?" Allie asked.

"That's how it looked to me, sir," Clayworth confirmed. "It looks like a giant box, three times as wide as it is high and deep, with six internal doors that are now external. They're protruding from the top. From here, I can see them edge-on, so they look like smokestacks or thick antennae. Or as if the box were a giant, rectangular metal insect lying on its back, with its six legs in the air."

"What else could you see up there?"

"Well, I could see that the outer, taller rectangle of the machine is open towards the inside. And the doors themselves are not rigid, but the frames are. The doors have a series of sections that are coupled with hinges about every two inches. The frames are on tracks I guess to roll the doors out. If I had to guess, the doors surround a sphere of some sort. That's my impression."

"Six doors in all," Allie noted, "semi-flexible and made of lead."

"Yes. Flexible because—they're made of metal that's sort of woven. Thicker than chain mail and not as flexible—maybe an inch thick. Much denser than chain mail."

"And you think it was built to cover a ball or sphere?" Allie asked.

"That's right," confirmed Lance Corporal Clayworth. "I wasn't able to see in, though. Nevertheless, this thing is definitely a bomb." Clayworth's serious voice had become grave, raspy. "Why else would these Germans fight to the death to weld the ports around these doors?"

Allie's blood was cold in his veins, but at the same time, it was racing. His mind was racing, too, as he reviewed one after another of the schematics he had memorized, considered, and discussed on his recent visit to Cambridge. "It's a bomb for sure, and we know that they loaded it with a tremendous quantity of TNT surrounding an inner box or core, probably in the shape of a sphere, and the entire sphere shielded with lead," Allie whispered half to himself, horrified by the familiarity of the layout. Then he addressed himself aloud to Clayworth. "The clock that's counting down—what does it say now?"

There was a pause during which Clayworth must have darted back around to look. Another burst of gunfire sounded from the apse, and a voice from that direction shouted something about "*Schnell*" and the "*Gefahrenzone.*" German had been a popular choice of foreign language for young engineers to learn, but Allie's was only passable. He strained to hear more, but the voice seemed to have receded into the general commotion. Then Clayworth was beside him again. "Thirty-five minutes 'til noon," he said, and then added: "My God, that's the countdown to detonation, isn't it? Please tell me thirty-five minutes isn't all we have to disarm this monster."

"It's more than enough for well-trained men like us," Allie said with a confidence he didn't feel. He just prayed Lance Corporal Clayworth couldn't sense his doubt and fear. "Let's go back to those panels—those flexible sliding doors that the Nazis were welding in place—were effectively welding open, right?"

"Right," Clayworth replied.

"Did they finish the job? Are all six doors welded open?" Allie asked.

"Four of them are. Four of six! They must correspond to the four green lights! Don't you think so? The frames of the doors must complete a circuit when they're welded open." Clayworth's voice sounded momentarily boyish with the pleasure of figuring things out. Allie couldn't help but grin and nod encouragement as he recognized Clayworth's realization as one of his own favorite pleasures. "The other two are kind of ... locked in place. By mechanical means, it seems like. It'll take some doing, but if it helps, I think we can close those two."

From the eastern end of the Abbey came the German voice again, clear this time: "*Halbe Stunde Fahrt, um aus der Gefahrenzone zu sein!*"

"He can't have just said what I think he said," breathed Clayworth as a few more shots rang out, and then the gunfire ceased.

"A thirty-minutes' drive to get outside the blast radius," confirmed Allie. "And that blast radius confirms what I've been afraid of ever since you mentioned those lead panels. This isn't a conventional bomb, or a biological one either. It's atomic."

CHAPTER FIFTEEN:
THIRTY MINUTES

Minute by minute they live:
The stone's in the midst of all.
—W.B. Yeats, from "Easter 1916"

A MOMENTARY SILENCE descended on the Abbey. Maggie could hear her heart beating in her ears like a great bass drum; she wondered whether every man still alive in the church could hear it, too. Then it seemed as if all the Royal Marines were moving at once, shouting orders and information to one another back and forth across the sanctuary. They swarmed across the space with no care for cover, and since no further shots rang out, Maggie judged it must be safe for her to come out, too. Standing in the center of the aisle, she surveyed the room aghast: littered with bodies, the floor slick with black blood. Tears welled in her eyes. After a moment, she realized that most of the bodies were clad in the Army brown that the Germans had been wearing—from where she stood, she could see six or eight of these, but only three in the blue of the Royal Marines. She dabbed her face with a handkerchief and wondered if this was what victory was supposed to feel like.

She was so absorbed in her reflections that a gentle hand on her elbow startled her, and she gasped. Then, turning, she collapsed with tearful gratitude into Ian's arms. "There, there, darling," he comforted her. "It's all over. They've gone, and the Royal Marines are here to take care of things. We've done our duty and we can be proud, and now it's time to go home." With his right hand he smoothed her flyaway hair. "You've been awfully clever, my love, and awfully brave." He kissed her brow and then, gently and swiftly, her lips. "Let's go and find our boy," he said after a moment, releasing Maggie from his arms but taking her left hand in his right.

"But you've been shot," Maggie said. It was true: the left arm of his jacket was blood-soaked from lapel to elbow, and its left shoulder was torn out raggedly. Ian's left hand looked pale and felt cold to the touch, though he could move his fingers. And now that she noticed, his breathing was shallow and a bit irregular.

Ian winced. "I'll need some attention for that," he conceded. "It doesn't half tickle. Still, though, I've lived through worse." With a wry smile, he lifted his bad leg and swiveled its ankle. "Let's find Allie, and then can find a medic." His smile vanished and he wrapped his arm back around his wife's shoulders as the Abbey's windows rattled at a sound like thunder that came from the sky above. The thunderous noise receded for a moment, then returned accompanied by the sound of distant machine-gun fire. "An air battle," Ian said, looking up uneasily. "Come, darling," he urged, and with his habitual limp, led Maggie by the hand to the south aisle, where he retrieved his cane; their progress was smoother from there to the shadow of the monster machine that still stood in the center of the church.

The sound of the battle raging outside, above their heads, was nearly as loud as the gun battle in the nave had been. Clayworth reassured Allie once or twice that the fighting was outside and he needn't take cover, but even so Allie had to keep reminding himself. It helped when brisk steps approached and Mr. Bloom's voice asked for a full report on the German machine. Allie forced himself to stand confidently and to keep his eyes turned, as he explained the evidence that suggested the bomb must be atomic, towards the place where his ears told him Bloom's face must be. "I feared as much," Bloom responded when Allie completed his report just as two more sets of footsteps approached, one of them with the characteristic syncopated gait he knew as his father's. "I've already had the Marines radio for a bomb squad," Bloom continued. "They're on their way, provided they can get through the lines of the Bf 109s the Luftwaffe has sent to stop them." Bloom gestured towards the racket overhead, then remembered that Allie couldn't see him. "At any rate, the R.A.F. is doing its best to give them a chance. Until then, keep learning all you can so that you can brief them when they arrive. They'll be less familiar with a weapon of this kind than you are, I expect. Meanwhile, I'm going to Ten Downing Street and from there to the palace. Churchill and His Majesty should be briefed in person. I'll radio ahead with your preliminary conclusion."

"Shouldn't we evacuate the city?" Ian asked. "I thought a radioactive bomb ... "

"Not necessarily," Allie said, "not immediately. There will be a shock wave dangerous to planes flying within, oh, thirty or fifty miles, so we should get our airmen down or away. The blast will endanger buildings within three to five miles and human beings within, let's say, seven miles. So we want to get people within that radius into shelters. The radiation kill zone could be ten miles in radius ... but we've got no time. We'll have to figure out afterwards how to rescue people from the shelters, but for now, let's focus on keeping them safe from the initial blast—or, with God's help, on keeping the blast from happening at all. That's what you should tell the Prime Minister and the King."

"I'll come with you," Ian said to Bloom impetuously. Then, clearing his throat and regaining his air of dignity, he added, "Surely two witnesses are better than one?"

Bloom inclined his head in assent. "Mrs. Brooke, will you stay and assist Flying Officer Brooke and Lance Corporal Clayworth in their investigation?" With a certain grim humor he added, "I'm concerned you might not be able to resist giving the personages in question a piece of your mind." Resuming a more serious tone, he added, "I want all our best minds, expert or otherwise, on the problem of disarming this bomb. And you've amply demonstrated that our best minds include you." Turning, he strode towards the north transept door and was gone; despite his limp and his new injury, Ian showed no difficulty keeping up.

Maggie turned to Allie and Clayworth. "How may I assist?" she asked.

"I'm going to climb back up to the top and see if I can describe the mechanism in better detail for Flying Officer Brooke," Clayworth said. "If you can help talk it out with him—"

"Nonsense," said Maggie. "I've got no munitions training or technical expertise of any kind. I'll be no help to Allie down here. I'll climb up with you—four eyes are better than two." And without any further ado, she proceeded up the ladder, somehow contriving both to climb deftly and to preserve her modesty despite the knee-length Home Guard skirt she wore. Lance Corporal Clayworth made to stop her, but anticipating his motion, Allie stayed his hand.

"You don't know my mother," Allie explained. "She's got a sharp eye and a strong will. If she says she's going to help you, then that's what she's going to do—and you'll end up being glad later." He grinned and shrugged. Clayworth shrugged, too, and followed Maggie to the top of the bomb.

The truth was, though, that they couldn't see much. The raised lead panels obstructed their views into the bomb's outer hull. By peering between them, Maggie could glimpse stacked parcels marked TNT, but it was impossible to see in any detail how the bomb was wired. She was impressed, however, with the methodical calm with which Clayworth reported these dispiriting facts to Allie. Her own insides were wound to the breaking point with frustration, and Rooney's nervous barks showed that she felt the same way. Clayworth was, at least, able to tell Allie about how four of the doors had been welded in such a way as to keep them permanently open, and he was able to indicate to Allie which two—the southern panel and the southwestern one—had not been welded. "That's what our strategy must be," Allie asserted. "The atomic bomb depends upon a powerful, completely symmetrical conventional explosion as the triggering mechanism to begin its cascading chain of nuclear reactions." Allie couldn't see the puzzled expressions on his mother's and Clayworth's faces, but just as if he could, he simplified: "If the core is somehow shielded from a portion of the TNT explosion—if we can get even one of those panels down, even partway—then the nuclear core won't detonate. Even an inch of lead can make the trigger force unequal by fractions of a percent. That's all we should need."

"Didn't you say there was nearly ten thousand pounds of TNT in this steel hull?" Maggie asked, and both young men nodded as if it weren't a guess. "That's quite an explosion. Shouldn't we focus on preventing that?"

"Ideally, of course," Allie assented. "But we can't get at the wiring or the trigger mechanisms—not without closing those lead panels, and maybe not at all. I'm afraid that at this point, the TNT's detonation is inevitable. I'll do what I can to save them both—but the difference between the TNT going and the nuclear core going ... well, it's the difference between losing the Abbey and losing London."

Maggie went white. "Surely you're exaggerating, Allie. Surely you are? One bomb can't destroy the whole of a city. It can't. Can it?"

"Without being able to see the bomb's inner workings," Allie admitted, "I can't be sure. But based on its size and what I learned this fall at the Cavendish lab, I would estimate this bomb's blast radius at upwards of three miles."

Now Lance Corporal Clayworth went white, too, with a bilious undertone of green. Only for a moment, though. He was a man of action. "We can't let that happen," he declared, "so let's get to work. Mrs. Brooke, can you help me figure out these door panels? Some sort of latching or locking mechanism seems to be holding them in place. I guess the welding was just an added safeguard against meddlers like us." He knelt down at the bomb's inner edge to peer down at the slot in the core's cover through which a lead panel thrust up like a gravestone.

Hardly had he begun his examination, though, when a new group of Royal Marines, arms loaded with a variety of odd-looking equipment, entered. "You must be the bomb squad," Maggie greeted them. They gawped up at her with varying degrees of confusion.

Allie stepped forward and put out his hand. "I'm Flying Officer Allister Brooke of the R.A.F.," he said. When one of the bomb squad shook his proffered hand, he continued, "I was a bomb aimer in France, but I was wounded in action and lost my eyesight just before Dunkirk. However, I have studied defense engineering and have some particular knowledge of proposed designs for nuclear weapons. I believe that this is such a weapon. I would like to make myself useful to you in any way I can, but I must insist that you begin by initiating an evacuation of all civilians within seven miles of this spot."

Clayworth descended the ladder, and the men huddled together, discussing. One of the bomb squad climbed the ladder, peered through the gaps between the lead panels, climbed down, and rejoined the huddle. The building shook, and peering out the western door, Maggie could see that a Messeschmitt Bf 109 had been shot down on the grounds to the north of the abbey. Its nose had broken against the pavement, and one wing had been sheared off by the bell tower of St. Margaret's Church beyond. Flames engulfed the plane. Maggie was suddenly gripped by a pang of sadness at the waste of it all: the rubber and fuel that were burning there in the street; the damage the crashing plane had done to the lovely old Anglican church; the young German lives that even now were being sacrificed to the flames.

Inside the Abbey, it took the huddled men only two or three minutes to reach a decision, and then the Royal Marines began rushing about, radioing for evacuation teams, making measurements, and placing bundles connected by wires in the crypt beneath the Abbey's floor. Maggie heard members of the squad using the terms "critpit," which meant nothing whatsoever to her, and "bomb disposal pit," which made a bit more sense. Calling for his mother to take his arm, Allie led her to the apse, out of the Marines' way. Maggie marveled once again at the ease of Allie's movements with Rooney by his side. The two of them sat with their backs against the gothic brass altar screen, their fingers curled in Rooney's silky fur, as Allie explained what the bomb squad were doing. After he had finished, Maggie knew not to be alarmed when, a minute or two later, the Royal Marines all came running to the apse and crouched on the ground. She and Allie, too, pressed their faces to their knees and covered their heads with their arms. For a moment, the group collectively held its breath, a bubble of stillness beneath the clamor of the air battle that still raged above. And then, a moment later, the apse rocked violently.

Maggie felt her mouth fill with dust; the back of her neck prickled as fine particles of plaster and cobwebs cascaded down it. When she looked up, the Abbey appeared the same as before, only messier. Dust dulled the gleam of the brass fixtures, embroidered hangings, and richly painted statuary. A couple of the stained-glass windows were cracked. Only when she followed the men back to the nave west of the choir, where the German bomb had stood, could she see the real effects of what the Royal Marines had done.

Where the menacing, odd-shaped box of steel had stood, a ragged hole now gaped in the Abbey's ancient stone floor. "Don't get too close to the edge," Lance Corporal Clayworth warned. "We don't know how much of the floor has been undermined." Still, Maggie was able to see that the crater was deep—Allie had told her that the crypt's floor was forty feet below the nave's. Now, in the event that they couldn't disarm the bomb, at least it would detonate underground, where some of its force would be absorbed and dissipated.

"I've asked them to drive one of those enormous lorries the Germans stole into the hole to help seal it, too," Allie explained to his mother. "It won't contain the explosion, but at least it'll dampen it—very, very little in the case of a nuclear explosion, but considerably if we're just dealing with the TNT. They'll be able to absorb a great deal of the energy due to their mass. At any rate—would you mind helping to direct the drivers?" Turning to Clayworth as Maggie edged around the hole towards the western door, Allie went on, "In a few minutes that'll be done, and then it'll be safe for you to show me around the crypt. You did say that's what you reconnoitered this morning before we got here, didn't you?"

"Yes, sir," Clayworth responded; "I personally secured the underground emergency escape route by which our dignitaries would have left in case of an air raid. We can make sure it's still intact and that you know the way to it."

"Tip-top," said Allie as a three-ton Biological Warfare Unit lorry plowed its way up the western stairs and into the nave. Once he cleared the doors, into the hole with a great resounding crash. Clayworth led Allie back towards the south transept door, where, behind a railing of wrought iron, a spiral staircase wound down into the crypt. Down and down they plunged, Clayworth pulling out his small electric torch and reflecting that in the dark, Allie would have the advantage. Rooney navigated the steps with ease, her velvet paws whispering against the iron. The staircase seemed impossibly long.

Finally they reached its foot. Clearing his throat in the dankness, Clayworth advised, "Right now we're facing west. The easiest way to find the exit from here is to stretch out your left hand and touch the wall—that's it. Now, just follow that around as it curves—good—and now we've turned around and are facing east. Perfect. Keep following that wall. All right, now, you seem to have come to a dead end, right? And you can feel that tomb coming up about waist-high in front of you? Just wedge your shoulder in there to the left of it, between the tomb and the wall you were following—you've got it—now give that a good shove."

Allie's face lit up as the tomb moved, fairly easily as if on a hidden track. "It's a bona fide secret passage," he said, "just like I used to put in all my adventure stories when I was a kid."

"That's right," said Clayworth. "Just feel what that step feels like—now, you've got it. That passage will lead you right under Saint Margaret Street and into the Palace of Westminster."

"Jolly good," grinned Allie. "I feel like a real spy now." He began retracing his steps to the foot of the stairs. "And from where we started, the bomb will be west northwest, right?"

"Exactly," Clayworth confirmed, leading Allie and Rooney through the gloom, over new rubble and beneath ancient stone arches, to where the monstrous German bomb lay, partly sunk in a crater its impact had created. The device—somewhat to Lance Corporal Clayworth's private disappointment—was intact, its lights just as before and its clock still counting backwards. The whole thing was now on a bit of a slant, though, and between that and the rough steps created by the explosions' debris, Clayworth spotted a route by which Allie could climb fairly easily to the bomb's upper surface as if via a set of rude stairs. If Clayworth hadn't been able to see much of the bomb's workings before, here in the crypt's gloom he could see even less. He oriented Allie to the unwelded panels and, as Allie got to work alternately fiddling with the ports through which they might retract and attempting to push them down by brute force, he excused himself. "I need to check in with my commanding officer and unit," he explained.

"Thank you, Lance Corporal Clayworth," said Allie warmly. "I believe I'm all right on my own for the moment. Go to your unit and get them clear of the Abbey."

"Yes sir," Clayworth assented.

"And Clayworth?" Allie added as the Marine turned to go.

"Sir?"

"If you could think of an urgent mission that will send my mother rushing away from London," Allie joked darkly, "that would be much appreciated, too."

CHAPTER SIXTEEN:
TWENTY MINUTES

Minute by minute they change;
A shadow of cloud on the stream
Changes minute by minute ...
—W.B. Yeats, from "Easter 1916"

STOUT HERO OF A THOUSAND VOYAGES on the Liffey, general of countless hundreds of battles at Port Meadow and Bagley Wood, man who had tumbled from the Belgian sky and lived to tell the tale, yet Allister O'Hare Brooke found himself flummoxed by German engineering. The bomb's design was ingenious: there was simply no way to get into its hull, to get at its wiring. Even if the Royal Marine bomb squad had used their blowtorches to breach the steel hull, what Allister had learned at the Cavendish told him that attempts to disassemble the mechanism would be more likely to detonate the device than to disarm it. Inelegant as the solution struck him, the only chance of saving London was to insulate the radioactive core as far as possible from the TNT trigger. Nuclear weapons, he knew, depended upon cascading nuclear reactions; to begin such a cascade required a perfect TNT implosion. Best would be if he could close the two unwelded panels entirely, but if he could move either one of them to shield the core from that segment's complement of TNT—shield it even partially—then there was a prayer that the TNT trigger would not achieve its function of triggering a nuclear cascade.

In the darkness of the Westminster Abbey crypt, moldy and nitrous as a wine cellar, Allie's long, slender fingers probed the ports into which he hoped to make the lead panels retract. He felt for any locking mechanism he might unlock, any track along which he might coax the panels to slide, but he found nothing. The panels' slide-and-lock mechanisms must have been too deep within the bomb's steel core for his inquisitive fingertips to find. Despite the crypt's chill, Allie wiped a sheen of sweat from his brow. Swift exploration with his sensitive fingertips revealed that the massive Army lorry resting atop the bomb had somehow narrowly missed the unwelded panels. Allie wasn't sure whether he should curse it for not landing on the panels and pushing them in for him or bless it for missing the panels and thus not shielding them from his ministrations.

He was keenly aware of the swift passage of time, a stream he wished fervently he could dam. The bomb's clock made no noise as it marked its backwards seconds, but Allie could feel the frantic ticking of his heart, and he willed it and the clock to slow. "Saint Patrick, patron of Ireland and of engineers, intercede for me," he prayed under his breath, leaning his face into the sun-warm silk of Rooney's back. His heart continued to race, his head to spin, and so he reached out for something his mother had taught him long ago. "I will arise and go now, and go to Innisfree," he began. He chanted to slow his pulse and clear his head; without consciously thinking about it, his right hand closed around a block of granite, the size of a largish brick, that lay amongst the rubble at his feet. It was square and solid in his hand.

"And *I* shall *have* some *peace* there, for *peace* comes *drop* ping *slow*," he chanted, slamming the brick sledgehammer-style onto the top of a leaden panel's frame with each of the line's accented syllables. "*Drop* ping from the *veils* of the *mor* ning to *where* the *crick* et *sings*." The vault resounded with his heavy, regular pounding, repeated in andante sets of six. And when he came to the lake "lapping with low sounds by the shore," the miracle he had prayed for came—a tiny increment, but unmistakable: the panel receded by half an inch or so into its slot in the bomb's steel shell. It was all he could do not to whoop his victory, but he reminded himself that he must direct every ounce of his strength into the task at hand—and so with a silent *thank you* to his double patron saint, he resumed his pounding, feeling a quarter-inch of movement at every stroke: "*While* I *stand* on the *road* way ... "

The polite clearing of a throat interrupted his meditative progress. "Sir," a voice that was not Clayworth's addressed him. Allie saluted in its direction. "The area is secure," the Marine reported. "My unit is waiting for your orders."

The words that sprang from Allie's mouth came unplanned, unsummoned, surprising him. "My orders are: Go. Get away from here. Take my mother with you, against her will if you have to. Drive at least five miles away, and then take shelter in a bunker or cellar. But at least five miles away."

"Sir, no sir!" the Marine refused, but Allie could hear uncertainty threading his voice. "We were sent to defuse the threat to Westminster Abbey, and we will stay here until the threat is defused. To do otherwise would be desertion."

"It's not desertion if you're following orders," Allie pointed out. Then he sighed. "What can be done here to avert the threat is very little, I'm afraid. I'll do what I can, and then our fate is in the hands of God. But what there is here to do can be done, succeed or fail, by one man. And should I fail, the lives of any who stay here will be squandered. You cannot help me, so I'm ordering you to help your-selves."

The Marine was silent for a moment. Allie could hear him shift-ing his weight subtly from one foot to the other. "Sir, no sir," he repeated. "This squad will not abandon its post."

"I believe you are an enlisted man, correct?" Allie queried.

"Yes sir," the Marine responded.

"And your entire squad is composed of enlisted men?"

"Yes sir," the Marine said again.

"Then as an officer of His Majesty's Royal Air Force, I outrank all of you," Allie pointed out. There was a tremor in his voice as he began, but in speaking he gained confidence. "Take your squad, take my mother, and go to safety. There isn't a moment to lose. And if you stay here and we survive, I guarantee you'll be facing a court-martial for defying my orders. So go."

Tense silence reigned for a long moment. Allie added, "When I've finished my task, my dog will lead me to safety. You can come back and pick me up in an hour. For now, go."

The silence continued for another moment, and then the Ma-rine's voice said, "Sir, yes sir."

Allie saluted again, then listened as the man's footsteps retreated through the musty chill towards the spiraling iron staircase. After a moment, he hefted his granite block again and began, aloud this time in his bell-like tenor voice, from the poem's beginning: "*I will a rise* and *go* now, and *go* to *In* nis *free* ... " The soft lead of the panel swallowed any ringing the granite might have done, so his voice rang out alone, aloft above the stone's velvety thuds.

CHAPTER SEVENTEEN:
FIFTEEN MINUTES

He, too, has resigned his part
In the casual comedy;
He, too has been changed in his turn ...
—W.B. Yeats, from "Easter 1916"

AS MAGGIE BROOKE came back in through the western doors of Westminster Abbey, she couldn't help but be shocked anew by the crater that yawned in the Abbey's floor of immemorial stone. But then, she had seen so many shocking things that day, from the bodies in the cellar of the Hare House Dairy to the downed Hurricane that, moments ago, she had watched ripping a great gouge down the middle of Saint Margaret Street between the Abbey and Parliament. She had been helping the Royal Marines to surround the building with their brightly orange-painted sawhorse barriers, garish warnings that passersby must avoid the premises.

Passersby seemed unlikely, though: the streets of central London were eerily empty and silent. Maggie and the Marines had finished their task quickly before ducking back into the Abbey to check on Allie's progress. From the floor's hideous wound wafted Allie's strong sweet voice, reciting Yeats to the rhythm of a regular, soft, heavy thudding that Maggie couldn't so much hear as feel in her ankles and knees. Tears sprang unbidden to her eyes, and under her breath, she recited along with him.

"The Luftwaffe are withdrawing en masse," she heard one Marine shout, and another shouted back, "they're all turning back east … "

Maggie thought about it for a moment. Had the R.A.F. beaten them so definitively? A suspicion rose in her chest and firmed towards certainty. "The Germans know this bomb is nuclear," Maggie announced loudly, "and they're expecting it to detonate in a quarter hour. They're moving their planes out of the way of the shock wave they're expecting. And in case our effort here fails, we must warn the R.A.F. to do the same." In the scurry of activity surrounding her, Maggie wasn't certain any of the Marines had heard her announcement, let alone given it any attention. She found the man with the radio, made eye contact with him, and repeated her revelation. He was a burly youth with sandy hair and a snub nose. For a moment the man looked as though he might argue—was he taking orders from the Home Guard now, and a woman at that?—but giving Maggie's words a moment of thought, he slowly nodded his big square head, adjusted his dials, and relayed her warning.

Next, Maggie made towards the southern aisle, intending to take the crypt stairs down and join Allie, but a dark-haired young Marine intercepted her. "We're evacuating the premises, madam," he informed her. "You too. Flying Officer Brooke's explicit orders, and he outranks any of us here." Maggie demurred and made to walk past the young man, but he caught her by the arm. "I'm sorry, ma'am. Officer Brooke insisted that we make for safety and take you with us. *Against her will if you have to*, he said, though I'd prefer not to have to carry you out of here. Let's do this the dignified way, please, ma'am." By the end of his speech, a note of pleading had entered the young man's voice, and Maggie took pity on him. It wasn't his fault her son was being pig-headed, nor did she want to delay his and the other Marines' flight to safety. Courtesy and compassion dictated that she comply for the moment. Giving a slight nod, she turned and allowed the young Marine to shepherd her to the western door.

The Marines swarmed around their convoy of open jeeps. Into each vehicle the men loaded some of their equipment, then a man or two, and then each jeep sped off. To her great dismay, Maggie watched as a pair of Marines loaded the limp, motionless, and bloody figure of Lance Corporal Clayworth into one jeep's back seat. Following her eye, Maggie's dark-haired young Marine said, "Clayworth? I think he got the last bullet from the last Bf 109 to turn back. Back of his head took it, just below the helmet. Looks grim." Maggie walked over to Clayworth's inert body and felt for a pulse along his neck. It was there, though impossibly weak. "He's alive!" she exclaimed. The young marine bellowed, "Medic!" and then escorted Maggie to a waiting vehicle and made sure she was seated comfortably behind the driver, next to a large crate of something or other.

Two more Marines piled into the passenger's seat, and they were off. As the jeep sped along Victoria Street, one of the young Marines in the front remarked, shaking his head, "I just don't know how I'm going to tell my Gran that I blew a hole in Westminster Abbey."

Before they reached Christchurch Gardens, though, the jeep slowed to check in with a passing pair of Marines who were making certain that the area was clear of civilians. This was Maggie's chance: While the men were focused on their colleagues off to the left, Maggie swiftly and quietly hoisted herself over the right rear door of the jeep and made for Perkin's Rents as fast as her legs would carry her. Once round the corner, she peered out: the jeep was once again moving along Victoria Street—they must not have missed her yet. Maggie let out her breath—she hadn't even realized until that moment that she was holding it. She sprinted down Perkin's Rents and then up Abbey Orchard Street towards the Abbey as fast as her long, surprisingly nimble legs would carry her.

CHAPTER EIGHTEEN:
TEN MINUTES

In the nightmare of the dark
All the dogs of Europe bark.
And the living nations wait,
Each sequestered in its hate ...
—W.H. Auden, from "In Memory of W.B. Yeats"

AFTER CUTTING ACROSS THE DEAN'S YARD, Maggie arrived—slightly winded—back at the Abbey's western doors just as the last of the Marines' jeeps pulled away. Ducking behind a buttress at the cathedral's corner, she watched it go, and when the coast was clear, she hurried up the steps—only to find the cathedral's great doors locked. The north and south transept doors proved locked, too. Not knowing what else to do, Maggie circled back around to the western stairs and sat to catch her breath. She was just wondering whether she ought to break a window—after all, the structure had suffered worse insults today—when a gray-and-black Daimler DB18 purred up to the steps, brand-new and gleaming. The musclebound chauffeur, his gray wool uniform immaculately pressed, dashed around to open the rear passenger door. A stout, bulldog-faced figure—familiar from papers and newsreels—emerged. He was followed by another musclebound fellow, this one in a sharp navy blue suit and carrying a journalist's camera bound in wine-colored leather; despite their different clothing, this man could have been the chauffeur's twin.

Maggie stood. "Mr. Prime Minister," she said. "I hope you've brought your key, as I seem to find myself locked out—and my son locked in. With, as you may have heard, a German nuclear bomb that's due to blow any minute now."

"Madam, I must humbly confess that my retinue and I have no more power to open these doors than you do," Churchill boomed in orator's tones from several steps below Maggie.

"And these are all the men you could muster, are they?" Maggie mocked. "When poor Harold went to Hastings to meet William, he at least was able to bring seven thousand men. You bring two against the fury of the Third Reich?"

"I am powerless, madam," Churchill repeated. "I place my fate entirely in the hands of the brave Royal Marines who formed the bomb squad here today, in the hands of the R.A.F. pilots who expelled the Luftwaffe from our skies, in the hands of the capable men of MI-5—and, I believe, in your hands, too, madam. Unless I miss my mark, you are Margaret O'Hare Brooke, and if I live to fight another day, I will have your sharp eye and quick wits to thank."

Out of the corner of her eye, Maggie could see the man in the navy-blue suit setting up a camera tripod on the southern edge of the Abbey's steps. Another woman might have been mollified by the Prime Minister's recognition and gratitude, but Maggie was too alive to the peril her son was in—peril that could have been avoided had Whitehall listened sooner to her warnings. "Bollocks," she snorted, her rudeness surprising her. She was suddenly aware that she was perspiring heavily—from her run, no doubt. The armpits of her Home Guard uniform were horridly humid. "You're here for one last photo opportunity. You needn't have bothered, though. The Marines have evacuated this area. You're free to flee to safety, Mr. Prime Minister."

"Hardly," he said—laughed, really. For a moment his voice lost its stentorian quality and became simply that of one human being addressing another. "There wasn't time for me to get from Number Ten to any real safety." He quickly recovered his sense of public moment, however. "Besides, you cannot think that I would abandon London, this bright jewel, on what might be its last day. A captain must go down with his ship."

"I'll take advantage of the circumstances to be bold, Mr. Prime Minister," Maggie said. "A captain who steers his ship wisely—with eyes wide open, alive to pertinent news from any quarter—need not go down with his ship. Such a captain's ship need not go down. But you have ignored good intelligence in favor of the romance of the moment, and now all you can offer Britain in her hour of peril is one more grand, empty gesture." The wind picked up; as it wicked the perspiration from her uniform, Maggie shivered. She hugged herself with both arms.

"I am sorry if my decisions have not met with your approval, madam," Churchill intoned, his voice steely. "To be honest, MI-5 did suspect Hitler might be capable of detonating an atomic bomb, but since no plane invented is powerful enough to carry and drop it—" He sighed. "I'm afraid we underestimated the Nazis' cunning. Today, though, I am prepared to remain with my beloved city in the hour of its need." A flash snapped, dazzling Maggie's peripheral vision. "The Americans call it dying with your boots on, facing the enemy. Today I show London, and the British Armed Forces, that I am with them. We hold one another's fate in our hands. Today I demonstrate my trust in them as they have shown their trust in me—and trust is the foundation of the great British nation. Without it, pardoning the expression, madam, we none of us stands a blind Irishman's chance in—"

"Mr. Prime Minister," Maggie interjected, her voice like the chimes of Big Ben. She looked down with hard eyes on a man who had so often let her down, so often been, she felt, on the wrong side of history. "You have left the fate of London," she intoned, "in the hands of a blind Irishman and a golden retriever." She paused for a moment to let her barb sink in. A shiver ran through her, this time nothing to do with cold; she was possessed by a mother's righteous fury. She wished she could claw his eyes out then and there. Had she been a man, she would have slugged him. As it was, she drew herself up to her full impressive height. "While my son, an Irish citizen who sacrificed his eyesight in the service of your nation, labors in the dark below our feet to save the people of this city, you stand here posturing for your precious camera, trading witticisms with an American matron. Even as it waits to be atomized, the Churchill public-relations machine rolls on. What kind of leadership, Mr. Churchill? What kind of leadership do you call this?"

The Prime Minister's eyes remained hard; it was evident to Maggie that he was unmoved, but he spread his arms wide. "What would you have me do?" he asked, and in her bones she knew it for a challenge.

"The time for action is past," Maggie said. "When I called you to action, you were deaf. We must commit ourselves now to God. Let's kneel and pray." She knelt where she was, lining her long shins up on the frosty stone step, facing north. *My kingdom for a cushion*, she thought as her knees protested, but outwardly she gave no sign of distress.

Churchill mounted the steps until he reached Maggie's stair. Then, with the halting movements of a man unused to the action, he went down first on one knee, and then the other, until he faced her. "For London and for the British race," his voice unrolled in its full oratorical glory, "let us pray."

"Go ahead," Maggie said simply, aware that her voice was so quiet that only Churchill could hear her. "I'm praying for my son." And then, closing her eyes, she began, "Hail Mary, full of grace; the Lord is with thee. Blessed art thou—"

But just as she began her prayer, the Prime Minister had begun to sing—not magisterially, as for an audience, but almost under his breath: "And did those feet in ancient time walk upon England's mountains green?" Maggie recognized Sir Hubert Parry's strange, haunting melody, composed during the anguish of the Great War. It caught her short, as her prayer, apparently, did the Prime Minister: he, too, broke off. Their eyes were level with one another, and now, for the first time, they looked at one another honestly, not as adversaries nor means to their ends, but as human beings, imperiled and afraid. Maggie stretched out her hands towards the Prime Minister, and he caught them in his, big, doughy, and warm. Neither of them noticed the continued snapping of the flashbulb. "Can we meet on common ground?" Mr. Churchill asked. "As Our Savior Christ has taught us, we are bold to say—"

He caught her eye, and then they bowed their heads and recited together: "Our Father, who art in Heaven—" Maggie noticed for the first time that London had fallen absolutely silent. No aircraft droned or roared overhead; no automobile traffic hummed down Victoria nor Saint Margaret Streets; no children or bobbies shouted in the distance; no boats blasted their horns or rang their bells on the Thames. The only sounds were Churchill's man's insistent flashbulb, their two voices in prayer, and her own pulse throbbing in her throat. "—hallowed be Thy name," they prayed. "Thy kingdom come, Thy will be done, on Earth as it is in Heaven." Big Ben's chimes began to peal forth their clear, booming rendition of the familiar

"Cambridge Quarters," readying all those with ears for the coming count of the hour. It was almost three; the decisive moment was nearly upon them. Maggie let the sequence of e, g-sharp, f-sharp, b pour over her as they continued together, "Give us this day our daily bread;" e, f-sharp, g-sharp, and e became the setting for their "Forgive us our sins as we forgive those who have sinned against us." "Lead us not into temptation" was nearly drowned out by g-sharp, e, f-sharp, and b, but "deliver us from evil" was buoyed aloft by b, f-sharp, g-sharp, and e. The chimes fell silent for a moment; the Prime Minister and the poetry don caught their breath as one, and as one, their eyes fluttered momentarily open, caught one another, and then closed. They squeezed one another's inside hands, then raised their arms above their heads, palms up. "For thine—"

But the rest of their prayer was swallowed by a concussion that rocked the heavens and the earth. Maggie Brooke's skull became itself, for a moment, the Great Bell of Big Ben—it shivered, it shook, it resounded with one prolonged bass note. The world was dark—was darkness itself—somehow she had forgotten how to open her eyes, had forgotten *up* and *down* and even *Maggie Brooke*—the one long bass note was all she knew or had ever known.

Then, slowly, she came to herself. Below her the earth was pillowy-soft and smelled of cedar shavings, port, and tobacco. No. That wasn't right. Light filtered into her field of vision, but no shapes; then, slowly, the world resumed its focus. A musclebound man in a gray wool uniform had both of her elbows and was lifting her gently. Another musclebound man, identical though dressed in a navy-blue suit, approached, a scarlet flower blooming at his temple. The world's one bass note throbbed in her ears; on the pavement, behind a handsome gray-and-black Daimler, lay a scatter of fine-gauge springs, cogs, and gears, spilling from a small, wine-colored leather box.

Beyond these things, an enormous panel of dark lustrous wood leaned against the Westminster Column; in Victoria Street beyond that, another panel lay shattered to splinters. Maggie returned her attention to the man in the gray wool uniform; his mouth was moving for some reason, and he looked angry. Lowering her gaze, it dawned on Maggie that what she had taken for the cedar-and-tobacco-smelling ground was in fact a portly man in a luxurious black suit.

"Are you all right, madam? Can you stand?" the chauffeur's voice reached her. Maggie marveled: at the beginning of his first question, the man's voice had been coming to her from miles and miles away—but by the end, he was standing right next to her, his hands under both her elbows. Suddenly she realized that she was sprawled atop Winston Churchill.

She scrambled to her feet and began straightening her Home Guard uniform. "Yes, thank you, I'm just fine," she said, though it was hard to hear herself over the deep, booming bass frequency at which the world was still resounding. She looked up the great western stairs: there was the façade of Westminster Abbey, minus its windows, its doors blown cavernously open—but there was Westminster Abbey, as far as she could see, still standing. She held her hands in front of her face, then pressed them to her cheeks. If her senses could be trusted, she was alive. Alive! It was all she could do not to whoop with joy. As it was, she turned back to the Prime Minister just as he caught her in his arms and whirled her around. His two musclebound underlings looked too dazed to be shocked or alarmed.

Apart from the little party on the steps of Westminster Abbey, Central London was empty of people. The Royal Marine evacuation force had done its job well. But had any innocent fisherman bobbed down the Thames that bright, cold afternoon just at two minutes past three, he would have seen a curious sight: an enormous British Army lorry marked "Special Biological Warfare Unit," bobbing along on the waves until, bit by bit, it sank out of view.

CHAPTER NINETEEN:

DIRTY

The years to come seemed waste of breath,
A waste of breath the years behind
In balance with this life, this death.
—W.B. Yeats, from "An Irish Airman Foresees His Death"

"HERE WERE ARE, Mrs. Brooke, here we are," the Prime Minister chanted joyously. "In my understanding, this would seem to suggest that no atomic detonation occurred. Is that your understanding, as well?"

"It is," she confirmed, unable to suppress a broad and genuine smile. "My Allie's efforts must have succeeded, at least in part." She looked over her shoulder towards the Abbey's gaping, doorless western entry. Wisps of smoke and dust curled forth from it. Her heart drew her to that forbidding darkness: she must go to her son. Her mind, though—well-trained to take advantage of the serious attention of fickle, powerful men—whispered that she must wait.

Churchill released her from his embrace, but still held both her hands in his. He fixed her gaze with his. "Mrs. Brooke, I hope that you can find it in your heart to forgive me. How can I make things right?" His face was grave.

Maggie saw that this was her chance. "I do forgive you, Mr. Prime Minister," she said, "unconditionally. But—" and now she knew she must tread carefully; she chose her words without haste— "if we are to avert future calamities, sir—if we are to defeat the Nazi menace— then we must meet his evil with our full resources, as a nation and as a world. We must exclude no intelligence, no talent or skill, based upon the gender of its possessor."

Churchill's eyes widened, and then he gave a chuckle. "You mean that we must include women in the war effort," he said.

"Just so," Maggie confirmed, then pressed on: "and not as auxiliaries and nurses. Was it not Queen Elizabeth who smashed the Spanish Armada and presided over England's golden age? Mr. Churchill, you lead a nation full of strong, intelligent, highly educated women, and you offer them nothing more challenging to do than sit home knitting scarves. Sex discrimination hamstrings this nation's aspirations to greatness. We must not suppress our next Elizabeth or Mary, our Madame Curie, our Joan of Arc. If you would defeat—if you would *humiliate*—Hitler, then women must be admitted to scientific research institutions, government, and military, even at the very highest ranks."

Churchill's face was grave, his brows drawn together, but as she spoke he began slowly to nod. Finally he said, "Come and see me about this, Mrs. Brooke. We shall have a series of appointments. Your help will be vital in giving us a start."

Maggie's face was equally grave as she intoned, "Agreed." Churchill leaned forward and kissed her on both cheeks, then turned.

"And now, my good woman," he said, facing her over his shoulder as his body moved away, "I must leave you and prepare my radio address. The Third Reich has nuclear weapons—and yet even that fearsome fact has not made them invincible. This is news the world must hear!" With that, the Prime Minister made for his Daimler, where the gray-suited chauffeur stood at the rear passenger door. As Churchill walked away amongst the scattered shards of all the Abbey's windows, Maggie could see that he was limping and that the knees and elbows of his handsome suit were much the worse for the past few minutes' wear. Still, as he walked, he pulled a cigar from his breast pocket; the man in the navy-blue suit, apparently unaware of the blood dripping from his brow, was resting a smaller, brown-bound camera on the automobile's roof and snapping pictures. The Prime Minister flashed his signature V for victory. Somehow, even from his back, Maggie could tell that he was smiling.

She noticed, now, despite the ringing that persisted in her ears, that the sounds of life were returning to London. A distant siren began to howl, and then another and another, like dogs barking one to another across a neighborhood.

She waited until the musclebound chauffeur had gently closed the Daimler's door before she turned again towards the Abbey. Down low, just at the foundation line, Maggie could now see an ugly crack that hadn't been there this morning. It seemed to run all the way around the building, and it sent a chill to her very heart. She bounded up the stairs, her balance uncertain, only to realize that the perimeter of floor she had used half an hour ago to skirt the crater was now gone. Looking up, she could see that most of the gothic-arched ceiling above the nave was gone, too, torn raggedly away; caught among the upper buttresses she could see what looked like the axle and wheels of a lorry.

Admitting to herself that this was not a viable entrance, Maggie circled yet again, at a sprint, to the south transept entrance. The thick oaken door that had barred her way just minutes ago now sagged, attached to the frame only by its lowest hinge. She pushed it easily aside. To her right the spiral crypt staircase still hung onto its stone anchors; she flung herself onto it to find that it swayed nauseously. What had once been a firmly fixed stair now functioned as a woozy, swaying ladder down into the dark.

To it she clung, and into the dark she descended. The atmosphere in the crypt was warm and sulfurous. Beams of daylight picked out details from the rubble here and there: a stone, a wooden curlicue, the toppled head of an angel. To her left and behind her as she stood at the foot of the dangling helix of iron, several life-sized marble funerary statues lay or leaned upon one another as if drunk; nothing else lay in that direction but a wall banked high with rubble. Before her and to the right, the vast space of the crypt opened out, lit by afternoon sun that filtered in through the Abbey's ruined ceiling high above. Nothing in it moved; nothing in it seemed whole. Here and there, small tongues of orange flame consumed isolated bits of wooden wreckage. From somewhere to her west-northwest, broad scorch marks radiated across the litter; toward their source she stumbled, perspiring, calling out raggedly for her son.

Just below the spot where the Nazis' infernal machine had stood on the nave floor, the scorch marks converged on a crater some thirty feet in diameter. Maggie stood on its edge and leaned in to look. Its floor was littered with twisted sheets of steel, red-hot and mottled with ash, a fine metallic powder scattered over all of them. As Maggie watched, a warm breeze found its way into the crater, lifting the metallic powder in swirls. "Allie!" she called, her voice as tattered as the sheets of metal below. "Allie!" She strained with listening for his voice or for the friendly bark that so often accompanied his approach. Her eyes scanned the crypt's walls and floor, but found no sign of life, nor any sign of a hiding place. Nausea began to rise in her belly. Despite the heat of this hellish scene, Maggie shivered, chilled to her core.

The shriek of fatigued metal made her jump. Turning, Maggie could see the spiral staircase shuddering dizzily as two figures descended. "Hullo?" one called. In a moment they reached the crypt floor. "Is that you, Mrs. Brooke?" Maggie turned away from the crater and made her way back towards them. She was suddenly weary all the way down to her bones. The events of the day crowded in on her consciousness. Her foot caught on a jag of stone, and she stumbled.

The figures rushed forward and caught her, one at each elbow, steadying her as she regained her footing. She could see now that they were two of the young Royal Marines from the bomb squad. "Thank God you're alive," one of them said. "When you made a break from the evacuation vehicle, ma'am, we feared the worst."

"My son," Maggie said, her voice oddly weak. The two Marines seemed far away, even though they were supporting her elbows. "Flying Officer Allister Brooke of the R.A.F. was working to defuse the bomb. I've got to find my son ... " She trailed off.

The two Marines exchanged a look. "There's no telling what kind of contamination we're exposing ourselves to down here," one said quietly. "Let's get upstairs." Wrapping their arms around Maggie's waist, they half-hustled, half-carried her to the staircase. One of them lifted her in his arms and carried her up the perilous stairs, the other following them. Halfway up, her face leaning over the soldier's shoulder, she vomited down the back of his uniform.

The ringing that had died down in her ears had returned, and now it was as if a deranged blacksmith had set up shop between her ears. "I'm sorry," she murmured to the Marine who was carrying her, "I'm so sorry." Somehow she couldn't muster the strength to feel properly humiliated. Gaining the top of the stairs, the Marines took Maggie outside and settled her in a patch of sunshine, her back against the wall of the Abbey's chapter house, her eyes towards the statue of King

George the Fifth that stood at the Saint Margaret Street curb. She closed her eyes for a moment, and when she opened them, they were tucking a blanket around her shoulders and closing her hands around a mug into which they poured tepid tea from an insulated flask.

"Are you feeling any better, ma'am?" a young man asked her, and she had to admit that she wasn't. Still, she persisted in asking for her son. "We're doing all we can to locate Flying Officer Brooke, ma'am. But right now I want to take you to hospital. Is that all right?" Maggie didn't want to go to hospital, but the truth was that she was too tired to argue—and she hoped that a moment's shuteye might quiet the blacksmith hammering in her brain. She felt herself lifted again in the young man's strong arms, felt herself laid carefully in the back of a Marine jeep. To her chagrin, the jeep's motion increased her nausea, and she wasn't able to keep down the tea she had drunk.

At last the jeep came to a halt and the young man lifted her not to his shoulder as before, but onto a gurney that felt, in comparison with the jeep's seat, deliciously comfortable. She closed her eyes and prayed to fall asleep, but all that came to her was a stupor in which her skull was Big Ben, striking three over and over as a signal that Allie should come, but he never did. Light and darkness flickered beyond her eyelids, but they were too heavy to open, and muffled conversations floated into her ears, but understanding them would have required too much effort. She was aware that she was moved from the gurney, then moved again; she was aware of hands against her skin, cool and gentle, and yet she was hot—parched and foul. In the parched, foul darkness she floated on wave after wave of reverberating pain.

At great length, she became aware of a new voice—a voice she knew—speaking nearby. Mustering all her energy, she fluttered her eyelids open. She was in a small room whose walls were a clean pale green; white curtains shaded the window, and the only light came from a great milk-glass globe above. Hanging from a stand near her shoulder, a bottle dripped clear fluid into a tube that led to her bandaged right wrist. She was covered to her chest in crisp white sheets and soft white flannel blankets, and her Home Guard uniform seemed to have been replaced by something flimsy and yellow. She looked around for the source of the familiar voice, but someone else was speaking now: a nurse, standing to her right, on the side away from the window. " ... afraid I must insist that you return to your bed," the nurse said.

"*I'm* afraid, young lady, that it is I who must insist," said the voice Maggie knew. She felt strong, warm fingers pressing the palm of her left hand. The last words she heard before the blessed darkness claimed her were, "If you really are concerned for my recovery, you may set up a cot for me right here, but I will not leave my wife's side."

CHAPTER TWENTY:

MEANWHILE

For all things turn to barrenness
In the dim glass the demons hold,
The glass of outer weariness,
Made when God slept in times of old.

—W.B. Yeats, from "The Two Trees"

THREE IN THE AFTERNOON in London was ten o'clock on Thanksgiving morning in Hyannis Port, Massachusetts. Ambassador Joseph Kennedy, relishing this rare day of rest and comfort with his family, was still wearing his pajamas, slippers, and dressing-gown when a peremptory knock came at the front door. The Ambassador was lingering over coffee and conversation at the breakfast table with the two eldest of his handsome, bright sons. Both boys were in their twenties—one at university, the other in law school—and it was a rare treat to see either of them, much less both at once. From the family room, the sounds of the two youngest children's laughter wafted in. The autumn's fiery leaves had fallen, and remnants of snow from the Armistice Day blizzard remained here and there on the ground, but today's morning sky was blessedly high, clear, and bright. "Dear," said the Ambassador's wife Rose, ducking her head in at the door, "I'm sorry to tell you this, but Hans Thomsen is at the door. I told him it was most irregular to call unannounced and at home, but he insisted that it was beyond urgent. Would you like me to give him coffee while you dress?"

"That's not necessary," the Ambassador said. "If he drops in on me at home before noon on Thanksgiving Day, he can meet me dressed as I am. Send him to my study, please." The Ambassador waited for her to go before he stood. He wanted to make sure it would be Thomsen waiting for him in the study, and not the other way around. "Boys," he said, nodding to his sons, "don't ever go to work for Uncle Sam. Never a day off 'til you're dead, and maybe not even then." He retied the sash belting his dressing gown, took his coffee cup with him, and headed up to meet the German chargé d'affaires, leaving Jack and Joe Junior chuckling ruefully over their cornflakes.

In his study, the Ambassador found the German chargé standing, hands clasped behind his back, and admiring the richly-bound volumes of law that graced the bookshelves. "Herr Thomsen," Kennedy said, extending his hand.

"How do you do," the German responded, shaking it. His voice was soft and refined; his meticulously-groomed face would have been handsome but for a certain jowly softness at the jawline, despite the slenderness of his figure.

"It's awfully early on a cold morning for you to be this far from Washington," Kennedy said, pointedly not inviting Thomsen to sit down.

"I can assure you nothing but business of the highest urgency could have persuaded me to intrude upon your holiday, Ambassador Kennedy," said Thomsen. "But a film has reached me which the Führer insists you see without delay." From an inner pocket of his double-breasted jacket, Thomsen withdrew a film reel. "This is one of several copies the Führer had made," he explained.

Suppressing an impatient sigh, the Ambassador opened a cabinet to reveal a film projector on a shelf that he drew out on runners; crossing the room, he pulled down a white screen across from the projector. He motioned towards the apparatus and allowed the German diplomat to feed the film in himself, making no move to help him when he appeared flustered, then realized the reel was on backwards. Finally the German nodded that he was ready, and Kennedy flipped the light switch. In the sudden darkness a test pattern leapt into visibility on the screen, then was replaced by the image of a cheerful young Heer corpsman pointing to a copy of the *Völkischer Beobachter* dated October 17, 1940. "What is this?" the Ambassador growled.

"Keep watching," murmured Thomsen, his face grim.

Now the film showed a hand-lettered placard reading *Przerośl, Poland—Pop. 4,163—Viewing Station 10,000 Yards from Detonation Site*. The camera swung to an idyllic, bucolic scene, then showed a Central European-style tin alarm clock, its hands indicating 7:59. The camera watched its second hand sweep past the six, past the nine, and towards home ... but precisely at 8:00 the picture abruptly dissolved into static, which then rolled into bright whiteness for a second or two. "What the ... " Kennedy breathed, leaning towards the screen. Out of the corner of his eye, he could see his son Jack leaning in the doorway of the study, watching too.

Over the next ten minutes of film, the Kennedy men's interest gave way to shock, then horror, then silent fury. As the images gave way to a white screen and the projector's steady clicking became the flapping of the reel's end, Thomsen said softly, "So you see that Przerośl, Poland, is no more. And I am informed that as of—" he consulted his pocket watch— "seventeen minutes ago, London, England, has suffered the same fate. The film you have viewed was of a small test detonation; the Luftwaffe has targeted London in a megaton attack. Now—" The Ambassador was sputtering in disbelieving fury, but the German chargé held his hands up for quiet. "Now I know that you and I are diplomats. We abhor violence; we seek consensus, compromise, solutions that minimize bloodshed. For us, warfare is wasteful and inelegant—and this new style of nuclear weapons, well—" Thomsen's face and hands indicated that he regarded such weapons with the height of distaste. "However, mein Führer suggests that we consider the death toll that a land invasion of the United Kingdom would have incurred. Viewed from this perspective, the nuclear attack on London has saved a million or more English lives."

"Get out of my house," Ambassador Kennedy snarled.

"Ambassador Kennedy, I know that I have been the bearer of deeply disturbing news, but—"

"Get out!" Kennedy thundered, drawing himself up to his full height and stepping menacingly close to the German chargé.

Thomsen bowed slightly, his face grave. "As you wish," he murmured. Leaving the film in the projector, he strode swiftly to the door of the room. "I will show myself out," he said, "but the record will show that I left you with this." Thomsen produced an envelope from his jacket's inner pocket. "This document is nearly verbatim the agreement negotiated by Molotov and Von Ribbentropp in Moscow." And slipping past Jack, who still stood in the study's doorway, Thomsen was gone.

The Ambassador sank into a chair. "How much of that did you see?" he asked Jack.

"The whole thing, I think," Jack said, coming in and sitting across from him. "Do you think it's true? That London has been hit with an atomic bomb?"

"I don't know what to think," the Ambassador said wearily. The day had begun so beautifully, with such security and hope; now it felt as if anything could happen, and the worst probably would. "I hate the idea of sending you and Junior over to fight another of Europe's wars," he sighed. "It's simply better for America if we stay out of this business. But I don't like Hitler thinking he can keep us out of the war by bullying us, and whatever our differences, I know Franklin's not going to like it either." He reached for the telephone. "Let's hope he's not in a messenger-shooting mood."

The President was no happier than the Ambassador had been about having his morning interrupted, and he was even less happy when he heard Kennedy's voice on the line. "We have no confirmation of that," he snapped when the Ambassador reported that London had been the target of a nuclear attack. When the Ambassador finished relating the tale of Thomsen's visit and the film he had brought, the President was silent for a long moment. Then he said, "And your boy saw the film, you said? He overheard the conversation?" When Kennedy affirmed the he had, Roosevelt said, "Stay in Hyannis Port, Joe. Enjoy your Thanksgiving. But you get your boy, with that film, onto a Navy plane down here. I want him to brief me by lunchtime." Ambassador Kennedy heaved another great sigh. It was turning out to be that sort of day. Still, he reflected—as disappointed as he was not to have all his children home at once for Thanksgiving dinner, letting Jack deal with Roosevelt for him would be the best thing for all parties involved, America included.

In London, Cardinal Hinsley, too, received an unannounced visitor. He had been sitting in his study, alone but for the maid who, every quarter-hour, brought a log for the fire and a new hot water bottle for his back, which was stiff and sore from the hours he and his staff had spent huddled in the bomb shelter in East Dulwich. He had been sitting in his study, nursing his poor abused back, watching various military officials cordon off his beloved Abbey, and then other officials in special protective clothing that made them look like deep-sea divers go in and out with equipment to measure God-knows-what. He watched them until the thin November sunlight failed, and then he watched their torches bobbing through the dark. He watched them because as long as he watched them he needn't think, needn't allow the grief and confusion at the corners of his mind to come flooding into its center. He wasn't certain he could bear that flood; he feared it might crush and drown him. He watched them intently until—

"Arthur?" A light rap at the frame of his open study door accompanied the sound of his name spoken by a dear familiar voice.

"Cosmo," Cardinal Hinsley said, rising to his feet to greet the Archbishop of Canterbury. "Cosmo, come and sit by the fire. May I offer you a drop of port?"

"Thank you, yes. I think a little port would do us both a world of good just now," Archbishop Lang assented. He sank into an armchair by the fireplace while Cardinal Hinsley poured them each a drink. When they were seated across from one another and each had tasted his wine, Archbishop Lang leaned towards his friend and asked, "Arthur, how are you?"

The Archbishop's question hung in the air for a long moment, and then the Cardinal said in a voice like one asleep, "I hardly know." He gazed for a long moment into the fire. "Was it lust that made Samson blind to the evil in Delilah's heart?"

"What?" Concern furrowed the Archbishop's brow.

"Was it pride? Did he think God's favor made him invincible?" As the Cardinal stared into the fire, his cheeks flushed and his lips began to tremble, and the Archbishop understood.

"Samson was a holy man, Arthur," the Archbishop said, taking the Cardinal's hand in both of his. "And as holy men, our calling is to trust. Samson trusted Delilah because trust was his nature. God called him to trust from the very moment of his conception. His trust made it possible for a deceiver to deliver him into the hands of his enemies. But his trust is also what made him God's own." A single tear streamed down each of Cardinal Hinsley's cheeks. "You mustn't blame yourself, Arthur. Hitler's agent deceived you, and you trusted her because your heart is full of the Lord. She has hurt you deeply. But that same trustful heart is what will be required as you care for your flock during this darkest of hours." The Archbishop held the Cardinal's hand for a long moment and let him weep. Then he murmured, "Arthur, let us pray."

In Washington, D.C., Thanksgiving morning was chilly, overcast—and nearly as busy as usual. In the Oval Office, Ambassador Joseph Kennedy's telephone call caught President Franklin Roosevelt in the midst of being briefed on the Supreme Court's recent decision in Hansberry v. Lee. The case had implications for residential development and race relations across the country. Across the Atlantic, Europe was paying the price for allowing its last great war's flames to smolder and the President prayed that the recent flare up of housing conflicts wasn't a sign that the U.S. could be facing a similar re-ignition of old hostilities. As annoyed as he was to hear Joe Kennedy's voice this morning—and as deeply troubled as he was by the Ambassador's news—

he wondered whether Hitler's latest outrage would finally show Kennedy the necessity of supporting Britain with more than just the sale of munitions. That was Kennedy's trouble: for him, Yankee business shrewdness was the end-all and be-all. But to be an ally, after all, was about more than making a buck.

Hardly had the President set down the receiver when the telephone jangled again. This time it was Winston Churchill on the line. "Winston," Roosevelt said. "It's a relief to hear your voice. I've just had a very disturbing telephone call from Joe Kennedy. How bad is it in London?"

"Listen for yourself," said the Prime Minister. Roosevelt strained his ears; in a moment, the breathing of the British statesman was replaced by the distant, joyful pealing of hundreds of bells. "Could you hear that?"

"What does it mean?" Roosevelt asked in awed and mystified tones.

"It means we've had a narrow escape, old chap, and it's a beautiful thing to be alive. It means we've spit in Adolf Hitler's face." Churchill sounded jubilant, even giddy.

"Hans Thomsen told Joe Kennedy that London was destroyed today by an atomic bomb," the President said.

"That was the plan," Churchill confirmed. "Agents of the Luftwaffe smuggled a megaton nuclear device into Westminster Abbey, and I'm chagrined to admit that Britain's official intelligence community entirely failed to uncover the plot. One tenacious American expatriate living in Oxford managed to piece the signs together and alert us just in time, and her son apparently decoupled the nuclear fuel from its triggering device. Westminster Abbey is a wreck, and I've got teams working around the clock to analyze the German device's remains and report on just how grave the Nazi nuclear threat is. But for the moment, I join the citizens of London in abject gratitude that tonight we are still here."

"Tell me how I can help you now," Roosevelt asked, mentally filing away the information that an American citizen had saved London. That fact could prove invaluable. And had Churchill referred to that American as *her*?

"First of all, information," Churchill said. "What else did your Ambassador learn from Hans Thomsen?"

"All I know is what I learned in a short telephone conversation—I'll be fully briefed in about an hour. But it's my understanding that Thomsen showed Kennedy a film of a nuclear test detonation in Poland. Presumably, this film—coupled with the destruction of London—was intended to cow the United States into signing a non-aggression pact."

"Then you must defy Hitler," Churchill intoned. "Franklin, the honor of your country is at stake. Join Britain now—you must declare war on Germany."

"Well, now, Winston, you know that's not up to me," Roosevelt hedged. "Only my Congress can tell me what the United States *must* do in terms of taking up arms against a foreign power. Ask for something I *can* give you."

Churchill was silent. Thinking, Roosevelt wondered? Conferring in signs with his advisors? "Franklin," the Prime Minister said after a moment. "I understand that some of Central Europe's most distinguished scientific minds have sought refuge at American research institutions. Short of military manpower, what Britain needs now is physicists and engineers to meet the nuclear threat. Can you send us scientists and equipment?"

"Done," the President declared.

"Thank you, Franklin." Churchill sounded genuinely grateful, and also weary beyond words. "And Franklin?"

"Yes?"

"It seems this American has become exposed to radioactive materials in the course of today's events and has become quite ill," Churchill said quietly. "Several Royal Marines may have been exposed too. Do you have people working on treatments for radiation poisoning?"

"We'll send you our very best," Roosevelt promised.

"Good man."

In London, Maggie Brooke's room was overflowing with flowers. The sharp, clean tang of mums and poinsettias almost covered the antiseptic pong of *hospital*. The nurses did their best to turn away visitors, but still Ian spent most of the day on Friday shaking hands and accepting congratulations and gratitude. With his shoulder bandaged and his arm immobilized in a sling, Ian's physical recovery was simply a matter of time. His heart, though, was breaking.

Near Maggie's bed lay telegrams of love and encouragement from Maggie's parents in Boston and her younger brothers in Amherst and Providence. Ian had read them to her during her few lucid, conscious moments during the day. He hadn't yet found the strength to let the American family know that Allie was missing again; nor, he suspected, did they truly understand how grave Maggie's condition was. He could hardly face it himself. After tea-time the hubbub of well-wishers finally quieted. Ian sat by Maggie's bed and held her hand while she slept. Her face twisted and twitched as if her dreams would give her no rest, and periodically she murmured their son's name. Her skin looked sunburned: on her hands and forehead, blisters were beginning to form. All Ian could do was comfort her and pray that the intravenous fluids and iodine treatments would do their work. Her life lay in the balance.

After a few minutes, Ian realized his own thoughts were no more restful than Maggie's. To distract himself, he leaned over and switched on the radio by her bedside. For a moment he was confused by the stentorian tones that filled the air in place of the gay dance music he had expected. Then it dawned on him that the Prime Minister was addressing Parliament and the nation. " ... of Commons together this evening while my remarks are broadcast to the nation," Churchill intoned; the booming quality of his voice was evident even though Ian was playing the radio quietly. "Not more than an hour ago I watched a film produced by Adolf Hitler and directed by his Luftwaffe leader Hermann Göring. The film depicted the complete destruction of a small Polish city by the name of Przerośl that formerly was the home of some seven thousand people, mostly Jews. What makes the film so utterly horrifying is that the city was destroyed by a single bomb—an atomic bomb. Hitler and Göring detonated the bomb inside the city to see if it worked. In this case the bomb did detonate, to catastrophic effects. I am grateful to Jack Kennedy, the son of Joseph Kennedy, the American Ambassador, and to aviators from the United States Navy for bringing this film to me so quickly ... " Ian allowed his attention to wander as Churchill's voice thundered on about the shocking extent of this attempted Nazi atrocity. What could he have done, he asked himself, to keep his family safe? Was it his protectiveness that had driven Allie to throw himself headlong into such ill-conceived heroics? Should he have put his foot down, insisted that his son obey him and that his wife stay home, out of danger? And yet it was her strength and independence, her tirelessness in the face of what must be done, that he had always loved and admired, and he was proud that his son had inherited those qualities. Something in Churchill's phrasing shook him from his musing to pay attention once again. " ... a family living in Oxford," Churchill intoned, "began to notice that certain German bombers ostensibly shot down by our Royal Air Force planes during the air battles of this summer and fall, may in fact not have been shot down at all. Rather, the planes, carrying the components of the atomic bomb, were deliberately crash-landed, their crews were killed, and the planes destroyed by the Nazi saboteurs after the bomb components were taken off." Ian couldn't help but chuckle ruefully at Churchill's attempt to include him, the man of the house, in the credit for Maggie's investigation. People so seldom believed that it was he who was helpless and befuddled without her—never the other way around. He leaned down and kissed her tenderly, careful not to awaken her.

"Adolf Hitler and Herman Göring," the Prime Minister's voice went on, "devised a secret plan to destroy London and the heart of this island nation with a single strike. They did not take into account the intelligence, resiliency, and courage of the great people of this nation, particularly the family from Oxford whose heroics have saved us all.

"The father is Ian Brooke, an Englishman and a graduate of Brasenose College at Oxford and a member of the faculty there for more than ten years. During the Great War, Mr. Brooke was seriously wounded in going over the top at Picardy; he was also wounded while bravely assisting the Royal Marines in yesterday's confrontation at Westminster Abbey.

"His wife, Margaret Mary O'Hare Brooke, is an American and instructor at St. Hugh's College, Oxford. Only through her dogged perseverance was the Nazi plot unraveled—working with powers of observation and deduction unrivaled by any Conan Doyle hero, she brought the plot to light and summoned the Royal Marines to take on the German saboteurs at the Abbey yesterday afternoon.

"Their son, Flying Officer Allister O'Hare Brooke, somehow was able to prevent the atomic detonation using expertise he gained at Caius College in Cambridge and as a bomb aimer in the Royal Air Force. The bomb's trigger, which was apparently composed of many tons of high explosives, did detonate, and the Abbey is very badly damaged: the foundation as well as to the precious stonework and artwork of that magnificent structure may need to be completely rebuilt. It will take many months to remove the vast amount of radioactive material in the crypt and elsewhere.

"Flying Officer Brooke has been missing since yesterday's explosion.

"Mrs. Brooke, the sole commander at the Abbey of his Majesty's forces aligned to defeat Hitler and to win the Second Battle of Britain, now lies in hospital, gravely ill with radiation sickness. She it was who helped us win this Second Battle of Britain, a battle fought on the ground in our capital city at the epicenter of our national faith. The annals of this great island nation will be filled with testimony as to the valor, sacrifice, and zeal of those who have done so much for so many. If the First Battle of Britain was won for us by the few, this one was won by even fewer. Today the few have become the two.

"We should take some comfort that we have for the third time in the past six months earned three great fortunes in this great conflict with Nazi Germany. The first I mention is obviously our valiant British army's rescue, and now the two Battles of Britain. Adolf Hitler's failure again to deal us a death blow makes clear that the Almighty must favor our cause. Why else would we, again and again, be delivered up from the grip of this great Satan?

"Before I promised you nothing more than blood, toil, sweat, and tears. Today I give you my tears, as I take yours from you. But these are tears of purest joy."

The end of Churchill's speech could hardly be heard over the thunder of applause, but Ian was no longer listening anyway. His eyes were fixed on Maggie's, now open and brimming with tears.

"Maybe the Prime Minister is weeping with joy for the British people," Maggie half-whispered, half-croaked in a voice that was obviously painful for her to muster, "but I am weeping with grief for this family and all that we have lost." Ian tried to shush her, but she went on, "Heaven help me, Ian, but if I had it to do again—if I had known yesterday morning what I know now ... "

"I know, my darling," Ian said, wiping her eyes with his handkerchief, then leaning in to cradle her in his arms. "But our Allie saved the lives of millions of innocents yesterday. It dishonors him to wish it otherwise. All we can do now is pray. And I can beg you to get better." Ian's voice became a whisper as the wind went out of him. "Maggie, I can't lose you, too. Do you hear me?" Ian leaned out to look her in the eye, but Maggie's eyes were closed.

CHAPTER TWENTY-ONE:

I HAD AN INKLING

Know, I would accounted be
True brother of a company
That sang ...

—W.B. Yeats, from "To Ireland in Coming Times"

ON TOP OF EVERYTHING ELSE, Ian's egg was underdone. He wondered why it was that a nation that could thwart Hitler at every turn still couldn't manage to produce a decent hospital breakfast. Maggie's skin was blistered awfully, but she'd had a restful night and was alert, if uncharacteristically quiet. He wished she could keep down real food, then looked again at the "real food" on his tray and wondered whether he didn't envy her I.V. fluids. Still, it did no good to complain. He squared his shoulders, wincing only a little as his wound gave him a twinge, and smiled at Maggie brightly across his teacup. Then a tap on the doorframe caught his attention, and he looked up to see Stephen Bloom standing in the door. He was wearing his customary inconspicuous, if slightly shabby, dark suit; he had the hint of a black eye, but he was immaculately shaved and his hair was freshly cut. He was an unassuming figure, but to the attentive eye, undeniably handsome.

"Don't get up, don't get up," Bloom said hurriedly as Ian fumbled to set down his teacup and rise in greeting. "I've only got a moment, and I don't want to interrupt your recuperation. I just wanted to look in on our heroine and see how she's getting along." He smiled gently towards Maggie.

"I'm all right," Maggie croaked weakly, but she wasn't very convincing.

Ian and Bloom exchanged a grave glance, and then Bloom returned his expression of gentle cheer towards Maggie. "You'll be pleased to hear that several R.A.F. fighter pilots have come forward to corroborate your findings," he told her. "They're reporting having seen Heinkels on fire and descending towards the Oxford area. Pilots who tried to follow and make sure they went down were set on so viciously by the Luftwaffe that they were forced to break off pursuit. Several of the men say it didn't sit right with them at the time, but they just chalked it up to combat or figured they were being paranoid."

"A fat lot of good their testimony does us now," Ian observed bitterly. "Nothing like a bit of shutting the barn door after the horses are gone."

"Well, yes and no," Bloom responded. "We're taking this as an opportunity to instruct our men to trust their instincts and err on the side of reporting. We're also restructuring our intelligence-gathering program for greater balance in the types of sources we consult. And that," he added, leaning down and gently taking Maggie's hand, "is thanks to you, Madam. I hardly know how to express the magnitude of the debt England owes you."

"Thank you, Mr. Bloom," Maggie whispered.

"Please, my dear lady. It's Stephen." He looked back to Ian. "I am infinitely honored to count you as my allies—and friends. But I'm afraid I must dash. I've got testimony to record, and you're due for a visit that's a bit above my pay grade. I'll just ask—whatever you may think of them personally or of their policies in the past—that today you think of them as representing me, and millions of regular Joan and John Bulls like me. Even imperfect people and imperfect nations can feel perfect gratitude." And with that—before Ian could articulate a question—he was gone.

"It doesn't sound like we're in for a very restful morning, my dear," Ian sighed. "I suppose I ought to take this as my cue to shower and shave." Standing, he set aside his breakfast tray and tried to pull his plaid flannel dressing-gown more securely about his tall, spare frame, but the sling around his injured arm made it an awkward fit. He fumbled for a moment, then wiped his eye. "Do you remember when Allie broke his arm falling out of Eugenia's pear tree?" Ian gave a half-chuckle and avoided his wife's eye. "That cast didn't slow him down a bit. The little monkey was climbing trees again within a day, one-handed. He made it look so easy ... " There was a pause, and then Ian wiped his eye again and cleared his throat. "I'll be back as soon as I'm dressed, my dear," he said, leaning down to kiss his wife gently, but when he stood again, he found more visitors waiting: red-uniformed Royal Guardsmen stood on either side of the hospital room's door.

"Prime Minister Winston Churchill and His Majesty King George the Sixth of Great Britain," one of them announced in a firm young voice, his accent as pure and upper-crust as Waterford crystal. Then the dignitaries entered: first the stocky, bulldog-faced Prime Minister, then the taller, slimmer, long-faced King. In the bed, Maggie made weak motions to rise or acknowledge her visitors in some way, but she soon fell back against her pillows, exhausted. For his part, Ian managed an awkward bow despite the constraints of his limp, his recent injury, and the small and cluttered hospital room, but the King placed a hand under his good elbow to indicate that he should rise.

It was Churchill, however, who spoke first. "On behalf of His Majesty's government and the people of England, Scotland, and Wales, I must formally thank you both from the bottom of my heart for the wisdom, courage, and selflessness of your recent actions. And on my own behalf, it's a great personal pleasure to have the opportunity to thank both of you face-to-face for rescuing me, both politically and bodily. Mrs. Brooke, you really saved my—bacon." Churchill winked at Maggie and chuckled mischievously; dutifully, Ian chuckled with him, and Maggie managed a weak smile.

The King, who had been beaming beatifically around the room at no one in particular, stepped forward now. "It is my sincere honor," he intoned, looking Ian in the eye, "To present you, Ian Bates Brooke, with the George Cross in acknowledgement of your extreme devotion to duty, even decades after your honorable discharge from service, and for extraordinary valor in the face of the enemy." Tenderly and without a trace of irony, he reached out and pinned a dark-blue ribbon bearing a silver medal to the lapel of Ian's dressing-gown.

Ian's heart swelled and a train of emotions chased one another across his face and through his heart. He was enormously honored, primally thrilled at the touch of his King's hand, awed and humbled by the awareness of how many others had played their parts in the events at the Abbey. Nearly at the same time, though, the involuntary thought arose: *Won't Allie be astounded.* At the thought of his brave, bright, and beautiful boy—lost, then recovered; estranged, then so nearly reconciled; now once again presumed dead—Ian found he could not contain his grief. His breath came short; hot tears carved tracks down his cheeks. Still, somehow he found the grace to say, "Your Majesty, I am touched to my very core." The King shook Ian's hand; *the King is shaking your hand,* he thought, *remember this moment,* but in truth all he felt or could feel was the absence of his son. He labored to control his sobs.

Turning to Maggie, the Prime Minister presented her with a gorgeously illuminated vellum scroll. She moved her fingers, but was too weak to lift her hand and accept it; in truth, although she struggled mightily to stay alert, her heavy eyelids kept closing. Grateful to be distracted, Ian reached towards the scroll. "May I?" he asked Churchill, and the Prime Minister inclined his head affirmatively. Ian took and read the scroll. "Mags," he said gently, and she opened her eyes for him. "Mags, it declares you an honorary British citizen." Her eyes closed, then opened again and seemed to focus; she smiled, and he smiled back. Deep down Ian was aware that were she stronger, she would be rolling her eyes: after decades of resisting his pleas to apply for British citizenship, she had it now, like it or not.

King George stepped forward again, drawing a gleaming, richly-engraved steel sword from a scabbard at his side. "Margaret Mary O'Hare Brooke," he said, and she fixed him with her mild, heavy-lidded gaze. Touching each of her shoulders and her crown with his sword, he gravely pronounced, "I dub you a Dame of the Most Excellent Order of the British Empire." Sheathing his sword, he pinned a brass cross on a scarlet ribbon to the collar of her hospital gown. Maggie's eyes grew brighter and it was evident that her cheek muscles were working, as if to produce a smile. Her lips moved, but no sound emerged. The King bent close to her and murmured, "I beg your pardon, My Lady?" He remained bent thus for a moment as if listening, then stood and clasped both of her fragile hands in his. "Thank you from the bottom of my heart, Margaret Brooke. Thank you for your insight and tenacity." He stepped back once again, the soul of discretion.

"Professor Brooke," Churchill not so much said as announced, making eye contact with Ian. "Dame Brooke. It is also my distinct honor and privilege—though mingled with grief at the loss of this valiant young warrior—to inform you that the rebuilt Westminster Abbey's main floor will prominently include your son's grave marker. Moreover, I sincerely hope, My Lady, that you will accept the Victoria Cross—our Empire's highest military honor—on your son's behalf." Reaching towards Maggie's poor blistered hands, Churchill attempted to place a bronze cross on a crimson ribbon in them.

Somehow, though, Maggie found the strength to clasp her fists convulsively and shake her head in refusal. Her whisper was painful, yet distinct: "He will accept it for himself." Ian looked as if he had been struck. His face colored; more tears coursed down his cheeks, and his eyes rolled toward the ceiling.

Gently, the Prime Minister took Maggie's hand in his own. "My dear lady," he said. "I am overawed by the courage and intelligence your son displayed yesterday. And you know my own Marigold is just his age. I cannot imagine how it would feel to lose a child so young and so promising."

Maggie sputtered, and the Prime Minister had to bend low to understand what she was saying: "Not ... lost ... for certain. Can't accept ... a posthumous ... medal. It's too ... soon ... to say," she whispered, her voice quiet and harsh.

The King understood. "To accept the medal, she would have to accept his death, Winston," he said quietly. "Let's leave it for now. She needs to believe."

Mr. Churchill was still holding Maggie's hand. "I see," he said, but his face was concerned, unsure. "Well then, it only remains for me to tell you both," he said, looking from Maggie to Ian and back, "that Franklin Roosevelt is sending us his leading expert on radiation poisoning and its treatment. Dr. Robley Evans will be with you before dawn tomorrow morning, Mrs. Brooke. Just hold on." The

Prime Minister's voice took on a note of pleading. "Hold on," he repeated. Looking at Ian, he said, "You're both exhausted and need to recover. We'll leave you now." With smiles and handshakes, he and the King withdrew along with their guard. In the hospital corridor, Churchill remarked to the King, "She *has* to live, you know. She *has to*." King George raised his eyebrows inquisitively. "Just think of the effect it would have if she could lobby Roosevelt on our behalf. She could singlehandedly secure the United States's full military might to the cause of defeating Hitler."

"A good point," the King agreed. "I do hope that she's strong enough to help, though, old chap. If radiation sickness doesn't finish her, I worry that her son's death might. And that will be a grave loss, for the British war effort and for the future of England's young women."

"We've committed everything we can to helping her recover, Your Majesty," the Prime Minister observed. "It's up to her now to be strong, and by God, if anyone can do that, I believe it's Margaret Brooke."

Ian and Maggie spent the day arguing about whether she would live. At first Ian wouldn't listen, but by tea-time he had dutifully made a list of her favorite hymns, her favorite tweed skirt suit, the signed first edition of *The Wanderings of Oisin* she wanted tucked under her arm, her preference for a plot shaded by rowan trees. "It's good to be prepared for the worst," Ian admitted, "but now that you've expressed your wishes, kindly agree to postpone putting them into practice." He kissed his wife's fevered brow; her preparations complete, she had sunk into a relieved half-doze among the pillows a devoted nursing staff had kept plumped and turned to their cool sides. Her eyelids fluttered open and she murmured something unintelligible; he took a chip of ice from a glass on her bedside table and pressed it to her blistered lips. "Hold on, my darling," he murmured. "Mr. Churchill has promised you the world's very best care; the American specialist will be here in a few hours. And if anyone in this world is strong enough to hold on, Mags, I know it's you."

Maggie moved her lips again, but the only word Ian could make out was "Allie ... "

Ian's face was hot and dry: he had wept himself out. Instead he said, "Do you remember the time we went to see your folks and we lost Allie at Walden Pond?"

"Do you remember," Maggie whispered, her eyes closed, "the time ... Allie slipped down the waterfall ... at Aillwee Cave?"

"Do you remember the Boy Scout hike when Mr. Murphree broke his ankle and Allie organized the boys into shifts to carry him down?"

"Do you remember ... Allie's ... pineapple plantation?"

"Do you remember when Allie was toasting marshmallows and set Anne's curtains on fire? Or," he chuckled, "or when Allie rowed Colin over to that little island and then couldn't coax him back into the boat when it was time to come home?"

Maggie was silent for a moment, and then—with evident effort, her eyes closed and brow furrowed, she quoted, "*Something drops from eyes long blind, / He completes his partial mind, / For an instant stands at ease, / Laughs aloud, his heart at peace.*"

Ian's eyes were distant for a moment, misted, and then he quoted back, "*Cast a cold eye / On life, on death. / Horseman, pass by!* Is that how it went?"

Maggie opened her eyes, surprised that Ian should have committed to memory one of her hero's final poems. "That's where our ...

baby boy was wiser ... than Yeats," she managed. "Yeats's eye ... was never as cold ... as he wished, thank Heaven. But ... Allie never ... even aspired to coldness." Her eyes dropped closed again, and her fingers' grip loosened on Ian's.

"And that's where I failed you both," Ian murmured, "isn't it?" But Maggie gave no answer. "Mags," Ian said, alarmed. "Mags."

"Let me rest," she whispered, eyes closed, barely audible. "Let me go to Allie ... "

At that moment Ian became aware of two familiar voices, locked in companionable debate, approaching up the corridor. After a moment, awareness flickered across Maggie's face too, and she opened her eyes. "Water," she whispered, and gratefully Ian held the glass to her lips as she sipped. The voices grew near, then fell silent; there was a rap at the frame of the open door. Ronald Tolkien's sweetly smiling face appeared around it, and above his, Jack Lewis's, his eyes serious and kind.

"How's our favorite great lady of letters doing?" Tolkien asked in a tone of quiet encouragement.

"The faculty have been praying for your recovery, Mrs. Brooke," Lewis added. "I can't even begin to list all the dons who asked to be remembered to you by name."

"'Mrs. Brooke' is M'Lady to you, Jack," Ian said in a weary, melancholy attempt at jocularity. "Our young George popped 'round just this morning and dubbed her a Dame of the Realm. How about that?"

"Well, that's nice and everything," Lewis countered with a wink at Maggie, "But *we're* here with an invitation to join a *truly* exclusive company."

"You've been telling us and telling us, Maggie," Tolkien confessed soberly, "but we lads can be pretty thick. It's taken your recent heroism to get us to see how daft we've been to exclude you."

"Which is not to say," Lewis added, "that we endorse your engaging in any more heroics. We'd like to see you home in the Bodleian as soon as ever you can." He produced, from behind his back, a large framed document ringed with signatures. "But in the meantime, know that you're the first Inkling to receive an engraved invitation to join us. Everyone's signed it, Maggie. Please come to our meetings. We could use your insight."

Maggie's eyes misted, and not with pain. For just a moment, healthy color returned to her cheeks. "I'm touched," she murmured; "your friendship means more to me than you can know." She squeezed each man's hand in turn.

"There won't be any M'Ladying there, though," Lewis laughed. "Our meetings are all cigar smoke and first names, so prepare yourself." Regaining his seriousness, he added, "Truly, Maggie, you awe me. I'm honored to know you."

Touching his friend's shoulder, Tolkien said, "We oughtn't overstay our welcome, Jack." He nodded to Maggie and to Ian. "I know you need your rest. You know where to find us if there's anything we can do—anything at all. You know we're at your service—and in your debt." And leaving the framed invitation in Ian's hands, the two scholars took their leave. Ian turned to offer Maggie another sip of water, but she was asleep—breathing evenly, a smile upon her lips.

CHAPTER TWENTY-TWO:
GÖRING S LAST GAMBLE

Whether man die in his bed
Or the rifle knocks him in the head,
A brief parting from those dear
Is the worst man has to fear.
Though gravediggers' toil is long,
Sharp their spades, their muscles strong,
They but thrust their buried men
Back in the human mind again.

—W.B. Yeats, from "Under Ben Bulben"

THE REICHSMARSCHALL REMINDED HIMSELF to enjoy the sound his beautifully shined shoes made in the spacious, marble-paved hallways of the New Reich Chancellery. He must remember to enjoy the familiar tightness of his crisply pressed uniform, the dignified weight of the medals pinned to it, the heavy ivory baton—as long as a man's thigh—he carried to mark his rank. Passing the many stately windows that lined the hallway, he must remember, he told himself, to enjoy the way the early winter snow dusted the street that still bore his name. He paused outside a particular door and checked his watch: he was precisely three minutes early.

He spent sixty seconds reviewing the words in which he would analyze the failure of Oberstleutnant Cordesmann's deployment strategy and the promise *that Direktor Schumann's device still held out for the Fatherland's victory. The Führer would be skeptical, but he was a rational man. The Reichsmarschall hoped that his faith in the Führer's rationality was not misplaced.*

Next, he spent thirty seconds meditating upon the meaning of this meeting's venue: the Führer's marble-lined office, not his private study. The Reichsmarschall couldn't help but have qualms: did the increased formality signal a loss of intimacy, a fall from grace? On the other hand, remembering the repair job he'd witnessed in the Führer's study, he reflected that the office's expensive marble walls likely ruled out plans for the deployment of firearms. He could feel fairly certain of surviving this interview, for which he was grateful: though he preferred to retain his dignity, he had come face to face in the past few days with the uncomfortable truth that he was not too big a man to beg.

Finally, the Reichsmarschall spent thirty seconds thinking of nothing at all. He took the chancellery's stuffy, overheated air into his large sturdy lungs and let it out again. He squared his big broad shoulders and stiffened his ramrod spine. He ran his thumb over one of his baton's diamond-inlaid gold-and-platinum end caps and let a sense of his own innate power and importance—independent of the Führer's whims—suffuse him like the warmth from an excellent Eiswein. Thus fortified—and still ninety seconds ahead of schedule—the Reichsmarschall opened the door; with a nod to the lovely Frau Schroeder, he crossed the anteroom, opened the inner door, and did a thing he enjoyed less today than usually: he made an entrance.

"So kind of Herr Göring to join me," the Führer murmured in that voice, which though quiet, somehow carried crisply across the fifteen meters between them. The Reichsmarschall had the sudden, disloyal thought that this sonority was in fact not a quality of the Führer's voice at all, but of the imposing marble room. Silently, he confirmed that his watch was still synchronized with the enormous built-in wall clock over the door he had just entered; he saluted, and then he noticed something that flummoxed him utterly: the chair

that the Führer occupied was no longer the room's only one. A folding camp-stool had been set up across the Führer's desk from him, and with a sweeping motion he indicated it: "Bitte."

On the Führer's desk lay a few scattered English-language magazines and a box, intricately carved, of a richly-grained wood the color of golden wheat, polished to a high gloss. The box's edging appeared to consist of tiny backwards swastikas; on each face was carved, with painstaking detail, a scene from the American frontier: buffalo grazing in the shadow of a butte; an American native in feathered headdress riding, bareback and barefoot, on a handsome stallion; the main street of a new-sprung Western town.

The Reichsmarschall's eye returned to the magazines fanned next to the box. The topmost was the latest edition of Time; *on the cover, a smug Winston Churchill, cigar clamped firmly between his teeth, displayed his trade-mark V-for-Victory hand gesture as Westminster Abbey rose majestically in the background. A handsome middle-aged woman in a Home Guard Women's Auxiliary uniform stood on its steps; large black letters declared, "Churchill Foils Hitler—Again!" From beneath* Time's *red edging peeked a somewhat tattered-looking journal entitled* Collier's; *the Reichsmarschall noticed it was an issue from 1937. In the dry dull climate of the artificially-heated chancellery it was difficult to breathe. The Reichsmarschall could feel moisture under his arms and hatband and across his back; he was suddenly self-conscious that the moisture might become visible through his pale blue uniform. He took a seat on the camp stool as directed.*

"Are you familiar with my friend Charles Lindbergh?" the Führer asked quietly, pleasantly. Before the Reichsmarschall could remind him of the many times he and Lindbergh had admired one another's aeronautical prowess, of the tours they had offered one another of their facilities, the Führer continued, "This box is made of American cottonwood, crafted by a Bavarian woodcarver in 1891 in a place called Wounded Knee. Mr. Lindbergh presented it to me as a gift. Would you care to see what's inside?" The Führer opened the

box's silver clasp with infinite care; the Reichsmarschall could see that it was lined with rich chestnut-colored velvet within. He reflected that the Führer's pretense that he might not know Charles Lindbergh was an alarming show of cruelty—the Führer knew full well that Neville Chamberlain's "Peace in Our Time" policy was the direct result of the Reichsmarschall's having convinced Lindbergh that the Luftwaffe was invincible. And now the Führer was erasing the Reichsmarschall from the story: it couldn't mean anything good. The Reichsmarschall's virile blood froze like a maiden aunt's. The Führer drew forth a long, greenish-black revolver with a plain dark wooden grip. "This is one of a pair of .44 Colts. A thing of beauty, no? Mr. Lindbergh tells me they were used in cleansing the American wilderness of its ... undesirables. Take a closer look." He handed the pistol to the Reichsmarschall, who hefted it in his hand. It was heavy, gorgeously balanced, center-fire with a swing-out six-chamber cylinder: a beautifully crafted weapon, antique and modern all at once.

"Open it and take out the bullets," the Führer instructed. The Reichsmarschall complied, lining up the chunky brass cartridges along the edge of the Führer's desk. A lump rose in his throat, making it hard to swallow and impossible, it seemed, to speak. He breathed with difficulty. "Are you interested, Hermann, in Anglophone literature?" The Reichsmarschall shook his head, perplexed by this new turn in the conversation. "And yet you do speak English, do you not?" The Reichsmarschall indicated by a nod and a shrug that he did, more or less. "Anglophone literature, Hermann, is a curious thing, strangely direct and artless. It is like the writing of children," the Führer asserted. "Take our Mrs. Brooke, for example," he continued, gesturing towards the figure behind Churchill on the Time *cover.* "What could she have done being what she is?" *he quoted in English.* "Was there another Troy for her to burn?" *The Führer paused, then leaned forward and spoke even more quietly, as if imparting confidential information. "That's William Butler Yeats, Hermann. Mrs. Brooke's poet of choice.*

"But that's not the writer who interests me most at this moment. Have you ever heard, Hermann, of the disgusting American genre called pulp fiction?*" When the Reichsmarschall indicated that he had not, the Führer held his hand out casually; the Reichsmarschall placed the revolver in it, and the Führer caressed it absentmindedly as he continued, "Listen to this." He plucked the* Collier's *magazine from his desk, flipped it open to a dog-eared page, and leaned back in his chair; in English he read in almost a singsong,* "One night, after we had finished dinner, Burkowski takes out his revolver, a '92 model, and looks at me." *The Führer's eyes snapped up from the page and focused sharply on the Reichsmarschall. "We have here only a '91 revolver, you understand. But we make do as best we can." He settled back, lowered his eyed to the page again, and resumed in his singsong English,* "'Feldheim,' he says, 'did you ever hear of Russian Roulette?'" *The Führer's eyes snapped up again. "Well, Hermann?" he asked. "I assume you have not."*

Somehow the Reichsmarschall found his voice. "I'm afraid I haven't," he agreed somewhat hoarsely.

The Führer relaxed again and went on, "The Russians. Like children, too, but in a different way from Americans—maybe more like sullen adolescents. Don't you think? At any rate: 'When I said I had not, he told me all about it. When he was in the Russian Army in Rumania, in 1917, and things were cracking up, some officer would suddenly pull out his revolver, remove a cartridge from the cylinder, spin the cylinder, snap it back in place, put it to his head and pull the trigger. There were five chances to one that the hammer would set off a live cartridge and blow his brains all over the place.'" *The Reichsmarschall winced involuntarily.*

"'Sometimes it happened, sometimes not.' And as he explained, Burkowski removed a cartridge from his gun, spun the cylinder with his thumb, snapped it shut without looking at it." *This time as he described the actions the Führer set the open magazine on his desktop and* demonstrated, *miming removing an invisible cartridge, then audibly spinning the revolver's cylinder.* "He said something about me never understanding the thrill of it, put the muzzle against his temple, and pulled the trigger." *There was a click as the Führer performed each action he narrated; then he continued in English,* "There was a click."

By now the Reichsmarschall knew for certain that perspiration, despite the chill he felt, had ruined his uniform, probably beyond all cleaning. He drew forth a handkerchief and dabbed ineffectually at his streaming brow, and even as he perspired, he shivered. The Führer lifted his eyes from the page again, this time lazily. He watched the Reichsmarschall for a moment. "Aren't you enjoying my story, Hermann? This cheap American thrill, made for adolescents? Perhaps you are like the protagonist Feldheim. The Russian gambler Burkowski calls him* methodical, not speculative, *and chalks it up to his German nature. But I think, Hermann, that you* are *speculative. You have gambled with my Teutonium bomb, have you not? And the world has seen the outcome of your speculation."*

He closed his eyes again. "But I digress. At the end of the story, Burkowski's tour of duty is nearly finished, and he has inherited a large sum of money. He has won, it seems, at the game of life. But still he cannot resist gambling." *The Führer read on,* "This time he took out five cartridges and left one, reversing the order of chances." *The Führer's eyes snapped up once again, and he leaned forward over his desk, gnashing his teeth ferociously. He snatched one of the cartridges from the edge of his desk, knocking the others over. Two or three clinked onto the floor. He shoved the cartridge into the revolver's chamber, snapped it shut, and then thrust the pistol towards the Reichsmarschall.* "You were my friend once, Hermann, and so I will give you the better odds. Take the pistol. Take it!" *He held it out with trembling hands, and with trembling hands the Reichsmarschall reached for it—then hesitated. The Führer drew the revolver back and eyed the Reichsmarschall appraisingly.*

"Perhaps you do not realize, Hermann, what I am doing for you in the name of our long friendship," the Führer explained in a weary voice, so quiet it was difficult to hear him. "Your trial for treason is set to begin tomorrow morning. The plans are in motion already. That's right, Hermann, your trial—and it will not be a quiet affair in my study. It will be a matter of national interest—of national spectacle. You will be convicted, of course, and publicly hanged. Much though it pains me to point out the baser aspects of human nature, Hermann, I must remind you that everyone enjoys seeing the mighty brought low. The Gestapo—well, such true-hearted Germans deserve, every once in a while, a feast and circus. What they will do to Emmy and to little Edda, I hesitate to guess. I will not be able to protect your dear ones, Hermann, though it pains me to admit it." Once again the Führer held out the revolver. "Take it, Hermann. After all we have been to one another, I cannot deny you a chance—a desperate wager, a slim hope—of dying like a man." With the horror of one handling a live cobra, the Reichsmarschall reached slowly forward and grasped the pistol in his hand.

Fumbling with a lower drawer in his desk, the Führer produced a bottle of fine Marillenschnaps from Wachau and one small glass. Pouring himself a swallow of schnapps, the Führer directed, "Spin the cylinder, Hermann." As he did so, the Reichsmarschall could smell the delicate scent of apricots spreading through the chill, stony air of the tomblike office. "Hermann, you know I don't take drink," the Führer observed. "But for an occasion as painful as this, I must make an exception. You gambled the future of the Reich with your Operation Über. You failed. Now it's time for you to gamble again. Hold the pistol to your temple, Reichsmarschall. Perhaps you will be lucky and die a man's death." Slowly, as if moving underwater, the Reichsmarschall lifted the pistol to the side of his head. It felt impossibly heavy; he steadied its muzzle against the point where his cheek- and jawbones met. Tears stood in his pale eyes: he did not want to die, he thought furiously, he did not want to die. In this moment, everything in the Reichsmarschall's field of vision stood out sharply, as if he were looking at the world through high-quality binoculars: the warp and woof of the German flag in its stand behind the Führer; each button and medal on the Führer's uniform; one whisker, high up on the left cheek, that the Führer had somehow missed in his morning shave; a single drop of schnapps trembling on the outside of the Führer's glass as he raised it and growled, "The moment is now, Hermann. Five against one. Pull the trigger."

The Reichsmarschall knew it would do no good to stall. He simply prayed for this cruel farce to end, one way or another. He tightened his grasp on the trigger, feeling its action move smoothly towards the point of no return, and then—

The Reichsmarschall was a young man again, a protégé of Manfred von Richthofen, the Red Baron. Surrounded by British gunfire, his Jasta—each man in a red Albatros D.III—frolicked like songbirds among cloud and sunbeams. They were untouchable; the British artillery might as well have been playful fireworks. He was a god, sporting on wooden wings over the Alsatian countryside. His pulse came fast and wild as a young lover's; his body was light, light, a feather carried on a spring updraft—

With the pistol's click, loud in his ear as an explosion, the Reichsmarschall felt all of the muscles in his body release their tension at once. He felt a warm sick wetness spreading in his trousers; after a moment, it turned icy as the perspiration on his body. He retched at the stink of himself. The Führer's face was heavy with disgust; his motion as he poured another swallow of schnapps was angry. "You can't make things easy, can you, Hermann?" He held the liquor to his nose. "Let me spare you the humiliation of a public trial, Hermann," the Führer said as if pleading. "Let me protect your little family. Help me help you—spare me the agony of putting my dear friend through such a vaudeville." The Führer lowered his schnapps and sat contemplating the Reichsmarschall as if waiting for him to make the next move.

"What shall I do, mein Führer?" the Reichsmarschall heard himself ask in a pitiful and wavering voice that couldn't possibly be his own. He felt as if, *in a dream, he were watching himself from somewhere near the ceiling. The revolver lay on his lap, his nerveless fingers still tangled in it.*

"Spin the cylinder again," the Führer directed wearily. "I am a merciful man. I will stay with you all day if that's what it takes to avoid a trial. Lift the revolver. I will drink when you fire."

This time, the Reichsmarschall felt numb, mechanical, as he complied with the Führer's directions. This time, rather than thunderous, the revolver's click sounded distant and hollow. The Reichsmarschall became a robot, spinning, lifting, and firing on command, over and over. At last the Führer's bottle was empty. The Reichsmarschall sat still for a long moment, not understanding. His head was empty of thoughts; his hands and feet were blocks of ice. Something foul was dripping from the seat of the camp stool to the marble floor below, but he hardly noticed. Dazed, he kept his eyes on the Führer and waited for his cue. After a long moment, it occurred to him to wonder whether his trial by fire were over. Might he be allowed to live? He dared not speak, but pleaded with his eyes.

The Führer reached down with infinite heaviness and fumbled once again in his desk drawer. "What's this?" he asked in mock surprise, and leaned back, setting another bottle of Marillenschnaps on his desk. Heavily, he started to work the cork from the bottle, then stopped and slowly stood. "Hermann," he said, "I need to use the latrine. We will take a five minute break, and then I will open my second bottle." As he moved to the door, some lucid rear corner of the Reichsmarschall's consciousness was astounded at how unsteadily he walked. His hand on the door, the Führer threw over his shoulder, "Use your morphine if you want—but don't overdo it. This is my revenge and I will savor it."

EPILOGUE

Had I the heavens' embroidered cloths,
Enwrought with golden and silver light,
The blue and the dim and the dark cloths
Of night and light and half-light,
I would spread the cloths under your feet:
But I, being poor, have only my dreams;
I have spread my dreams under your feet;
Tread softly because you tread on my dreams.

—W.B. Yeats, from "He Wishes for the Cloths of Heaven"

IN THE PREDAWN HALF-LIGHT, the sky above Peterhead Bay was still scattered with a few dimming stars. Only because the water was salt was it not scummed with ice; a chill night wind still poured over the cliffs and across the water. The gulls were not awake yet; ashore, the docks were already coming to life, but along the bay's south breakwater the only sound was the suck and slap of waves against the stone. Just outside the breakwater, two well-muscled Bloomoggan-ners, rime glinting on their oilskins and in their broad sandy beards, rowed a fishing skiff southwards. The people of Peterhead had heard last week's news from London, and they were glad in an abstract way that the city had survived. But London was a long way off, and almost nobody in Peterhead had ever been there, so the story of an atomic bomb in Westminster Abbey was mostly repeated in the pubs as trivia or incredulous folklore, and in the rest of town life went on as it always had, fishermen setting out before dawn and hauling all day on their heavy nets, the felons at Peterhead Convict Prison breaking rocks for the north breakwater.

Around the big men in the skiff were heaped their nets. In the stern of the skiff, hunched against the cold, rode a third figure. His form could barely be distinguished from the nets heaped before him; he was swathed in oilskin, his face invisible within a voluminous hood that swallowed it like a monk's. The skiff continued its laborious progress southward until the lights of the bay were hardly brighter than the smattering of stars in a sky swiftly turning from black to midnight blue to a gray as thick and soft as the breast of a dove. Cold gave a sharp edge to the smells of salt and scale and seaweed. The two big men were ruddy-faced, their long sleeves rolled up, warmed by their hard labor, but the figure in the stern must have been freezing. He drew his oilskins tightly about his compact body, but he did not shiver. Instead, with eyes lost in his deep hood's shadow, he scanned the southeastern horizon for something.

Presently his search was rewarded. Just at the water's surface, several hundred yards to their south southeast, a blue light winked. The big rowers made towards it. The blue light's winking resolved itself into a pattern of longs and shorts; the figure in the skiff's stern waited for the pattern to repeat in full, and then he lifted his electric torch and responded with a winking pattern of his own. As the skiff drew nearer in the half-light, the blue light's source came into soft, dim focus: it was a lantern mounted on the turret of a U-Boat. The hooded figure with his electric torch and the U-Boat with its blue lantern continued their silent exchange of messages. Gazing into the stern as they rowed, the two big fishermen could see blue lantern light glittering, revealing one side of the deep shadow of the other figure's hood and the long thin silvery line of a scar on his face.

Meanwhile, some five hundred miles to the south, repair and containment squads swarmed over Westminster Abbey in the thin light of December dawn. The radioactive decontamination team, in head-to-toe rubber suits reminiscent of those worn by divers or bee-keepers, lent a surreal air to the scene. They were nearly finished, though, sponging up and disposing of the pale atomic fuel dust that had lain thick in the bomb crater and clung in a thin film on the wreckage of what had been the Abbey's crypt. Mostly now they crept among the rubble with their Geiger counters, scrubbing a spot here and there, confirming that the scene was safe for standard cleanup and repair crews. Already, some hundred feet above them, workmen were busy erecting a temporary roof and boarding up its windows to protect the nave and apse from the elements while the foundation was shored up. When the structure was once again sound, the roof would be entirely rebuilt and the glorious stained-glass windows re-stored. Cardinal Hinsley would not have believed how quickly the donations had poured in from every corner of the globe—massive grants from aristocrats in Europe and industrialists across the Americas and the Commonwealth, yes, but also pennies from the poor of the world in their millions, all accompanied by well wishes and prayers. He found himself touched most by modest gifts from kind souls who revealed that they were not Roman Catholic—he received them from Protestants and Greek Orthodox, and even from Jews, Muslims, Buddhists, and Hindus. The human family were connected at their hearts after all, and even Hitler's venom and his minions' guile were no match for the overwhelming compassion of God's chil-dren, in all their varied glory.

As the otherworldly decontamination team withdrew, announcing the all-clear, teams of workmen trooped like ants down the ladders and scaffolds that now connected street level and crypt more safely than the rickety, much-abused iron spiral staircase, which workers early on the scene had removed as unsafe. Now they swarmed all over the main crypt and throughout its warren of adjoining rooms, setting up floodlights, clearing away debris, and cataloguing fragments that might be whole enough to be restored. Smashed grave-markers mingled with bricks, splinters, charcoal, and faces, visors, hands, and wings fashioned in marble and ancient gilded wood. In places, gorgeously-carved granite arches and columns still held the crypt ceiling—the Abbey's main floor—aloft; in other places, the stone supports lay in ruins, and workers hastened in with iron braces to ensure that the structure was sound.

The crypt's southeastern corner was in much the same condition as the rest of its edges, and better than some. It demanded no undue attention, and so the day was quite advanced before workers turned their attention to the life-sized marble funerary statues that lay or leaned upon one another there, blocking access to a wall banked high with rubble. Methodically they numbered the relatively intact statues with grease pencils, logged them into a ledger, and hauled them up to be transported to a storage facility. Methodically they sifted through the smaller cobbles and pebbles for anything recognizable, then bagged the rubble to use as infill in the foundation repair. Dust was swept away: before repair triage could begin in earnest, the engineers, preservationists, and restorers must examine the site clean.

"What's this, then?" one workman asked his fellow as they were finishing with the corner. "Look: this tomb don't fit quite flush with the wall."

His companion looked and had to agree that along the edge of a waist-high tomb in the corner, a crack or tiny gap was apparent. "You reckon it's part of the foundation damage, Joe? We oughter report it so the builders can patch it up."

But Joe had crouched in the corner, shining his torch intently on the crack. "I don't think so, Eddie," he responded. "See how the gap only goes up the height of the tomb, not above it? See how even it is? I think it might be how this wall is made." He pushed into the small space between the protruding tomb and the adjacent wall to get a better look, and as his broad shoulders, not finding space to accommodate them, shoved at the tomb, it moved away slowly but smoothly, as if on a track.

"I'll be!" Eddie exclaimed with a low whistle. "Joe, I believe you've found a secret door."

"What do you reckon's back there?" Joe asked. "Lost treasure? Arthur's tomb?"

"Final resting place of Excalibur, I shouldn't wonder," Eddie said. "Come on, then. Shine a light and let's have a look."

Joe complied, flashing his torch around the passage revealed by pushing the tomb away. He crawled in for a few feet, then stood up: the low passageway had opened out into something resembling a stone-faced corridor, spacious enough for a man to stand, provided he weren't unreasonably tall. Luckily, Joe wasn't. He flashed his torch around a bit more, but it didn't penetrate far into the underground corridor's velvety blackness. The walls here were rougher-hewn than out in the crypt proper. The air smelt of mold and faintly of sulfur, and from somewhere in the distance the faint sound of trickling water reached their ears. "Sounds like we might have a damaged water main somewhere ahead," Joe called back. "Need to report that, for sure. Fresh water, by the smell, not sewage." Looking again, Joe could see that these walls were cracked and that the floor ahead of him was strewn with small rubble. "Some damage in here from the blast, I'd say," he called to Eddie, "but it mostly looks superficial. Still, worth checking on. Don't want no cave-ins—I'd reckon this passage, if it continues, runs right under Saint Margaret Street. Be a real inconvenience to motorists if this turned into a sinkhole."

Joe turned back to rejoin Eddie and report his findings to the crew organizer—but as he stooped to crawl across the passage's threshold, a faint sound made him turn around. "Wait a minute, Eddie," he called, "Think I hear sommat." He held his breath, nearly, then, straining his grizzled old ears to pick a sound up in the blackness. For a moment all he could discern was the steady, distant susurration of seeping water, but then he caught again the noise that had made him stop. Faintly but unmistakably, from far down the passage, came the weak and muffled barking of a dog.

DANIEL O'ROURKE is a WWII history buff and nationally recognized, award-winning corporate lawyer with over forty years of professional experience. This is his first novel.

DATE DUE

PRINTED IN U.S.A.

19887953R10153

Made in the USA
Lexington, KY
30 November 2018